DREAMSLAYERS

J.W. Webb

Would you trade your soul to save your life?

The Crimson Lady knows that's the only way to find the man she wants to kill—the mercenary known as Corin an Fol.

Sign up for the J.W. Webb VIP Lounge newsletter and receive this exciting tale at the door! More details at the back of this book.

Acknowledgment for:
John Jarrold, for editing
Darcy Werkman, for copy editing & proofreading
Roger Garland, the late Tolkien artist, for the illustrations
Ravven, for the cover design
Map design by Stardust Book Services in collaboration with Chaim Holtjer
Formatting by Stardust Book Services in collaboration with Rae Davennor

This one's for Robin,
Shining Star that you are!
Thanks for putting me back
together so many times.

PART 1|FUGITIVES AND EXILES

CHAPTER 1 | THE
SPYMASTER'S DAUGHTER

Arraleen Caze watched the fools file noisily into the outer courtyard. It was early afternoon, and the soldiers looked nervous and sweaty, stifled by all the armor. Hardly surprising considering the heat. Were she in a better mood, she'd feel sorry for them. But not today.

Their captain was a pinched-face weasel. She could see him looking up at the balcony where she stood. He couldn't see her, but he would assume she was there, and she stared down at him with cold contempt.

Gosha, her favorite servant, appeared, her face glistening with sweat and eyes worried. "Mistress . . ."

Waving her to silence, Arraleen smiled and returned her gaze to the ugliness below. After a moment she spoke, her clipped tones directing the gate guards below. "Address those fools," she ordered Teraska, commander of her guard. He was a burly red-faced northerner and once a fighting-slave, but freed by her father.

"Hareshe, they are here on order of the Yanturi himself," Teraska called up to her using her formal name. "This captain has news concerning the Golden Villa."

"What?" *They wouldn't dare . . .*

For answer, her captain dipped his helmet. She saw the Yanturi's soldiers gripping their throwing spears. *This could get out of hand.*

"I'm coming down. Tell those fools to shut up and wait."

He bowed again. She turned and saw Gosha hovering.

"Well?" Arraleen snapped at her servant, who quickly made herself scarce. She left the balcony, her sharp mind irritated and distracted. Where was he? It had been two months, and no word. She was used to him being absent, but he usually sent word by coded bird. Something had gone awry in the east. He'd been so confident. The Sangala were missing too. And now the Yanturi's miserable guards were outside her father's country estate.

Father, what have you done?

Eyes blazing, Arraleen swept through the marble-columned halls like fury. She breezed down the velvet-carpeted stairs, casually glancing at her father's many trophies and weapons lining the walls. She stopped for a moment by the long oval mirror, as was her custom. There, she took a minute to study her features and cool her anger. *I'm already twenty-seven.* Some women would be past their prime, worn out by child-bearing and drudgery—even her sisters, spoiled kittens that they were. *Past their prime.*

Not Arraleen Caze. She'd barely got started. She gazed at her reflection. Dark eyes dusted by mocha skin stared back at her, the expression haughty. *Cold.* The face she wore with strangers. She looked sleek in her black, gold-laced tunic. A gift from her father, it almost reached her knees. From Shen apparently. A favorite. She wore her flared baggy trousers tucked neatly into black boots. Despite the summer heat, Arraleen always wore her boots. A lot of things could be hidden in a decent pair of boots.

Satisfied, she clicked her tongue and moved on. A servant dipped his head as she swept by without sparing a glance. A guard waited at the door and bowed. She ignored him too.

The shouting was back. The fools couldn't help themselves. Teraska had best keep his temper, those northerners being what they were. Barbarian oafs, though her father had said that Raleen, his homeland, was a civilized country. She didn't believe that. The few northerners she'd seen were ugly, with pale skin and coarse manner. Teraska was loyal, and that counted for something.

She walked through the doorway and across the inner courtyard. Teraska met her at the gate. He bowed and she glared at him. The shouting was heated. There'd be a fight at any moment.

He joined her as she strode briskly toward the outer courtyard and gilded gates, where the Yanturi's spearmen were jumping up and down like mountain baboons. They calmed down quickly when they recognized the High Califez's daughter. Their captain was sweating profusely in his ornate armor. He bowed curtly, his men following suit.

Teraska stood beside her as she stopped by the gates and swept the soldiers a cold angry glance.

"What nonsense is this?"

The captain stepped forward. "Hareshe, I—"

"Stop mumbling, soldier. Else I will cut your tongue out!" She barked the words, and he jumped visibly. She almost laughed at his bug-eyed stare. *You drew the short straw coming here, Captain.* "Well?" she added in a calmer tone.

"Hareshe, the Yanturi is most angry. He demands word of your father's whereabouts. He . . ."

"Stop dripping, man. There's more to this, isn't there?"

"Hareshe, forgive me. The Yanturi suspects your father of collusion with the easterners. He says Tulomon Caze must be arraigned, and—" The voice choked into a gurgle as Arraleen's hidden dagger sliced clean across his throat.

The captain staggered, clutched his neck, and tumbled. The men surrounding him gripped their spears, faces ashen. Beside her, Teraska unsheathed his long northern sword. Nobody moved except the prone captain, who kicked slightly as he lay bleeding on her father's expensive cobbles.

Arraleen glanced at a big soldier who stood closest to the dying man. He had hard pale eyes. A Dalcian. *So the Yanturi use foreigners too.* She stooped and wiped the knife clean on the dead man's cloak before sliding it back inside her tunic sleeve.

"You're the captain now," she told the Dalcian, who looked shocked but nodded stiffly. "Report back to the Yanturi, you and your men. That dolt was impertinent, prompting his demise." She nudged the dead man with her boot. They looked at her, lips pursed. Only the newly promoted captain seemed steady. Not a bad day for him, though that would change when he got back to the city. *Shame.*

"My father," she addressed the Dalcian again, "who that man dared name in person, is Vendel's loyalist servant. The Yanturi knows this. All know this. But my father has enemies spinning falsehoods in court. Lesser men who would see his fall. Fleas on a wolf's back. Understood?"

The big Dalcian nodded and bowed stiffly. His soldiers settled back, leaning on the spears. She heard Teraska sigh beside her.

"You wanted a fight, didn't you?" she whispered.

"I don't like these turds, Hareshe."

"You northerners don't like anyone."

She surveyed the soldiers again. "What was this fool about to inform me?" She kicked the corpse and stared coolly at the pooling blood seeping into the cobble cracks.

"The Sangala chief, Octaxa, is dead, Hareshe," the Dalcian told her. "It happened in the east. A disaster. In distant Shen. There was a battle—a siege, I believe. The Yanturi received word from Ran Genza. The Cardalan ruler suspects your father . . ." He glanced down at the dead man and chewed his mustache.

Arraleen raised a brow. "Continue."

He nodded. This one had courage. Almost, she liked him.

"The Yanturi suspects everyone, Hareshe. But none more so than the High Califez. The Sangala were assigned to your father. Most are rumored dead, alongside their chief."

"And the Yanturi's courtiers are implicating my father as the culprit? Why would he betray people charged with his protection? The Sangala are ferocious killers, they probably brought their fate on themselves. Whatever happened in that country has nothing to do with the High Califez."

"There is more, Hareshe." He looked worried for the first time.

I thought there might be. "Go on," she told him.

He coughed, his pale eyes flicking at his dead predecessor.

"Speak bravely, Captain, and you'll not share his fate. You will have heard that I despise cowards more than anyone."

"Yes, Hareshe. I have heard that."

She pressed her beringed palms together and held them to her chest. It was a sign for him to relax, though Teraska tensed beside her. But he had cause, having seen her in action too many times.

The Dalcian chewed his red mustache. "The Yanturi has confiscated the High Califez's residence in the city. Your father's Golden Villa. He has guards stationed outside. The . . . coffers were plundered when the mob got in . . ."

Icy calm, she said nothing, dropping her hands to her side. The man to the Dalcian's right coughed. Arraleen's slap struck the side of his face, knocking him back into another, his spear clattering to the ground.

"Cough again and I'll sever your throat," she told the trembling guard. The man would faint any moment judging by his sorry demeanor. Arraleen returned her gaze to the new captain.

"Your name, Dalcian?"

"Crastus of Kamor, Hareshe." He bowed again. She noticed one of the guards propping up the fellow she'd struck. She chose to ignore that.

"Well, Crastus of Kamor, I've not heard of your city. Is Dalcia as wide and remote as rumor states?"

"It is, Hareshe. A vast land. Jungle and rivers in the north. Temperate mountain forests in the middle. Cold in the south, and coastal strips where the city states lie. Kamor is one such, the furthest from the Reech."

"Fascinating," she said, crisply. *A simple yes, would have been sufficient.* "What happened to my family? My brother and half-sisters, their children?" She didn't mention the hundred-odd servants and slaves quartered at her father's famous villa in Omala City. Minions didn't count. Neither did the whore who'd given birth to her siblings.

"I believe they are in custody, Hareshe."

Beside her, she could hear Teraska grinding his teeth. "Stop that," she hissed.

She turned back to the Dalcian. "I will take carriage into Omala at first light tomorrow. You, Crastus of Kamor, will recover my father's pilfered property and deal with the reprobates. You will also ensure my family are well looked after and returned to their home, and recompensed for any inconvenience."

"The Yanturi ..."

She raised a finger, stopping him. "I will take carriage to the palace in person. Teraska here will accompany me. I will request private audience with the Yanturi and sort out this mess. Now leave us, and quickly, for my heart's hot with fury. And . . . take that with you." She kicked the graying body of the dead captain. "Lest I bid my slaves remove his armor and clothes, and feed the body to my cats."

The Dalcian's eyes widened in fear. They all knew about the three black panthers she kept in her forest at the rear of the estate.

"Hareshe, I will inform the Yanturi's vizier of your response. And I will send men to address the situation at the villa."

"Good. *Go.*"

Without waiting for them to depart, she turned briskly, snapping her fingers for Teraska to follow. Once back inside the villa, she ordered Gosha to fetch her a minted tea and prepare a hot bath. Teraska waited at the door as she stripped and stepped into the golden steamy tub. Gosha poured warm water over her body and scrubbed as she sipped her tea, her mind racing.

Gosha's nimble fingers and the water eased her worries. Now to address the issue. "What do you think?" she asked Teraska without turning.

He remained at the doorway.

"Well?"

"I counsel prudence, Hareshe. Until your father returns, even you are not safe from our enemies. Going to the city could prove rash. More than risky."

"Am I to let my family stew in Omala's oubliettes, or wherever those stupid guards have them held? And what of my father's belongings, and people? There has to be recompense for this outrage."

"But your father . . ."

She turned abruptly, water spilling from the tub. Gosha had finished and was standing back, head dipped lest Arraleen's eyes fall on her. They all knew how dangerous she was when her voice grew quiet.

Teraska looked uncomfortable in his armor and cloak. His brown eyes tried not to gaze at her breasts. She found his discomfort amusing. She'd have smiled if she hadn't been so angry.

"And where do you think he's got to?"

She placed the tea aside on a stool and stood, dripping. Teraska's awkward glance shifted to the tiles at his feet. Gosha rubbed Arraleen's shoulders with a towel until she bid her desist.

"Laregoza." Teraska stared at the tiles.

She snapped her fingers. Gosha finished toweling her off, and another girl brought her black silk gown. She slipped inside the garment and bid Teraska join her out on the balcony. He did so with a resigned expression.

She walked across and helped herself to more tea from the decanter at table. She didn't offer him any and he remained standing, wall-like at the doors. Ignoring him, she gazed down from the balcony, her keen eyes following the road leading from the estate. She scanned over the palm trees fanning either side of the road, and she took in the fertile tilled fields, with the slaves busy at work. Beyond were the hills and woods, and the winding brown river.

She saw the arch bridge almost a mile away, the stones lit by sunlight. The soldiers were crossing it in ordered file, trotting in step. Twelve miles to the city, they'd run all the way. Even the officers in the Yanturi's spear guard were refused horses, lest they grow idle.

"You think he's still there?" she asked eventually. "Why?"

He joined her and gazed down at the gates. "Grodu is missing."

"So?"

"He was meant to report back regularly after your father arrived in Laregoza. We've heard nothing. And yet Ran Genza suspects your father and sent word to our ruler. The Sangala were up to something out there."

"You *think?*" Her sarcasm cut razor-sharp. He twitched but held her gaze. The Sangala were twisted bastards, but her father knew how to handle them better than most.

She summoned patience and drained her tea. Finally, she turned and offered him a smile.

"Do you think he's dead, Teras?"

"I don't believe so, Hareshe. Any other man . . . yes. But your father, much like you, can weather any storm."

She flashed him a grin, genuine this time. "You're right, and I would know if he's dead. But what has happened to him? Two months? Things obviously didn't go to plan in the east lands."

"Grodu reports directly to me. The former gladiator's always been reliable. But he was assigned to Octaxa. The Sangala freed him from the slave pits, after all. Though your father arranged that, Octaxa always claimed Grodu was his man."

She shrugged, irritated again. "Forget Grodu. I'm talking

about my father. I mean, why stay in Laregoza?"

"Perhaps his meeting with the Shen didn't go as planned. The Sangala might have—"

"Keep guessing, Teraska. Truth is we won't know a damned thing until he gets back. Meanwhile, we'll need a plan. I'll work through that on the way. Forget the carriage, we'll ride out at first light. Once in the city, you'll cover my back as I deal with any nonsense from those courtiers and guards."

He nodded, looking uncomfortable, and she didn't blame him. The chance of them getting back with their skin attached was slim indeed. But if she didn't act, her father's enemies would. They'd already filled the Yanturi's ears with their filthy lies. He'd soon find a new favorite among them—the one who fawned the most, and poisoned and murdered better than his peers. They were maggots feasting on the Yanturi's rancid spoiled flesh.

She allowed the anger to pass as she studied the landscape. The soldiers were out of sight, and afternoon was fading fast.

"What do you know about the deal my father was making with those Shen?"

"It was most secret, Hareshe. Even the Yanturi was kept unaware. The Sangala leader, Octaxa, had duped the Cardalan ruler—*Ran*, they call him over there—into believing we were their allies. But the Shen official that Grodu met with had a better offer. With that in mind, your father persuaded the Yanturi to allow him to sail from Kulshana with the Sangala and interview the Shen in person. Their leader, Chulan, sent a servant. Grodu said he was an assassin. He was certain of it, and mentioned his concern in his last coded letter."

"You think the Shen assassinated my father?"

He shook his head. "Grodu said the Shen killer upset the Sangala and your father with his arrogance. They are strange folk, apparently, with odd customs. He said the Sangala sailed east on this Chulan's assurance of gold and trade. Your father stayed put in Soloza—that's a city on the coast. But something happened there unforeseen. The Sangala are powerful, but perhaps . . ."

"What of Grodu's assassin fellow?"

"He returned to Shen by road."

"I don't see the relevance."

"It's in his name, Hareshe."

"His name? What's special about his name?"

"Chulan's man called himself Gujun."

"So?" She was irritated again.

"Gujun the Slayer. A name well known among the Cardalan slave soldiers I fought against in the rings, before your father freed me."

"Slayer?"

"That's what they call him."

"Hmm, and they call me the Dreamslayer. Strange coincidence. Nothing more. And yet . . . you're worried, aren't you? Your primitive northern superstition. This Shen *Slayer* knows my father's whereabouts?"

The sound of dogs yelping excitedly interrupted her train of thought. Teraska looked alarmed and leaned out, gazing down from the balcony.

"More soldiers around the back?"

He shook his head. The dogs sounded excited rather than angry. She knew the difference.

Father.

Arraleen grabbed her robe and almost ran down the winding balustrade stairway to the back doors, Teraska stomping noisily beside her. She reached the pantries and kitchens leading out to the gardens beyond. The dogs were baying and whining. She saw servants rushing about in confusion.

They reached the back doors and stopped when a tall figure entered, his face swathed by a brown burnoose, the eyes haunted and exhausted.

Father.

Tulomon Caze, High Califez and Vendeli Spy Master, stared back at his daughter for a moment before collapsing to his knees.

"Fetch water," she shouted at the servants as she rushed toward him, her head full of questions.

CHAPTER 2|THE SHEN

They were amateurs. He'd heard them following half an hour ago. Gujun smiled. This city was a maze, and he was hunted. He was wanted in Cardalan and Shen. The price for his head was going up every day. He could have been worried. He wasn't. The fools following him through the lanes had no idea that they would soon be the victims.

The lanes were a tangle of hovel, slum, and side cut, reeking with a stale stench caused by clogged drains and effluence. They twisted, crossing into others. This lower city was a drunken spider's web. And it was cold. Raining. He didn't like this place. The shadow of the inky mountain brooded over the drab houses like an ominous storm giant.

Cardalis. The city in the clouds.

More like cold fog and drizzle. Early autumn felt like winter here. Caranaxis, it had been called in the so-called glory days. Back when the mad emperors ruled. Gujun had heard the stories in taverns on his journey here. He'd heard many things. He wasn't a drinker, but taverns had their uses. The man he was meeting would be in one nearby. High up, in the upper city. A privileged servant and spy for the Ran.

Gujun smiled. It would be good to see Grodu again. He didn't have any friends, but the former gladiator from Golt had come close. They'd shared a time in Laregoza on the coast, a land he'd like to know better. Once he'd spoken with Grodu, he'd return there.

The footpads were closer. Three of them, probably more coming the other way. Word must have got out that a Shen renegade had dared enter Cardalis. The Shen were despised here, especially after Cardalan's ignominious defeat outside Ta Shen last summer.

A tangled mess. Gujun had fought for the wrong side. It was the reason he was here. They wanted his head back in Shen. Even someone with his skill couldn't stay ahead permanently. There'd come a time when he slept, or was trapped, outnumbered. He'd kill many, but in the end, they'd take him to the saw. The new warrior emperor, Lin Gu, was not big on forgiving.

He reached a corner and waited. The sound of footsteps entered the alley behind. Armed only with a knife, Gujun crouched, his breath slow and easy. Shadows grew and angled toward him. He glimpsed a glint of steel. They were almost on him. Noisy, clumsy fools. Gujun jumped out and walked out to greet them.

There were three large men, two armed with cudgels and the third hefting a spear. He saw that one looking, and knew others were approaching down a side lane. He dropped his hands to his sides, smiling. The three scowled back. One laughed.

"Fucking Shen." The footpad with the spear spat on the cobbles.

Gujun stepped toward them. "You're in my way." They looked confused. Why wasn't he running? A small man, trapped, and a despised foreigner. Worse, a Shen.

The nearest one laughed. "He's a simpleton. We can have some fun here." He walked forward quickly, the cudgel swinging.

Gujun sensed two men approaching from behind. He smiled and watched as the heavy stave whistled toward his head. He leaped forward and caught the cudgel, trapping it in his left hand while jabbing his fingers up into the assailant's eyes.

The man fell backward. Gujun grabbed his collar and spun him about in time to receive a tossed dagger in his gut. A second one struck his chest. Gujun shoved the corpse to the ground and slipped his dagger free. The knifemen behind were hanging back, horrified that they'd killed their comrade.

The second cudgel bearer was backing off, but the spearman meant business. This one must have been a soldier. He was confident, angry. Gujun sensed he knew how to use the weapon. His stance was strong. He crouched carefully and lunged quickly, jabbing at Gujun's midriff.

Predictable thrust. Gujun shifted his weight onto his left leg and turned, the spear sliding past his chest. His foot hooked behind the spearman's ankle and lifted, causing him to lose balance. He lurched forward, tugging at his spear. Gujun's knife sliced open his throat.

He was done playing. The thug with the cudgel had turned to run. Gujun's tossed knife stopped him from getting far. He yelled and tumbled as the blade struck the back of his skull. Gujun watched him crawl. He'd finish him soon.

Time for the knife men, still hovering at the corner. Gujun scooped up the spear. The first turned, brandishing a second knife. Too slow. Gujun tossed the spear and skewered him in the chest, pinning him to the wall. His accomplice ran.

Gujun grinned, enjoying the sport. He sprinted after the runner, gaining on him in seconds. The man panted and tried to dive into another alley. Gujun leaped and twisted his body, launching both feet into the side of the runner's head, knocking him against a building. He crumpled, and Gujun stamped on his neck, snapping the bone.

He walked back to the one mewling and crawling with Gujun's knife protruding from his skull. A shallow wound, not a killing throw. He needed answers.

Gujun stood behind the crawler and kicked him hard in the groin, knocking him prone.

"*Please*, leave me be."

Gujun leaned forward, grabbing the man's filthy hair at the base of his nape. He twisted the blade, yanking it free. The man cried out for mercy.

Gujun laughed. "Can you guess what they call me in Shen, Card?"

"No ... *please* ... spare me."

"The *Slayer*. Gujun the Slayer."

"Please ..."

"You've a choice, Card. Assist me, and die quickly. Or, I slit your guts and string them out. Choose quickly!"

The man sobbed and nodded.

"Where do I find the inn called Scarlet Girl?"

"It's a tavern in the upper city. Not safe. I ... soldiers there."

Gujun nodded. Sounded right. Grodu would be stationed near the barracks and stables.

"How do I get there?"

"There are gates, the wall. You'd have to—"

"Just tell me where."

"It's close to the barracks. On Conqueror Avenue. Past the temples to the old gods." The man choked back a sob.

"How far?"

"Half a mile, no more. But the gates ..."

"Hmm, you said that."

"*Please* ..."

Gujun turned the wretch around so that he could look into his terrified eyes. *Time to die, old son.* He was choking, swallowing bile. Gujun sliced the knife along his throat.

He stood, looked about. The lanes were quiet but wouldn't be soon.

Dangerous coming here, even for him. And without his Jian blades. He'd left them buried under an ivy-oak stump outside the city. Shame, but he'd be spotted right away with the swords strapped across his back.

Besides, a man needed to keep his edge. That meant challenging yourself. He wiped his hands on the corpse's tunic and started walking briskly toward the street corner where he'd confronted the footpads. He knew the way to the upper city gates.

He'd studied the maps back in Shen, before he'd left Chulan's villa with most of his former master's gold. Chulan no longer needed the money. The late magister's decaying bones were fox food outside the walls of golden Ta Shen. Lin Gu had made a point by dismembering the traitor's body, sometime after Gujun slew him. Not that he'd stayed around to watch the show.

Strange decision that had been. *Career changer*. But he'd been unusually emotional that day. He laughed at his sentiment.

I'm getting soft.

Gujun approached the gates warily, his hood covering his features. Keeping to the eaves and shadows hemming the streets, he saw a guard seated, dozing, on a bench at the right gate. Two more were dicing at a table, a lantern lighting their faces through the gatehouse window. They seemed absorbed with their game. Gujun saw no reason to interrupt.

His eye on the sleeping guard, he reached the nearest buttress supporting the fifty-foot walls. He eased his dagger through a gap in the stones above his head and pulled his slender body up. The climb took some effort in the darkness. After twenty minutes, he caught his breath back and crouched low, becoming one of many shadows in a wide lantern-lit square.

Different feel up here. *Clean*. The streets ran broad and

straight in five directions. He saw a sign glinting under lamplight as the night wind buffeted it to and fro, the hinges creaking. It was colder up here, away from the slum fug. He approached the street sign, eyes scanning. No one was around, just the grumble of breeze and drip of rain from a gutter. A dog barked close by. He stopped, waited. Silence. He moved on.

The sign read *Conqueror Avenue*. He was in luck. The letters had been crudely painted over the original unreadable script. Must have happened when Carda the Cruel sacked the city, killing the mad god emperor and announcing the Cardalan Republic. Three hundred years ago. Not that he gave a shit about that. History was for scholars—idle folk who slept in beds.

A short careful walk revealed another sign, indicating the *Scarlet Girl*. A dull lantern flickered above twin doors painted red. He heard voices inside. Someone was singing badly. He checked the hood, his cloak. Slipped a finger over his dagger and pushed open the doors.

Several faces turned his way as he entered. A couple of soldier types stared hard but soon lost interest. They'd see him as yet another street beggar coming for scraps. A few were tolerated in the upper city in return for cleaning the sewers and other such tawdry work the soldiers and respectable citizens disdained.

Gujun chose an empty corner farthest from the fire. He counted a dozen men in the tavern. Nine were soldiers. One looked like a nobleman, with his lush garments and ermine cloak. He appeared almost asleep. The other was clearly a merchant. Cunning eyes, with a hooked nose and diamond studs in his ears.

A shabby-looking girl worked the taproom counter, and a portly innkeep chuckled with a soldier at the fireplace. Mostly he was ignored, though the nearest two soldiers glanced at him from time to time.

Gujun waited for the inevitable confrontation. *Here we go* . . . One of them, the biggest, stood wobbling, half drunk. He walked across and glared down at him.

"You fucking staring at me?"

Gujun said nothing, but matched the drunk's glare.

"He's a simpleton." The big fellow turned and laughed. His friend shrugged, not interested.

The soldier grinned. "I think I'll throw you outside." His sword hung at his belt. He reached across to grab Gujun's cloak, but he stopped abruptly as Gujun's dagger pricked the soft flesh below his right eye.

"Go away," Gujun told him.

The big soldier blinked with the other eye. He backed off, face red with fury.

"You're a fucking Shen." He reached for his sword, stopping again when he saw Gujun flick the dagger deftly between his fingers.

"What's this, Dorask? We don't want trouble in the *Girl.*" The innkeep had noticed them, as had everyone else, except the noble now sprawled on the table by the girl. The soldier glared at Gujun, and his friend stood and joined him. That one had a crossbow. The innkeep came over and placed a hand on both their shoulders.

"Please," he said. "Lads. Go, sit and sup. The ale's on the

house tonight. Let me deal with this ugly fellow."

The big one nodded, but before complying he fixed Gujun a hard stare. "I'll not dirty Reinad's tavern. But once outside, you're dead, Shen." He moved back to his stool and the companion followed, after a long hard stare at Gujun.

"What's a fucking Shen doing in the upper city?" the big one muttered to the other.

The innkeep pulled up a stool. "You'd best leave while you breathe, Shen. I don't know how you managed to enter the upper city, but I doubt you'll get out alive. Beyond foolish, your coming here."

Gujun matched his stare until the innkeep dropped his gaze. He looked flustered, wanted to move on, but needed his patrons to know he had things under control.

"Did you hear me, Shen?"

Gujun placed the dagger on the table, spinning it between his fingers. The innkeep watched it glint in the lamplight. Outside, the sound of rain patted the dirty windows.

"I'm not here to cause trouble."

Beneath his false bravado, the innkeep's rheumy eyes looked relieved.

"You'd best go," he muttered. The two soldiers were watching again, but the smaller one had lost interest, while his friend chugged another ale. Other eyes were distracted by a newcomer. A huge bear of a man had entered, shrouded in a heavy woolen cloak and hood. A warrior. His dark eyes flashed Gujun's way. The giant pulled up a stool, and the girl poured him a frothing ale before he spoke. A frequent customer.

The innkeep had seen the newcomer and used his arrival as an excuse to leave Gujun's table. The soldiers were quieter. Even the coarse, drunken fool seemed subdued by the newcomer's presence.

Gujun watched the innkeep whisper something in the cloaked man's ear. The man turned and looked Gujun's way, his hooded features hidden by shadow. The innkeep pointed at Gujun and looked agitated. He nodded at the quarrelsome pair, and at Gujun a second time.

The cloaked figure said something and placed a huge, scarred hand on the innkeep's arm. He stood and walked over to Gujun's table, pulling up a stool.

For long moments they stared at each other. Finally, the man laughed.

"You've got sand coming here, Slayer."

Gujun grinned back. "I go where I please, Grodu."

The former gladiator shook his head free from the hood. Gujun studied his scars, the shaven pate, and his dark-olive skin. He came from Golt, a place Gujun had never heard mention of before. He looked well fed and stronger than ever, the clothes fine beneath that heavy cloak.

Grodu studied his face. "I know this man," he told those watching on. "He has some news for me. Enjoy your ale and leave us be."

The prying eyes withdrew, apart from the big lout who looked angrier than before. That one met Grodu's glance and reluctantly dropped his gaze.

"You might have to kill Captain Dorask and his friend," Grodu whispered. "They appear upset with you."

Gujun shrugged.

Grodu grinned and clasped his hands together. "And here you are . . . in Cardalis. Astonishing. What to ask? I don't know where to start." Grodu rubbed the stubble above his ear.

"At the beginning?" Gujun suggested.

"You returned to Shen, did you not? Were implicit in the fall of that city. We received word that things didn't turn out as expected over there."

"Situations change," Gujun said.

Grodu motioned the innkeep, noticing Gujun was without. "Bring us more ale, Reinad, good fellow. This man's dry."

Reinad hurried over and placed a heavy tankard in front of Gujun. "We don't serve Shen usually," he muttered. Gujun suspected he'd never seen a Shen. Few of his people journeyed to this shithole, even in the truce days. Reinad departed quickly, offering a sly glance at Grodu.

"You're not thirsty?" Grodu asked when Gujun didn't touch his drink.

"I don't drink much ale."

"You Shen should relax more." Grodu chuckled. He drained his tankard and reached across for the other. He took a long slow sip and gazed hard into Gujun's eyes. Satisfied, he nodded. "Things must have gone badly wrong for you, Slayer. I thought you had it all worked out, when last I saw you outside Soloza."

"I did. But the circumstances changed."

"Chulan promised you the slaver's villa."

"He did."

"And yet—please deny this—I heard a rumor it was you who killed the Shen Magister. I didn't believe it, of course. Knowing you're not stupid." Grodu stared hard at Gujun's face and shook his head. "You did it?"

Gujun nodded.

"What happened, Slayer? You stood to gain everything. And why are you here, of all places? Where the Shen enemy are hated even more, since Ran Casca's army broke on their second city's walls?"

"You once called me an ally. Hinted we could be friends."

"So . . ."

"You're the only man who has called me that."

Grodu rubbed his eyebrows. "I saw virtue beneath the villainy. What do you need? *Gold?* Swords?"

"I have sufficient of each."

"Then what, man? Why risk your skinny Shen hide coming to Cardalis? The spider's web. If Ran Genza knew of your whereabouts, he'd string you up by your gizzard. You know his brothers all died out there?"

"I've heard he wasn't overly sad about that."

"No, ha! It worked out well for him. First his father gone, next the troublesome brothers moved off the board. He gets to sleep at night. But still . . . you're Shen. He'd make an example, and enjoy doing so."

"Best you don't tell him."

Grodu's face darkened. "Careful, Slayer. You forget to whom you speak."

Gujun raised a brow. "I came here because you wanted a useful ally. And I'm currently open to options."

Grodu took a slurp and wiped his mouth. "Still do. But my patience runs short. Explain what happened out there, and what you want from your only *ally*."

"Find and secure me lodging in Laregoza."

Grodu scarce contained his laughter. "*What?*"

"I liked it there. The sea, the warm sunshine. A man needs to retire somewhere he likes."

"You are deranged, Slayer. Did the Sangala devils cast a bone at you? Clearly you're touched, man."

"You have contacts in Soloza?"

"A few."

"Put in a word for me. I have a place in mind."

"You do?" Again, Grodu slurped and chuckled.

"You know it. The villa where we met the Vendeli spymaster. When both Tulomon Caze and that Sangala serpent Utuxla were vexed by my appearance."

"You were impertinent, I recall."

"I didn't like them."

"You're serious, aren't you?"

"I had to leave Shen in a hurry. There's a price on my head there."

"Why? You killed Chulan. He wasn't popular, I heard, after betraying your empress. I would have thought you'd have been honored as a hero."

"Chulan stabbed Empress Rasnei."

"You're an assassin. I thought that was your job."

Gujun shook his head. "That may be so. But it was a black deed done that day."

"I don't understand. You killed Chulan the traitor, and yet you're an outlaw in Shen, and a hated foreigner from the winning side over here. What makes you think they'll prefer you down in Laregoza? The place is overrun with Cards from Talimi Garrison. Ran Genza was born in Largos."

"Because, born there or not, I've heard that the Laregozans are dissatisfied with their Cardalan overlord. There's been talk of rebellion, a break for independence."

Grodu stared at him for a few long moments. "I've heard that too. As has Genza. He's anxious. His general, Dranan, was killed down there, during a fight in that same villa you like so much. When I returned there with a Northman and his woman."

"A Northman?"

"Never mind that. Genza's nervous. Dranan was popular with the troops at Talimi Garrison. Genza suspects his second, the capable and ambitious Cama, is planning a coup. The Ran wants me down there next week."

"I'll have some questions for you when I arrive."

"First, you've got to get out of this city with your head attached. You're not worried?"

Gujun shrugged. "No. Just bored."

"It's all a fucking game to you, isn't it?"

Always has been—a cruel one. He smiled crookedly. "Life

is unpredictable."

"You've a death wish, like most easterners I've met."

Perhaps I have . . . Gujun shrugged, and Grodu drained the ale. He snapped his fingers for another. The inn was quiet, the hour late. The big soldier, Dorask, still watched them on occasion.

"Find me a safe house, Grodu. Somewhere close to the ocean where I can lie low until I plan my next move."

"Maybe I can help you with that. But I'd need something in return."

"Go on."

"You mentioned Tulomon Caze."

"The Vendeli spy master who saved you from the slave pits. He didn't care for me."

"That was Octaxa the Sangala chief. Caze didn't save me, but rather instigated my original capture. Long story. Caze escaped the fight at the villa. The Yamondon king wants his head. Ulani knows that while that jackal lives, the strife with Vendel will continue indefinitely. And he needs it tidy to secure trade with the Shen . . . and Genza, if needs be. Ulani's pragmatic too."

"I recall that the Yamondon was your real master." Gujun guessed there was more to this than Grodu gave out.

"The king, yes. I owe him."

"You want me to kill Tulomon Caze?"

"Maybe. But you'll have to find him first. The snake escaped from the docks in Soloza. Genza will want me in Laregoza keeping an eye on Cama's people. He'll be suspicious if I head south. But you, Slayer, can be invisible."

Gujun swept the room with cool eyes. *An interesting proposal.* He'd give it due thought. "You think Caze has returned to Vendel?"

"In secret. Their despot ruler, the Yanturi, will be wanting answers, with half his beloved Sangala missing. I suspect Caze will keep a low profile until he can figure out a way to get back in his master's favor. The Yanturi is a volatile prick."

"I didn't much care for the Vendeli I met. Why should I go there?"

"You want that villa, and your name cleared? Perhaps a new identity? You could be a retired merchant who left Shen in years gone by. No questions asked. With servants and slaves aplenty."

"That could work."

"Then find Tulomon Caze and bring King Ulani his head. He'll give you all that, and more besides."

I'd count on it. "King Ulani has scant influence in Laregoza."

"So? Ulani III is the greatest warrior of the modern age. And a guileful strategist. The Yamondons will destroy the Vendeli hold on the east coast. It's only a matter of time. The Yanturi is weak, his Sangala fanatics badly damaged, and the court nobles corrupt and quarrelsome. No grit. The Yamondons are warriors born. It's their time, Slayer. Cama knows this. That's why he's secretly asked for Ulani's help against Genza."

And there it is. Gujun steepled his fingers and leaned forward on his elbows, staring deep into the big warrior's eyes. "I was planning on retiring."

"Men like us don't retire, Slayer."

"That's true." *But I can always dream . . .*

29

"You'll think on my offer?"

"I shall."

"Good. You'd better leave soon, while you've skin on your back."

"What about that ugly fellow?" Gujun glanced casually at the soldier, Dorask, leaning heavily on the table where he diced with his surly companion.

"I'll see that he loses interest in following you."

It was Gujun's turn to be angry. "He insulted me. I'm going to kill him before I leave."

"You're not. The fool's not important. And he's one of Genza's cursed Immortals, his favored fighters. Why draw unnecessary attention?"

"The fields outside Ta Shen are full of rotting Immortals. Very well, I'll let that pass and expect to see you in Laregoza."

"Next week, no later. Do you have a horse somewhere? Weapons?"

"I'll acquire a horse. And yes, I've a good Chiang spear and my diamond-studded Jians hidden outside this city."

"Good. It's a four-day ride on a swift horse. I'll meet you by the docks. That's if you survive that long."

Gujun stood slowly. He swept the taproom with a final cool glance and smiled briefly at Dorask. The drunk Immortal stood shakily, but Grodu motioned, and he slumped back in his chair. Gujun turned and left the *Scarlet Girl* without a backward glance.

CHAPTER 3|THE VOW

Arraleen Caze shouted at the dogs until they scampered off. She helped her father up. His face was stained, dirty. There was a blood stain above one eye. He stood for a moment, shaking, until a servant ran for a chair. She made him sit and rest, and bid her retainers clean his face and give him water.

He drank long and slow. Belched, coughed, and drank some more.

"Daughter."

"Don't speak. Recover." Her mind was racing. What had happened to him?

He nodded, drained the water gourd, and was offered a second.

"Are you hungry?" He was so thin.

He shook his head. She bid the servants leave them. Teraska hovered, but she ordered him stay put. "Who's minding the gates?" she asked him.

"Darayez and Slinor," Teraska said. "I ordered them stay sharp with both eyes on the road."

They'd better, else I'll remove their tongues. "Good." She nodded and turned to study her father. His clothes were torn and faded from sun and travail. He looked shattered, worn thin by worry and weariness. A concern. She'd never seen him like this. At least his dark eyes were needle sharp as ever. He stared back at her, the ghost of a grin on his lips.

"What is funny? Are you hurt? Can you walk?"

He nodded and stood again. "Only my pride is hurt."

"What happened? *The state of you* . . . and, by the gods, where have you been?" she asked angrily, as they walked through to the main anteroom, where Gosha and two others had wine and fruit hastily arranged on a table.

Arraleen reached for the nearest wine glass and poured two cups. She downed the first and offered the other to her father. He sipped carefully.

"Augh . . . I've missed decent wine. Laregozans . . ."

"What happened out there?" she pressed. "You know the Yanturi—"

"Yes. I saw them here, his soldiers. I deemed it prudent to stay hidden while they passed me on the road."

"The mob raided the Golden Villa on the Yanturi's orders,

Father. Can you believe it? Your ancient home has been turned upside down. And, worse, he's imprisoned your family. Your latest mistress, my half-sisters. I don't know about Cordeel."

"They are your family too, Arraleen."

The fuck they are, but I'm not going there today. She forced a crisp smile. "*So . . .* what's your plan, Father? You must have a plan—yours is the sharpest mind in Vendel."

He looked at her for long moments before replying. "Survival," he said eventually. "I'll write the Yanturi and see he gets the note. There're still a few men I can trust in the palace. That way, he can focus his rage on the messenger, and not us. Hmm, once he knows the truth, he'll calm down and release the girls."

"What if he doesn't?"

"I'll have to kill him."

"That will be my task. I'm the killer in the family, remember."

"That you are, Arraleen. But you can avenge me later." He sipped his wine while she stood over him, her eyes angry and face hot. "Yamondons," he said eventually. "Ulani's devils stole a march on us."

It's always Yamondons. "I thought Octaxa's witchery had those bastards curtailed."

"The Sangala let us down. Most went east and never returned. Utuxla was among those killed by the Cardalan soldiers who attacked the villa. I saw them at the docks before I escaped. There was a Northman there too. And more importantly, Grodu. Word of his involvement reached me when I arrived back in Kulshana." He glanced at Teraska, who nodded.

Grodu. That ugly name again. "It's been months since we heard from Octaxa's man in Cardalan. You were in Laregoza all that time?"

"No, I left hastily. Took the long way back. I procured a horse from an inn stable outside Soloza, found some food and grog, and rode west to Permio. After that I joined a caravan on its way to Omala, stopping off at Kulshana to meet with my people. It was there that I discovered the Yamondons were in Laregoza, meeting with the Cards. And Grodu was their contact."

"But Grodu was Octaxa's loyal servant," Teraska said, forgetting his manners.

Arraleen glared at the big northerner, but her father waved her to relax. "I thought so too, Teras. Seems Grodu's been working for Ulani for years."

"But we saved him from the slave pits, with Octaxa's help," Teraska said, clearly not wanting to believe his former comrade and fellow gladiator a turncoat.

"Does it matter?" Arraleen snapped. "He's a traitor and will pay. First, we need to placate the Yanturi. Stop this outrage."

"That's looking unlikely," Teraska said, his eyes on the door. One of his men stood there. Darayez, she thought. But it could have been Slinor. The twins were hard to tell apart. He looked distraught and nervous. Teraska walked over and questioned him.

He returned with his face set grim.

"They're back?" Arraleen asked him.

"Not them."

"Who?" her father demanded.

"A score of Dalcian mercenaries led by a Sangala."

"Sangala?" Caze stared at his daughter. "They're all dead."

"Apparently not this one," Teraska said. "He spoke to Slinor. Said he knew the High Califez was inside and had orders to fetch him—his words—for interrogation concerning his part in the betrayal of the Sangala."

"I'll go speak with the man." Tulomon Caze stood shakily.

"Sit, Father. Rest. I'll deal with this." *Time to get my fucking swords.* She kissed him lightly on the cheek. "Relax. Get your strength back. We might have to act quickly." Arraleen fixed him a stare until he nodded, his lean face angry.

She armed herself and accompanied her captain and guard back to the front gates. She stopped, seeing the red-cloaked, shaven-headed figure, recognizing a Sangala by his customary arrogance and warrior stance. She bid the men wait as she walked up to the gates, her hauteur matching the impostors.

The Sangala smiled as he leaned on a heavy spear, emblazoned with its dyed vulture feathers and tar. She saw pale-faced soldiers lounging in the rose gardens close by.

"You are trespassing." She kept her voice calm though she raged within. "And those Dalcian mercenaries are not welcome in our estate. How is it you Sangala employ such filth?"

"Needs must, Hareshe. These are hard times. And they're loyal enough for the right coin. Good fighters." His smile was broad, the voice strong, clear, and commanding. She hadn't met many Sangala, unlike her father who'd had to deal with the jackals for years. Warrior priests, and zealots. Cruel fanatics. Into sorcery and vile practice. The Yanturi loved them. His subjects feared and hated them almost as much as the Yamondon foe.

"My name is Olgasha," he told her with his beautiful smile. "I've come to collect your father, Tulomon Caze. I know he's here. The former High Califez has colluded with the Yamondons, resulting in the deaths of many of my order. The Yanturi has tasked me with his execution in the Omala oubliette tomorrow afternoon. I shall enjoy the honor."

"What villainy is this?" She spat the words out through her teeth, the rage brimming red. "You've corrupted our ruler. You fucking wizards. You had better leave quickly, else I kill you myself, Dog. Father's not here, you're out of luck. But when he gets back, he'll make sure the Yanturi knows of your treachery and lies."

"*Dreamslayer . . .*" He smiled again, his dark eyes mocking. "Prized assassin, trained by your father's guards. Indulged. Think you're a match for me? You're just a headstrong girl, spoiled by her wealthy doting father. Taught the sword and the bow on a whim because the only son proved a disappointment. You know nothing of battle, hardship, and pain—the real world. Its grime, misery, and toil hasn't shown its face to you yet. But no matter. You have till morning when we burn this villa to the ground, as we did your golden one in the city."

"You did *what?*" She looked down and noticed that her hands were shaking on her sword hilts. She wanted to kill this bastard so badly.

"Ashes, my dear. And your father's consort, your pretty sisters. *Dead.* Not sure about the brother. But if Cordeel's on the run, my people will soon scoop him up."

"You dared . . ." She clenched and unclenched her knuckles, forced her breaths slow.

"By order of the Yanturi. Your family doesn't exist anymore, Arraleen Caze. Your father's assets are taken. Lands confiscated. Fetch Tulomon Caze, and I'll let you go. The servants too."

"Fuck you."

She made for the gate latch to get at him, but stopped when Teraska called out a warning. Three Dalcians rose from the bushes hemming the gates. All carried bows, with red fletched arrows nocked and ready.

"Ready when you are, Dreamslayer." Olgasha smiled. "You've got till morning. We'll camp here for the night, ensure that you sleep well."

He turned and walked back to the gardens where the mercenaries lounged, the archers following at his signal.

Teraska joined her as she gripped the gate rails, her temper at boiling point. She wanted to kill all of them with her bare hands. *How dare they . . .*

"You must flee, Hareshe. Before dark. You and your father."

"I will not."

"You have to. Else everything is lost. We twelve can hold them off while you escape to the woods."

"I'm going to gut that Sangala bastard."

"Later. First, you must look after your father. Go, Hareshe, before that serpent sends men into the trees surrounding the gardens. He's overconfident. That will change if he gets bored. *Please . . .*"

She stared at him and nodded. "You've been a good servant,

Teraska. Loyal and dependable. Hear my last command. Sell your body well, you and your men. The gods will have rewarded you in Hyshanna, when next we meet."

"We shall, Hareshe. I swear it."

"Good. And thank you, warrior."

She turned, walking away without further word.

"I have to free the cats so they can hunt," she told her father as she supported him through the wildwoods. He hadn't spoken since she'd informed him what had happened in the city. His favorite mistress and younger daughters were dead. The son missing, most likely dead too. Her brother. She'd never cared for Cordeel, but he was useful. Clever. The others, not so much. Shame.

Of far more importance was the insult to their honor. Caze was among the noblest names in Vendel. Even the Yanturi's heritage wasn't as grand as theirs. Their family was old whereas he was an upstart, his warrior-courtier grandfather took the throne in one of the many bloody civil wars choking the last century.

They reached the cages. She heard her babies growl. He stayed put, his face raw with rage and sweat. He didn't look well. They had water, but not much else. She'd ordered Gosha prepare some fare and meet them at the other side, near the mountain rise. Once there, they could range south through the wild country.

The panthers were hungry, and they growled as she approached. She crooned soothing words, reaching a hand through the bars and stroking Clezelle's fur on her sleek belly.

She was the biggest, and cleverest. Mother of the other two, Halinki and Slazeasy.

"Clezelle, listen," Arraleen whispered close. "You and your daughters must fare for yourselves until I return. There are plenty Dalcians to eat out there, but don't get shot. And spare the Sangala in the red cloak. I'll prepare something special for him."

She pulled the bolts back, and the three slinked out of the cages. Seconds later they'd vanished into the thick steamy undergrowth. The cats knew her scent, and her father's. Gosha's too. Anyone else was warm meat.

She smiled fiercely, thinking of Clezelle's fangs tearing at a Dalcian white throat. She returned to her father, seated in a tree bowel. He looked a mess. "You up to this?"

"Of course. But first you get away, girl. I'm for visiting the Yanturi." He pulled his secret dagger from his sleeve and made a slicing motion through the air. "This abomination is not to be borne."

"Since when have you been a fool, Father?" She rounded on him angrily. "Getting yourself tortured and killed won't remove the stain to our family's honor. They're dead. We're not. *Yet.* And I plan to delay that occurrence for as long as possible. We'll make south, avoiding the city. Stay high in the jungle mountains. I'd sooner take my chances with wild beasts and Yamondon scouts than the Yanturi's spies and soldiers. They'll be watching all the roads. You know I'm right, don't you?"

He stared hard at her, but nodded eventually. He looked exhausted. Done for. The sight of him depressed her.

"We'll postpone our vengeance until we return," she said. "Agreed?"

He shrugged. "All right, Daughter, we'll do it your way. You're in charge until I have my wits back. But I'll handle the insult to this family. It's on me. But for now, lead on, *Dreamslayer.*"

A panting Gosha met them in the densest stretch of forest cloaking the slopes above the villa, a mile west in the shadow of the mountains. She'd brought a male slave who'd carried Arraleen's favorite diamond-studded scimitar, together with a short spear and a hunting bow, with a dozen green-fletched shafts tied and bundled in a sack. Her father took the spear. Gosha had carried the pack of supplies.

"You have family in Omala, do you not?" Arraleen asked the girl.

"I do, Hareshe."

"Take this man and seek them out. You'll be safer there."

Gosha nodded, failing to mask her relief.

"Your name?" Arraleen asked the slave. A big Yamondon captured years back. One of the field hands, by his rough sunburnt look.

"Scaro, Hareshe."

"Look after her, Scaro. You belong to Gosha now. You're fortunate; she has a kinder nature than mine. Listen well, both of you. If word gets out of our meeting here, I will find you and take your livers for my cats. Understood?"

They nodded, and Gosha showed a tear. The man looked

indifferent. But Yamondons weren't like normal folk. They were jungle devils, half crazed by the drugs they were given at birth.

"So . . . what's your plan, *Dreamslayer?*"

She hardly registered his irony as she struck the vines from her face. He was bitter, angry as her. Perhaps even more. Gosha and the Yamondon had departed an hour ago. Arraleen watched with her father, settled for the night as best they could be, as the sun set like an overripe orange, swallowed by the mountain. The long Vendeli summer was almost over. The rains would come soon. She hoped not for a week or so. Hard to move around in the rains.

Gloom shrouded the woods and stockades below. She could see the glint of armor and spears as the moon rose, and a silver calm spilled through the long-folded valley. Her home. When would they see it again?

"What's that?" She grabbed his arm and pointed, seeing a tiny spark of flame emerging outside the villa. "Bastard's broken his promise," she spat. Her father said nothing.

Arraleen saw more distant flames emerge like swamp gas. They must be brands. They were torching her home. The sound of clashing steel reached them through the quiet. Next came the rush of flame. Tall spiky flames flickered and raged, an angry orange glow. She watched with mouth dry, until darkness cloaked them in the forest. Something slithered past her leg. Arraleen ignored the snake as she witnessed the villa crack open and crumple, finally flaking into coaly ash.

Her father ground his teeth and jabbed his spear into a trunk, before twisting it and yanking it free. Arraleen bared her panther smile and mouthed a silent prayer.

Mighty Agarra. Oh, Thrice Cruel One. Goddess of Vengeance, and Lady of the Night. Witness my vow. I—your daughter, Arraleen Caze—will seek out and take the life and soul of the Sangala, Olgasha. He shall be my gift to you! Guide me back to him safely, and prepare me for that happy day.

She blinked. The flames faded as night deepened. Her father had sobbed himself to sleep. She listened to the night beasts for a while and closed her weary eyes. She slept for an hour, no more.

CHAPTER 4| LAREGOZA

Gujun watched the warm waves washing the sand. Almost a week had passed since he had slipped out of Cardalis, riding south on a fine destrier he'd stolen from a tavern stable a mile outside the city. Easy getting down here. Staying might prove harder.

Laregoza. Soloza docks. The soft surge of sea nudging the jetties close by.

I like it here.

Watching the waves, his mind relaxed and thoughts drifted pleasantly. He felt at peace. Calm. Unlike everything else in his life. In this city harbor, Gujun could escape the turmoil. At least for a short while, enabling him to work out a plan. These docks were a sanctuary, where he could recover from the ordeal of the last two months.

This older part of the docks was deserted. He'd found warehouses and huts frequented by the odd rat, nothing more. Plenty of places for shelter. The warm autumn climate enabled him to sleep without blankets or heavy garments. The small fire he kindled kept the rats at bay. He'd fished from the jetty at night and ate well enough.

What to do ... He could stay here for weeks, fishing, eating. Enjoying the sun. But he needed information and that meant a tavern. Besides, Grodu would be here in a day or so. He'd want to learn all he could concerning Tulomon Caze and Grodu's offer.

He waited for the sun to creep below the clutter of roof and crane, then gathered his Jians and dark cloak and made for the nearest lights, a half mile toward the city main. Soloza sparkled with torchlight beyond.

He entered streets, heard voices. Someone laughed, and a woman cried out. He moved on. A scabby-faced hound scurried off as he passed a midden reeking of dead fish and offal. He crinkled his nose and walked faster.

A yellow lantern revealed a tavern.

Torlo's Retreat.

The faded sign's hinges creaked with the evening breeze. The place looked clean. He approached the nearest shutter and looked in, making sure he wasn't seen.

Quiet, but not empty. He saw three fishers laughing in a corner, playing dice. A soldier leaned against a wall as he stroked a girl's dark locks. He saw a chubby fellow with an apron, sweating profusely and mopping his face with a checkered cloth. The innkeep, he assumed. A young woman was wiping down the empty tables.

This will do.

He entered. Eyes turned his way. Unlike Cardalis, these were friendly. Or indifferent. Honest fishers tired after their day at sea. The soldier had other things on his mind. The girl was giggling as he whispered in her ear.

The innkeep saw him and frowned. He said something to the girl cleaning the tables. She nodded and walked over.

"You're not from around here, are you?" She smiled, seeming likable. Kind honey-brown eyes. The kohl made them appear larger. Olive skin. Small in stature, like him. Musty scent. On first impressions, he liked her. But perhaps he was getting sentimental.

"I'm from the east." Gujun smiled back, surprising himself.

"You want a meal? We've good clams and eels."

"I'd sooner have fish."

"We've got that too, and potatoes."

"Just fish."

"Ale?"

"Is the water drinkable?"

"Only if you want the shits."

"Then ale will suffice."

She raised a quizzical brow. "Are they all like you in the east?"

"No one is like me."

She let that go and made back to the kitchen. The innkeep seemed flustered. Not about Gujun, but something the soldier was saying. He needed to get closer. The big man was drunk, the girl worse, and he'd worked the clasp on her blouse revealing most of her ample bosom. He stopped when the innkeep asked something angrily.

The soldier straightened and pushed the girl from his lap. She giggled and stood grinning. "Dazelle, let me talk with Torlo here. We've some business to settle." The man's voice was sharp, despite his drunk manner. An officer, Gujun surmised.

The tavern girl returned with a large mug of ale. Gujun sniffed it and thanked her. She hovered as he took a sip and nodded. "Good," he said. She smiled, but remained put.

"Can I help you with something?"

Gujun wanted to hear what the soldier was saying to the patron. He was out of luck, as they'd reduced their tone to secretive whispers.

The girl scratched an ear. "Why are you here—come off a boat?"

"No, I . . . *walked*," he lied. He'd sold the horse in a shady corral five miles out of town. Didn't want soldiers recognizing the beast in Soloza. Plenty more nags around when he needed to move on. "I like walking. You get to take in the sights."

"You are a strange man." She showed no sign of leaving.

"I've been called worse." Gujun decided he might as well be sociable. Learn what he could from the woman. "What's your name?"

"Kanemys." She crinkled her nose. "Yours?"

"Gujun."

"That's a strange-sounding name."

"And yours is lovely."

She frowned. "You're not drinking the ale."

"I'd sooner wait for the fish." He glanced at the door leading off to the kitchens.

"Cook's preparing it." She crinkled her nose again. "Which land are you from? It must be somewhere cold, as you're so pale."

"Northern Shen. I was born in a city up there."

"I don't know much about Shen."

"And I know little concerning Laregoza, and this city. Perhaps you can enlighten me?"

"Only if you tell me why you're here." She smiled and pulled up a stool, staring curiously into his eyes.

"I'm just passing through."

"To where, Largos?"

"Maybe." He shrugged. She didn't look convinced.

"You're on the run," she said, her big dark eyes excited. It was Gujun's turn to raise a brow.

"And you're overly inquisitive. Should I be worried?" He narrowed his gaze and saw the alarm in her eyes.

"I'm . . . just making conversation. I'll go see how the fish is—"

"No, stay. I like talking to you. I'm sorry, I don't trust many people these days. Old habit."

"That's sensible, if you're a fugitive."

Gujun held out his hands feigning exasperation.

She laughed. "Indulge me, sir."

"Gone on, keep probing." He sipped the ale. It wasn't bad, and he was enjoying the girl's company. She was sharp, but he

47

hadn't encountered many tavern wenches. In Pol, Shen people usually ran from taverns when Gujun and his gang entered.

"Those skinny swords look expensive," she said. "You don't appear poor. And you're certainly not worried about Lieutenant Garion over there, as most honest rogues would be. I think you're an outlaw in your own land. Perhaps a noble who fell out with the king."

"Shen has an emperor, not a king."

She shrugged, clearly not knowing the difference.

"A new emperor," he added. "The empress was murdered two months ago."

"That's horrible."

"Yes, it was."

"You were there? Involved?"

"Perhaps I was." Gujun wondered why he was so relaxed with this girl. Not like him to give anything away. Must be the sea air.

"You weren't the one who killed her?"

"No." He stared at her, and she dropped her gaze.

"I'll get the food, it should be ready." She walked away, her manner unsettled. She was well made, Gujun thought as he watched her sidle out into the kitchens. He turned to survey the innkeep and soldier. Still talking in whispers. Too bad.

Kanemys returned with a steaming plate of red snapper, which she told him had been caught this afternoon. Gujun thanked her, leaned back, and stabbed a piece with his dagger. It was hot and spicy and delicious. She left him to his meal, as more men were entering.

Gujun gazed casually at the two newcomers. Cardalan soldiers, similar in garb to the oafs he'd seen in Cardalis. Same army, different regiment. One of them caught his eye and frowned, and Gujun turned his gaze away. The two walked over to join the lieutenant, who looked up and nodded. The innkeep disappeared into the kitchen. Gujun pretended not to watch as Kanemys brought the two ale and then whispered something in the lieutenant's ear. One of the men lit a pipe.

"He'll be here in a minute," one of the newcomers said.

"Anyone follow you?" the lieutenant, Garion, asked the biggest. Gujun noted how he appeared sober. That one had been masking his drunkenness. There was no sign of the girl he'd been fondling. Must be a door out the back. Worth remembering.

"No one about," the big soldier responded.

"Except him." The one who'd stared at Gujun pointed to where he sat. Gujun chewed on his fish and waited.

"Are we going to have trouble with you, foreigner?" The lieutenant seemed aware of him for the first time. Again, an act. "Well? You're from Shen, by your look. A renegade. Kanemys says she likes you. That's why you're still alive. I suspect you're a spy."

"Suspect all you like, Lieutenant," Gujun answered evenly, matching the officer's gaze. "I'm merely a traveler enjoying this hostelry's excellent snapper."

Garion was about to respond, when another man entered the inn. Hard-faced and cloaked. He swept Gujun a quizzical glance and moved over to the three at the counter. The innkeep was making himself busy, trying not to eavesdrop.

"We'll get to business in a moment," the hawkish newcomer said, clearly a man of higher rank judging by his immaculate garb and manner, his keen gaze on Gujun. Gujun watched as he walked over and rested his scarred hands on the table.

"You're a long way from home, Shen."

Gujun nodded and pushed his plate aside. He wondered where Kanemys had got to. "Passing through."

"To where?"

"My affairs are my own, soldier."

The man smiled. "Of course you would say that. But even you are not safe here, Gujun the Slayer."

Gujun tensed. "How do you—"

The officer raised a hand. "We're not enemies today, Shen. I received word you were making for Soloza."

"From Grodu."

"No." He smiled. "From your new emperor, Lin Gu."

Gujun slid a hand over his dagger. "How does the emperor know my whereabouts?"

For answer, the officer pulled up a stool and motioned his men leave him be. Gujun noted they were watching intently.

"He doesn't, yet. Though, I suspect he'll know soon."

"You're going to tell him."

"No. But those three Shen I saw on the way here certainly will. They looked much like you, Slayer, with their dark leather, long pigtails, and silver trimmings. They were well-armed, confident fellows."

Gujun said nothing, his mind racing. Silver and black were

the gang code colors for the Silver Slayers—his old crew. Had Lin Gu sent his own people after him?

"Where are they?" he asked, masking his anger.

"Half hour's walk. In Soloza, scouring the streets. With full permission from Talimi Garrison. I know that because it was my secretary who granted it. You see, I hadn't met you then. And Grodu ..."

"What about him?" Gujun studied the officer's face. Calm, strong, a seasoned veteran by his steady dark eyes. Aquiline and handsome, a large gold earring in the left lobe. The dark beard was trimmed close. Ambitious. One to watch.

"I got word from him this afternoon," the officer said. "It's why I'm here, came to see these boys. And you," he added with a smile.

"You mean to do Lin Gu's dirty work for him, take the reward? It must be five hundred crannels by now."

"Seven." The officer smiled. "But no. As I said, we are not enemies. I don't care about what happened in Shen. Or your past, Slayer—I've heard the stories from men who served on the river campaigns. You weren't liked over there."

"Then what do you want?"

"Actually, to help you." He smiled, artfully. "You see, like Grodu, I've vested interest in helping King Ulani III of Yamondo get everything he wishes . . . in return for his aid."

Gujun nodded. "You're Cama, the rebel leader Grodu mentioned. You mean to topple Genza."

"I mean to free Laregoza of his scourge."

"Grodu told me that Genza was from here. That's his family's villa along the coast."

"Which we both visited, though I came later. He may be Laregozan, but Genza—the whole family—is hated here. Ever since their ancestor Carda escaped the Ptarni slave pits and led the revolution that brought a close to their depraved rule, those upstart Rans have treated their old countrymen like scum. Ran Carda bled Laregoza dry, as he put all his energies into conquering the lands surrounding and renaming them the Cardalan Republic. So, yes. Ran Genza is not liked here."

"And you cannot defeat him without Yamondon help?"

"Probably not. The southern army's turning against him. And most the river garrison was wiped out in your country, thanks to his lunatic brothers. That leaves the Tseole Warders, some two thousand, scattered here and there. And the main regiment in Cardalis. Ten thousand strong. The Immortals are his men. Cardalan's a touch volatile these days."

"Like Grodu, you want me to work for you. With the Yamondon."

"Grodu's left for Vendel."

Gujun masked his surprise. "He told me he was coming here."

"He asked me to seek you out and convince you to join him, sail to Kulshana."

Gujun didn't like the sound of this. "He said Genza needed him in Laregoza seeking Tulomon Caze. And keeping an ear out for your rebellion."

"That was before Tulomon Caze turned up in Omala City."

"He survived?" *I should have guessed he'd escape back there.*

"And the fool returned to his house. They burned it down, but Caze and his daughter escaped—a week ago. The word came via pigeon from Grodu's contact."

"Interesting. Where will they go?"

Cama shrugged. "The new Sangala leader was charged with apprehending Caze. He sent bird to Genza, promising aid against the rumored insurrection . . . in return for Grodu's scouting skills and further Cardalan support if requested. Genza agreed, thinking Grodu still works for him. Which he does." Cama smiled. "Though not in a trustworthy way."

"That's all fascinating, but I've decided to stay here in Soloza."

Cama's eyes narrowed. "I don't think that's an option for you anymore."

"Are you worried for my safety?" Gujun's sarcasm cut through the room.

Cama smiled. "I daresay you'll kill those three Shen hunters out there. But there'll be more. *And more.* Lin Gu was most insistent in his letters. And like Yamondo, we want to please the new ruler in Shen. He seems brighter than the last one."

Cama blinked in alarm as Gujun's dagger appeared under his chin.

"You know nothing of her," Gujun said, removing the knife slowly. His anger had nearly got the better of him. A mistake. *I should be more careful. She is gone, and words can't hurt her.*

Cama glared at him. "Best you hold onto yourself, Assassin. Seems to me, you're short on allies."

Gujun chuckled, feigning humor. "I never had one until I met Grodu."

Cama stood and grinned fiercely at him. "I'll ignore your

gesture. Call it a culture clash. A misunderstanding. I meant no offense. Think on what I've said, Shen. And once you've dealt with your friends out there, seek me out."

"What happens if I decide not to help you?"

"As I said, the new emperor is keen for your head. Least I could do was send soldiers out searching the dockyards of Soloza harbor. You know, be helpful."

Gujun smiled. "Let me think on this."

"Don't think too long, Slayer." He turned and rejoined the other soldiers, who all stared back at him.

Gujun seethed inside. He sipped the ale and watched those in the inn for a few moments. Once they were preoccupied, he slipped out and padded toward the distant lights of the city. Someone called his name in a whisper. He gripped a Jian hilt and turned.

Kanemys stood in an alley, a shawl around her shoulders.

"You work for Cama."

"I do, yes."

"And I thought you liked me."

"I might, yet," she told him.

Gujun nodded and turned away.

"Be careful," she whispered.

"I'm always careful," he replied and trotted out into the night.

The sharinga star caught lamplight as it flashed toward him. Gujun dived in a side cut. Here in the city there were many such. Footsteps approached from different directions. He glimpsed the throwing star stuck in the door where he'd been hiding. He smiled, recognizing the calling card of his gang.

"Gujun." The voice belonged to Sha Tan. That made sense. Sha Tan had always been ambitious. He'd joined the Silver Slayers five years after Gujun, and he had always resented Gujun's hold over the gang.

Gujun walked out into the street. Sha Tan stood smiling, a second star in his hand, a Jian glinting in the other. Gujun turned slowly and saw two shapes in the gloom behind. Seemed that nobody stayed loyal these days.

Gujun folded his arms. He scanned the street. There were metal bins with lids stowing food, maybe trash. He walked casually toward Sha Tan, who stepped closer. He could hear the other two closing the gap behind.

"You'd best throw," Gujun said.

Sha Tan hurled the sharinga. Gujun spun on his heels and grabbed a bin lid for a shield, knocking the weapon aside.

Sha Tan reached inside his cloak for a third. Too slow. He clutched his throat, as Gujun's tossed dagger pierced his gut. He staggered, crumpled.

Gujun swept his Jians free, and he whirled around. He sliced air and flesh, as the second attacker jabbed at him with a Chiang spear. The man's head rolled. He didn't recognize it. The third assailant lashed out with twin Jians. Another stranger. They were young. New crew members, he suspected.

Gujun met those blades with his own, parrying and probing, until he slipped a Jian past the other's guard and gutted him. He dispatched the dying man and walked back to where Sha Tan sat with his back against the alley, red hands failing to staunch the seepage.

"Seems like you made a poor choice," Gujun told him.

"Who can refuse seven hundred crannels." Sha Tan grinned as he coughed blood.

"Money isn't everything, Tan. We Slayers had our honor."

"You betrayed us, Gujun," he choked. "Abandoned us after you stabbed Chulan."

"I daresay you would have survived, Tan. Shame."

"There'll be others coming."

"I hope for their sake they're more efficient," Gujun said, and he sliced a Jian across Sha Tan's throat.

An hour later he was back in *Torlo's Retreat*. Cama and the other soldiers had gone, as had most the people he'd seen. The innkeep still looked addled, especially when Gujun returned to his table.

Kanemys appeared, her eyes worried.

"You killed them?"

Gujun stared at her. "I think I'll have another ale."

"We're closing, it's late."

"But we haven't finished our conversation."

CHAPTER 5| THE LEGEND OF DARK MOUNTAIN

Arraleen wiped sweat from her eyes as they struggled up the steep rise, the fierce sun blazing through the trees above. They hadn't reached the real jungle yet, but this bushy scrub and forest was a nightmare to navigate. Her father still hadn't recovered his full strength and they stopped often, their progress slow.

Nine days out from their escape had found them trudging higher through the eastern slopes of the Emerald Mountains, which separated Vendel from Yamondo in the west. Gone were the ordered fields, roads, and clean terrain, replaced by wild rivers, dark woods, and stifling heat. Briars tore her arms and vines tripped her. Her father's plan was to stay in the mountains as long as they could before reaching the southern Borderlands. After that, Dalcia.

They'd quarreled about that, but she knew he was right. They had to get away and regroup. And he had to recover. Once he had, they'd return to Omala. Or she would, and kill them all.

"How are you bearing up?" she asked him as they crested the last steep slope. He was panting badly, and even she was out of breath.

"Angry, and hungry."

"In that order? Me too. You want to rest?"

"Give me a moment, I'll be fine." He leaned the spear against a stump, slung the pack of supplies down, and perched miserably on the moist tangle of vine and fern, the flies buzzing around his face.

She stood watching him, her mind flashing back to the previous week. No point moping, but every time they stopped, the shadows pulled her back there.

She had the two scimitars and bow strapped across her back, the quiver of arrows and three daggers tied to her belt. He had his long knife and the spear. Gosha had done well. They'd enough dry meat supplies to keep them going another week, perhaps more. Water too, though that would run out quicker. They dared not drink from the mountain streams, else poison choked them slowly.

"Why are you staring at me like that?" His anger turned on her.

She shook her head. "Dalcia? That's the best we can do?"

"What other choice is there? Stay in Vendel? With the Yanturi alerting every garrison within three hundred miles? Cross the mountains to Yamondo?" He laughed bitterly. "Ulani would boil our heads and dance naked with joy."

"Why not north—chance the desert?"

"Permio? They'll expect that. Besides, there's nothing up there except hunger, drought, and camel thieves. You've heard what the filthy Permians are like?"

"We could chance a harbor, sail east."

"And we would be caught. Remember, I'm the spy master. I trained my people well."

"To save their own skins, while trapping yours," she scoffed. "They should be loyal to you, not that fat turd in Omala."

"A few will be. But you shouldn't judge them so harshly, daughter. The Yanturi and his Sangala can be most persuasive."

"You thought the Sangala were all dead."

"Seems I was wrong. About a great deal, I was wrong," he added afterward.

"So Dalcia it is." She sighed and sat cross-legged on a log, hoping the ants wouldn't bite. "What's our plan when we get there?"

"We need to get there first."

"No, Father, we need a plan. You always insisted on thinking months ahead. It was why you survived, you told me."

"True."

"Well?"

"We fare south to the coast, avoiding the Reech."

"What's that?"

"A strip of land in the far southwest of Dalcia. Occupied by the worst scum imaginable. Corsairs, slavers, and brigand lords. Dalcians are a hard race, but even their fierce warriors stay clear of the Reech. Once we're at the coast, we can find a ship. Maybe sail east, or north beyond Golt. There'll be options, once we get clear of the Yanturi's grubby fingers. The main thing is getting out of Vendel and staying clear of Yamondo."

You make it sound easy. She shifted on the log. "A journey like that could take weeks."

"Months, unless we get horses at a trading station or village."

"And risk the roads?"

"Once we're in the Borderlands, I'm confident of help. But much closer, there's a village south of the Deepwoods. I know a man there. Loyal. The Yanturi's father had his family executed for tax reasons. He escaped and scraped a living near the mountains, braving the constant Yamondon raids. He also worked for me. That paid better."

Arraleen smiled grimly. *I can imagine it would.*

"Nuosta will assist us," he assured her. "And he'll have horses. Once at the Borderlands, we'll swap for fresh ones and make some time up."

She sighed, letting her body relax. "You *do* have a plan. Good. Ready for more fun?" She stood and stretched her aching limbs.

"Always." He grinned up at her.

They continued throughout that day into evening, the terrain deepening. Clouds obscured the skies, and a soft rain dampened their resolve. The canopy was denser up here, and birds cried out, as skinny creatures slithered through the undergrowth. They found a shoulder of rock allowing a camp. She whipped out her flints. They'd risk a fire, keep the predators at bay.

High in the mountains. Exhausted. They shared the one blanket Gosha had supplied, having scant room for more. They sat huddled together as the warm rain spat on her tiny fire; the faggots fizzled and finally went out. At least she'd tried.

"Can you sleep?" she asked him.

"I'll probably never sleep again," he told her.

"You need your strength, Father. And self-pity is beneath you. You always told me that. Self-pity and tears are for lesser folk. We noble born lack the leisure for such fancies."

"I've lost everything, Arraleen. My home, my lovely daughters. Sorielle, my woman. And Cordeel . . . who knows, maybe him too?"

You forget to mention Anyarvana, your loyal wife. My sweet mother, Arraleen thought bitterly. *But why am I surprised—you never mention her these days.*

"You still have me, Father. And you have your vengeance waiting. You'll need strength for that, and that means sleeping."

He nodded. "I'll try."

They sat hunched for hours. Occasionally she got up and messed with the fire, but to no avail. The rain worsened as dawn approached. He must have slept for a time. She hadn't. He stirred and nudged her shoulder.

"You all right, girl?"

"Just thinking."

"Sleep any?"

"Nope . . . you?"

"Yes, a little. I feel better, and there'll be no more pitiful nonsense. I'm sorry."

She shrugged. "We'll get through this, Father. We have to."

"We will." His smile was genuine for the first time since he'd returned. She took that for a good sign.

"Do you know where we are?" she asked him, after a while watching the rain. They were both drenched, the blanket heavy and dripping over them.

"In the mountains," he said, and she cuffed him.

"That's not helpful."

He nodded, his face thoughtful again. "I've not been here before, but I know the region and its rumors. There are legends concerning the Dark Mountain. That lies southeast beyond the Deepwoods—a jungle area we'll need to cross."

"I've heard of the Dark Mountain." She shivered, and thought she was probably catching a chill from the rain.

He nodded, peering out at the veil of mist revealing dawn.

"Tell me about the legends. You always spun a good yarn."

"I did?"

"The few times you were around when we were young, Cordeel and I. But Mother did more often." She felt the trace of tears rimming her eyes. "I loved her fables about the Crystal Kingdoms long ago. The magical lands in the far north."

"Ah, yes. Heroes and villains and monsters. Good stuff. Vana knew how to thread a good yarn."

"She told us one tale about a bad-tempered warrior called

Corin an Fol, who became king. A rough northerner, and mercenary type."

"That's common in fables."

"This Corin had a big sword." She smiled. "Killed the monsters. I liked hearing about him and his rebel friends."

He snorted. "I didn't think you cared for men."

"I like killing them."

"I'd sooner you'd married and given me sons. Fine warriors they'd have been."

"I'm not a fucking brood mare." She felt her cheeks flush.

The old spark had risen. They'd talked about this often. His other daughters had failed him too. Miscarriage and stillborn. And Cordeel was . . . who he was. A drunken conniver, gambler, and womanizer. Not a man to trust. Their family had seen scant happiness since her beloved mother, Anyarvana, had succumbed to fever that winter. Father's line was dying out. Too bad. Her destiny lay elsewhere.

She shook the thoughts away, as they weren't helpful. "What about this mountain of yours?" she asked, relieving the tension between them.

"Strangely enough, it concerns your Crystal Kingdom stories," he told her. "About the same period in millennia past, when the old gods waged a war in the heavens."

She nodded, knowing the legends, as her favorite yarns concerned that war. She folded her arms and smiled, forgetting the damp, her eyes dreamy. "Go on," she nudged him.

He grunted. "You're right, it passes the time." He coughed,

sipped some water she offered, and continued. "They say that before that conflict, the Great Enemy had rebelled against the Weaver twice. For punishment, the one they called the Shadowman was restrained and His flesh hewed into nine parts, each section locked in a deep place on a different world. Ansu, our home and the first world, got His head. Guess where the old gods put that?"

"Beneath the Dark Mountain." She yawned and smiled. It was good to hear him talk.

"Yes, and with a fire demon guarding it. But the stain of His blood seeped out from that terrible cavern far below the jungle. It spread into Yamondo, corrupting that people into what they've become. Twisted devils, and headhunting cannibals."

She shook rain from her hair. "But they say the Shadowman wasn't destroyed, and somehow left the mountain." She sneezed. The rain had eased, though not enough to make any difference.

"He was helped by those who still worshipped Him. As a dark spirit, He waged a third war, aided by the Urgolais sorcerers of that time, and other cruel spirits. And many evil men. He was defeated a final time, in the far north. The people up there had sorcery too. The Aralais wizards helped them."

"Yes, I know that part, Father. The outcome led to the Happening, a thousand years ago."

"Common folklore. They're just stories, Arraleen," he said, wiping rain from his face. "But there is something evil lurking near that mountain. I traveled close once with your grandfather. He knew the rumors and wanted to test my courage. West of here lies a valley. A deep gorge splitting the mountains. I saw the

Dark Mountain from there. The sight terrified me. I don't know why, but I've never forgotten the feeling to this day. Like cold wriggling maggots chewing on my flesh."

She said nothing, staring at him.

"We stay clear of that mountain," he told her.

"And make for the Deepwoods, your village?"

"Deepwoods are thick jungle, but passable with care. We'll get closer to the road down there."

"It's almost light. Best we get started."

He nodded and stretched. She stowed the soaked blanket best she could, and shook her weary body into motion.

It took them two miserable, wet days to skirt the region that hid the Dark Mountain. It might have been her imagination, but the nights in the Deepwoods were filled with shadows and flying shapes. She heard moans and whispers, death cries and screams that must have been the night gangers passing through. On the third morning, they cleared the jungle. Arraleen grinned in relief seeing the sun spray gold on grassy fields, and in their midst, the ribbon of road leading off to a distant settlement.

"Your village?"

He nodded, and coughed. He looked pale, and she hoped the constant damp hadn't damaged his lungs. She couldn't allow him to get sick.

They dared the road, making good progress as the sun climbed higher in the pale blue sky. It was warm, not hot. Their skin dried, and their clothes steamed, as they approached the orderly huddle of huts. A circular stockade spanned the road and a gate blocked the way ahead.

They walked toward the gate and it creaked open. A young man bid them welcome. His eyes blinked in surprise when he recognized her father.

"Welcome, Lord," he said. "You do us great honor."

"I would speak with Nuosta."

"I shall fetch him, Lord." The young man turned and sped into the village.

She followed her father toward the largest hut, as a tall, tough-looking middle-aged man walked toward them, a beaming smile on his dark, bearded face.

"My Lord. *Lady.* This is an unexpected pleasure." He frowned when he saw their sorry state. "You have been attacked? My goodness. By Yamondons? It must be. Come, let us feed you and we'll talk."

Her father thanked the smiling man and they followed him inside the largest hut. Despite the warmth, a fire blazed in the center, its smoke smarting her eyes. Two women stared at her nervously as she sat cross-legged by her father.

The headman, Nuosta, fussed one of the women to bring stew. Half hour later, Arraleen and her father were sated and happy. She felt her stomach growl.

"We need your help, Nuosta," Tulomon Caze said, wiping his mouth.

"Of course, and it's yours without asking. But it's strange, is this, Lord . . ."

"What's strange."

"The man was here, just two days ago."

"What man?" Arraleen demanded, and Nuosta started at her forwardness.

"My daughter works for me too, Nuosta."

"You're Arraleen Caze." He looked edgy, and one of the women covered her mouth.

"What man?" she repeated.

"A slave, or had been recently, I suspect. Big ugly Yamondon, by his look. I'd have killed him, had he not mentioned your names. Called himself Scaro, and said he had a message for Tulomon Caze and his daughter, from the woman called Gosha."

"Where is the message?" Arraleen asked.

He nodded and stood. "It was sealed, so I didn't open it." He reached into a shabby teak chest and produced a crumpled parchment.

Tulomon bid her read it first.

Arraleen ripped open the golden dragon seal, her father's stamp. Gosha must have salvaged that too. She read the written words out loud.

"Lord and Mistress, we are safe for the moment in Omala City. But there is turmoil here too. The Yanturi is insane with rage, believing his High Califez has joined the Yamondons, and the devils in the east too. He believes that together they mean to usurp his throne. The Sangala, Olgasha, has vowed to find you

both, and bring the Yanturi your heads . . .'"

She looked at her father.

"To be expected," he said. "That it?"

"There's more . . ."

"'The spy Grodu has been seen in Kulshana, with a troop of fighting men. Foreigners. They're asking about you. My servant, Scaro, went to the palace taverns and heard that the Yanturi received word from Grodu, who is angry that the High Califez betrayed Octaxa, his master. Apologies, Lord. His words, I've copied. Grodu has sworn to find you too.'"

She passed the parchment across. He read it twice, eventually nodding and giving it back to Nuosta.

"Burn that," Tulomon Caze told him, and the head man placed it on the fire.

"You've horses we can use?"

"I'll have them groomed and saddled. Where will you go, Lord?"

"Best you don't know, old friend. That way they can't cut it out of you."

Nuosta nodded. "They'll get nothing from me. But I'll assume you're heading for the Borderlands. If so, be aware there are two large garrisons of Dalcians stationed along the road."

"When did that happen?"

"While you were away, Spy Master. Both the Sangala and those close to the Yanturi have been hiring mercenaries. He's planning an assault across the mountains."

"He's insane. I've kept the peace for thirty years, barring the constant skirmishing. Ulani isn't a fool. The mountains have always protected our countries from each other."

"I suspect the turd blames you for that too," Arraleen said, angrily.

"Stay the night please, both of you," Nuosta pleaded. "Get your strength back, and we'll find you fresh clothing. You'll need more blankets, and I've coin too. You have enough weapons?"

"I can always use more," Arraleen said.

They spent that evening talking by the fire outside the tent. Tulomon Caze had welcomed Nuosta's people into their company. Ale was shared, and even Arraleen laughed as the young ones danced to pipe music and told bold tales. It was late when she slept, inside Nuosta's tent, vacated for their personal use.

The death cry woke her immediately.

Arraleen rolled to her feet and slid a scimitar free from the scabbard by her belt on the hut's sooty floor.

Her father blinked and sat up. "Was that—"

"Someone hunts. I'll go see."

"Arraleen . . ."

"What I do, Father."

She heard shouts. Another yell. The sound of steel echoing through the night. Nuosta's village was under attack. Someone knew they were here. But how? Who had betrayed them? Didn't matter. They had to get away.

She pushed the door open, knocking the tossed dagger aside with a forearm. She saw a man running toward her, flames rising behind.

"Father!"

A brigand with shield and sword. He grinned and lunged at her. Arraleen danced to her left, and skewered him beneath the ribs, piercing leather and flesh.

More shouts. Men rushing. She heard Nuosta's angry yells.

"Father!"

"I'm here." He appeared beside her, looked down at the corpse. "Dalcian. Sent by whom?"

"We need those fucking horses." She spat on the body at her feet.

Dark and moonless, the shadows of hut and smoke mingled as a night breeze lifted her hair. More shouts off to the right. She ran, her father cursing beside her with spear held ready.

Two large Dalcians blocked their path between the huts. One carried a crossbow, the other a spear.

Arraleen switched her sword to her right hand and reached down with her left—her quickest—pulling the dagger free from her boot. She tossed it deftly as the man fired the crossbow. She slammed into her father as the bolt grazed her arm.

Tulomon Caze cursed. He recovered in time to skewer the second Dalcian with his spear, as Arraleen finished off the first. She grabbed the crossbow and found a couple of bolts in the dead man's belt. These she took, and cranked the weapon.

They ran. More screams. The fires were raging and the huts

crumbling. How many were out there? She couldn't tell. She heard horses whining and stomping, trapped in the stockade.

"This way," her father yelled at her.

They reached the village center where the road led out, the stables barely visible to the left. A big figure blocked their way. A Dalcian with sword and spear. This one wore ring mail, but it didn't save him. Arraleen shot him through the left eye as they crashed past.

"Lord, flee, both of you! I'll hold them back."

Arraleen turned and saw the shadow of Nuosta standing at the gate, a horse stomping on either side. He gripped the reins, shaking them up and down so they could focus on the brass-studded bridles.

They ran toward him. Beside her, her father cried out as an arrow struck his side.

Fuck.

Arraleen bit her tongue and tasted blood. She turned, cranked. Aimed and shot. A shadow disappeared.

"There are many," Nuosta shouted, as they caught up with him by the gate.

"Can you ride?" she yelled in her father's ear.

"Yes."

She helped him into the first horse's saddle. "I'm sorry we brought this on you," she said to Nuosta, as she vaulted onto the other horse. "Ya!"

She slapped both the mounts, and they cantered noisily into the gloomy moist night.

She heard the twang of bowstrings. Ducked as an arrow whooshed past her head. A glimpse at her father wasn't encouraging, the red-feathered shaft sticking from his side.

They reined in out of bowshot. The sound of fighting faded as the flames rose and crackled. So much for Nuosta and his village.

"Is it bad?" She tried to see where he'd been shot.

"Annoying," he responded in a half gasp. "Someone must have got to Nuosta's people. One of them betrayed him."

"Perhaps it was someone in the village."

"Never."

Doesn't much matter now. "You're not about to die on me, are you, Father?"

"It's lodged in my hip bone. So, no. I'll live. But you'll need to get the fucking thing out and deal with any shit inside."

"We'll need water and fire. I've plenty of knives."

"First we need to get out of here."

"You'll last for a while?"

"Till morning, yes."

"Good. *Ya!*"

They brought their mounts to a halt two hours later, as dawn broke, spilling crimson light over a huge lake glittering off to the east. Arraleen dismounted and helped him from his horse. He was barely conscious, the left leg soaked with blood.

She made a fire, not caring if eyes would see. No choice but to keep him alive. She heated her dagger and found a stick for him to bite down on. She cut away his trousers with another dagger. As he'd said, the arrow was lodged deep.

She cursed profusely and washed the wound area clear of blood best she could. Not good.

"You ready, Father?"

"Do it." He bit on the stick.

The knife was hot enough. She examined the arrow again. Bodkin or barb? One way to find out. "Here goes," she said, and yanked hard, twisting, pulling the shaft free.

He choked, spat the stick out, and fainted.

She examined the arrow. Bodkin. *Good.* No splintering of flesh. She washed the oozing blood clean, until she could staunch the flow, sealing the wound with the heated knife.

That woke him, screaming until he fainted again. She tore off a clean strip of her shirt and bound the leg. Not pretty, but it would suffice.

Job done, she washed her face, kindled the fire, and swore at the sparkling pretty lake. A beautiful morning, but where the fuck were they?

CHAPTER 6 |OUT OF CHOICES

G ujun stood on the quay, watching the sunrise above the distant cliffs. He could see the villa clearly, shining like a huge square pearl. It was the place where he'd accompanied Grodu, on Magister Chulan's orders. And where he'd met the Sangala, and their master, High Califez Tulomon Caze.

Chulan had promised Gujun a villa in Shen once he killed the empress and the magister took her place. Instead, he'd killed Chulan. And now Grodu said he could have this Laregozan villa. A second chance. If he aided the Yamondon king.

I want that place. But . . .

He was tired of working for other people. Too many rules. *I need to think.* He stared for an hour, as the light changed and the water lapped below his feet. Finally, he sighed and strode back to the hut where he'd been sleeping. He'd decide today, he determined.

Gujun was cleaning his Jians when soft footsteps pricked his ears. He approached the broken window and gazed out, swords ready.

Kanemys was walking toward his hide, her dark hair wrapped in a shawl. Gujun frowned, and decided to go out there. Seeing him, she stopped and produced a parcel she'd hidden beneath her robe.

"I brought you some fish." She smiled.

"You shouldn't come here. You know what happened the other night. That's just the start."

"Lieutenant Garion sent me on Cama's orders. I'm sorry."

Gujun shrugged. "No matter, I was going to speak with Cama later."

"He's left for Talimi Garrison, where he's meeting with the Yamondons." She unwrapped the parcel, and it smelled wonderful. "You want this?"

They sat on the dock, the sun on their faces. She untied the shawl and shook her long curls. He liked her face—dusky skin freckled, the soft-brown clever eyes.

"The fish is excellent. I like the spice."

"Cumin."

She'd brought ale too, which he sipped slowly, having acquired the taste.

"What will you do?" She was glancing at him sideways,

masking a smile.

"I've been thinking about that."

"Surely there isn't much to think about. I mean . . . you don't have any choice, the way I see it."

Gujun smiled at her. "And how do you see it?"

"Captain Cama is a dangerous man. Ambitious. Wants to be general, perhaps rule Laregoza himself. He needs you, as does his ally, Grodu. They've known each other for years. Genza sent Captain Dranan to that villa knowing it was a trap, and the Sangala were waiting for him. Dranan was killed, but so were the Sangala, when Grodu turned up unexpectedly with a crazed Northman. Cama was Dranan's Lieutenant before his recent promotion. He wants revenge and holds the Ran in Cardalis accountable."

"This I know, though I'm not sure how you do?"

She raised a brow. "I work in a tavern."

"You're wasted there."

"Cama will kill you if you refuse his offer, or more likely send men to do so."

"I know that too."

"And you already have so many enemies. Why make more?"

"Because I don't like threats, and I'm tired of being told what to do."

"But you're an assassin."

"Yes. But I'm thinking about a career change."

She shook her head. "I'm worried about you."

"Why?"

She chewed her lip. "I like you, Gujun the Slayer. I'd like

to be your friend."

My friend . . . Why would you want to be my friend, woman? That way lies only pain. He reached forward and brushed his fingers against her cheek.

"I like you too, Kanemys."

"Call me Kanny, it's my nickname."

"Kanny then. You're the second person who wants me for a friend."

"Who was the first?"

"Big Grodu of Golt."

"Oh, no. I've heard he's a terrible man."

"Aye, he's useful. But talks too much." He gulped a bite of fish down. "Listen, Kanny. You don't want to be my friend. I'm not the sort of person who has friends. I'm a killer, and that means people want to kill me every day. Deal with a pest. It's best that you stay away from me. Anyway, my mind's made up. I've decided to move on."

"Vendel?"

"I have no wish to go to Vendel, I've heard it's a shithole."

"But Cama? And . . . Grodu—"

"Will be disappointed."

"Where then? You'll be hunted."

"Always." He smiled. "Since you're my friend, I'll tell what I'm thinking."

"I'm not going to like it, am I?" She crinkled her nose.

"Probably not, but here it is. I'm riding north to Cardalis."

"Why would you do that?" Her eyes were anxious.

"Because both your Captain Cama and Grodu the gladiator-cum-spy have made me an offer. It's only right I should give Ran Genza a chance to make me a better one."

She looked shocked. "You're serious, aren't you?"

"Always."

She stood. "I can't persuade you, so I should leave. You'd best leave too, Slayer. And quickly. They'll be coming, and fast, once I inform Garion of your decision. And others from Shen, I'll bet."

"I'll be gone when they come."

She nodded. "You are a strange man, Gujun the Slayer. But not the villain you think you are. I've known far worse men. I'm sorry you'll die soon."

That I doubt very much, but thanks for saying it. He flashed her a grin. "We all die, Kanny. But I'm far harder to kill than most."

She shook her head, disappointed. Then she wrapped the shawl around her face and left him without further word. He watched her walking slowly and sighed.

Guess I've made my mind up. Best go get ready.

Three days later, Gujun sat his stolen horse at a crossroads, the warm wind whipping his hair. He'd cut it shorter before he left, freeing the customary pigtails. His conversation with Kanny had helped him change. A new look for a fresh perspective.

Largos sprawled three miles below. At the far side, a broad sluggish river wound around dockyards and jetties. The city appeared much bigger than Soloza, sprawling for miles. He could see a huge temple dome dominating the central region. He scanned the low walls, the distant gates. A short ride. Best he wait until nightfall.

Kanny's news should throw Lieutenant Garion off the scent, until Cama returned from Talimi Garrison, wherever that was. *Hopefully not close to Largos*, he thought wryly.

He studied the terrain beyond city and river. Brown arid hills folded and lifted into stubble haze. He preferred Soloza, but the city below would hide him until he deemed it safe to return. Perhaps Kanny was right? He had a death wish. The sensible thing would have been to agree to help Grodu and the Laregozans. Keep him busy, and rich. But he'd not been overly sensible lately, ever since his rash choice killing the former magister. The strange thing was he didn't really care. Such nonchalance would get him killed sooner rather than later.

But I'm enjoying myself, a free spirit at last.

He found a shady spot under the gibbet that creaked and rattled at the corner. Just old bones up there. Gujun chewed on some jerky he'd acquired with the horse. He was half dozing when the sound of hoofbeats had him jumping up and leading the horse into undergrowth close by.

He waited, listened. Those horses were well shod. Soldiers. Had to be.

He tied the steed to a thorn bush out of earshot and crawled on his belly back to the road. He chose a concealed earth bank where he could get a good view and hear any conversation, should they rein in. He was in luck. Two riders arrived ahead of the main squad.

The officers looked sharp in their conical-pointed polished helms and glittering armor. They wore scimitars at their belts, and a round shield hung from their saddles. Their manner was relaxed, companionly. One turned and gazed at the spot where Gujun lay. He stared for a moment, before returning his gaze to the city.

Gujun mouthed a silent curse.

Lieutenant Garion. He hadn't trusted Gujun's word to the girl. But maybe this wasn't about him? Coincidence? He didn't believe in them. The other officer was speaking as his horse cropped grass at the verge. Gujun crept closer. Quiet as a dormouse, he perched low, listening as the two waited for their men.

"Think he'll attack first?"

"No, Kem. Genza's a lazy sod," Garion replied. "He'll wait and see if the Vendeli do his dirty work. Thinks Grodu's off arranging that."

"He must suspect the Yamondons are involved. He's not stupid."

"Yeah, but what can he do? He's safe as a bed bug up in Cardalis, with those fucking Immortals smothering him with lusty kisses."

"Can we beat them, Gar?"

"Cama says we can. Captain Dranan had other views."

"Dranan was always Genza's man."

"And look where that got him," Garion snorted. "What's keeping them?" He guided his horse over to the gibbet and looked for his troop. "They're taking their time," he grumbled.

"What his next move?"

"Genza?"

"No. Cama, you daft twat."

Garion grinned and struck his friend's shoulder with a riding crop. "Dunno, Kem, but I guess he'll wait on news from that Yamondon king, Ulani. He's been at the garrison all week expecting messengers from there. Meanwhile, we're camping outside Largos. By the river. Hope you've brought plenty of wine, Kem Dorle. You're duty quartermaster for this trip."

"We won't run short." The younger officer looked irritated. "What about the fugitive? The Shen Cama told us to keep an eye on?"

"He's in Largos."

"You said he rode north to Genza, the treacherous dog."

"That's what the tavern girl told me. And of course the little shit would have told her that."

Gujun raised an eyebrow. He'd misjudged Garion. The man was on to him.

"But why lurk in Largos, when he's pissed off both Cama and Grodu?" Kem Dorle said.

Sensible question. Don't know the answer . . . Gujun smiled wryly.

"And me." Garion spat on the dirt below. "I didn't like the fucker. Cocky little twat. That's why I'm scouring the city while we wait for Cama and his new Yamondon friends. Give our boys something to do. We'll nab this Slayer fellow, and let Cama decide what to do with him. Should be fun, Kem."

"Hmm, heard he has quite a reputation in the east." Kem turned his head, hearing shouts. "Here they are."

"About fucking time," Garion said as the sound of hoofs traveled close. Gujun squinted and saw the dust rising above a large troop of steel-clad horsemen. The soldiers rode up and joined their officers.

Garion surveyed the road and city again and held up his hand, motioning they ride on. The troop trotted on toward the city in double file.

As the men passed by, Gujun counted two hundred strong. He sighed. Looked like Largos was off limits for the moment. Should he return to Soloza? He wanted to, but they'd expect that and have soldiers waiting. And Lin Gu would have sent more men, with maybe some of his Silver Slayers among them. He clicked his tongue. Perhaps he should ride north to Cardalis again. No, that's a shithole. Cold and wet.

I like the sun.

Southward lay the ocean, and fat chance he'd get on a boat. Besides, he didn't know much about boats. *I'm out of choices.* He gazed west at the fuzz of brown beyond the river. It looked uninviting, hard country over there.

He walked back to the horse and untied the reins, leading her back onto the road.

"Looks like we're making for Permio, you and I."

Gujun took the north road down a long slope for ten miles until it veered left, hugging the river. Largos was lost behind. He stared at that dirty churning water. No way of crossing here. He rode on into evening, then stopped and rested his mare, risking a small fire. He had a day's jerky, no more.

No problem. The bow and shafts he'd stolen would catch him some quarry. He had his Jians, and the Chiang spear was tied to the saddle. And his seven throwing knives were strapped to the front of his twin Jian belts. What else would a fighting man require?

Next day revealed rougher terrain. Dry. Colder. The wind had picked up, and craggy brown cliffs frowned from the far banks. The road twisted north as dust blew in his face. It was almost evening by the time he reached another turn in the road.

Gujun reined in sharply. Here the road dropped steeply down to the river, where it curved and slowed around another bend. Shallower, but wider. Recently dredged, the mud scooped into banks on either side. The road straddled the sand banks over to a grassy island in the middle. Beyond that a sturdy wooden horse bridge spanned the forty-odd feet to the far side.

More concerning was the large network of stone buildings wedged tightly against a dun-colored cliff. A fortress. The road led right up to its iron gates.

Gujun chewed his lips. *Talimi Garrison.* Had to be. And even from here he could spot armor, as the evening sun glittered off helmets and hauberks.

He swallowed a curse. How to get around that? He saw a dirt track leading off to the south, before vanishing in the fuzz of hills beyond. Dare he chance that goat path at night?

He waited, half hidden beneath a scrubby olive tree, as the sun dropped crimson behind the hills. He'd wanted to wait a while, but the sound of hoofbeats left him scant choice.

He laughed to himself. He'd never believed in the gods, but he wondered if one of the most spiteful ones had taken against him.

Fuck it.

He clicked his tongue and guided the mare down the slope toward the banks and bridge. He rode across at ease, the brown water gurgling as he passed. The fortress was quiet. The horsemen behind were lost to the growing gloom.

He reached the far bank and urged his mare trot toward the fortress. So far so good. He stopped by the cover of some pines and looked back, spotting a dozen riders descending toward the river. No going back there.

Talimi Garrison was a hundred yards ahead, the goat path, fifty. The riders would be on him in minutes.

Here goes.

"Ya!" He squeezed his calves, urging the beast forward. "Come on, girl." He slapped her side as his knees guided her toward the goat track. He heard shouts from behind, saw torches winking on the walls to his right.

More shouts. An arrow struck a tree, another stuck in his saddle. *Fuck.* Too close for comfort, that one.

"Gallop, damn you!" He spurred her on, and the mare raced toward the gloom of hills as more arrows zinged and skidded into the dirt behind. He heard horns, shouting, and more riders were coming from the gates. He rode at full tilt until the road skewered up into the deepening night.

At last he slowed her to a walk, as the sounds of pursuit faded. It was too dark to maintain any good speed anyway. He guided her best he could, until reaching a high area with a wide view below. Here Gujun dismounted and grabbed his flask. He held it to the animal's mouth, allowing it to drink. He took a sip himself, then led the mount over to the ledge.

He saw the fortress half hidden below, and torches twinkling somewhere nearer. A scouting party sent to ensure he didn't return? He climbed back in the saddle and bid the horse walk on since the track was treacherous and steep in places. He rode carefully until the morning light spilled gray on a desolate open country.

Gujun rested the horse and managed a doze, until the wind had him moving again. Sharp and dry. A different land to the one he'd left across the river. He could see the haze of marshes fading southward. In the other direction were jagged hills and strange rock formations, with colors ranging from pale blueish-gray to dull red and amber. Neither way looked promising. Ahead, the land fanned wide and flat, without break or rise in the monotony. He saw no rivers or trees.

Too bad.

He rode for most of that day, allowing the horse to rest and crop on any stubby grass they came upon. That night Gujun slept on a cold rock, the horse standing silent beside him. Another day, and his food had gone. The water was running out. The horse would die before him, but neither of them would last much longer. No choice but to keep riding, until she collapsed or they got lucky and he sourced a stream. He doubted that would happen. More likely, he'd walk the land until he did the same. He laughed at his recent choices.

No change by afternoon. He slunk in the saddle as the mare trembled beneath him. Finally, she staggered. He slid from her back. Gujun looked her over, shaking his head. He stroked her neck and allowed her to drink again. She shivered, her eyes glazing. *Too bad . . . but this is for the best, old girl.*

"I'm sorry." He sliced his dagger across her throat. "But it's better than starving."

Gujun untied the Chiang spear and bow and arrows, and he staggered on, best he could, leaning on the Chiang and bow until darkness closed around him, the Jians' diamonds sparkling in the moonlight. He contemplated cutting his own throat. As he'd told the mare, it was better than the alternative.

His mind was wandering. He thought he saw movement. *Probably fever.* He laughed, as a light flickered close by, then faded. A second glowed and somebody spoke.

"Come and claim me, djinni. But beware, I've still my swords."

He reached back for his Jians, but lurched, as something hard struck his head. Another blow followed. Gujun pitched face first into the dirt and a heavy boot impacted his side. He blacked out.

He woke to the crackle of a fire. His tongue was swollen, and he felt weak as a kitten. He hoped they'd kill him soon. He stirred, groaned.

"He's woken up," a deep voice said, cheerfully.

"Tough little bugger," said another. The accents were strange. Permians, he suspected. Desert devils.

The sound of boots scuffed his way. One nudged his side.

"Why aren't you dead, little fellow?"

"Because I'm enjoying myself too much."

A chuckle. He sat up and spewed vomit into the dirt. He squinted. "Why didn't you kill me last night?"

"You seemed harmless, despite all your odd weaponry."

"You could have robbed me."

"What sort of men do you take us for?"

"Permians."

The kick was hard, and sent him sprawling. He spat blood and slid over, raising himself to his knees. "Point taken. But who are you then?"

A face emerged before him. Bizarrely scarred on either cheek, the skin black, and dark eyes hard. A warrior. But from where?

"I'm Agashi, a Tarak of the Third—and you, stranger, are in our camp. You wandered in here last night like a drunken farm wench."

"You're Yamondon?"

"Of course."

Gujun burst out laughing.

"He's a madman, it's as we thought, Tarak."

"What is funny?" the warrior asked him.

"Life." Gujun chuckled, then blacked out again.

CHAPTER 7|THE BORDERLANDS

Arraleen's father was feverish for three days. His color was pale, his mind wandering. She kept the wound clean, her thoughts angry and anxious. She'd found plenty of food. Caught fish from the nearby lake. Hunted and brought down a hare. Even foraged for mushrooms and wild garlic. Anything to help him recover.

Part of her training had involved healing. A necessary skill for a professional killer. You can't afford to lie around bleeding when things go awry.

During the three tense nights they'd spent sheltered under trees, she'd listened to his ramblings and mutterings, trying to piece together what had happened in distant Laregoza. How things had gone so wrong. He'd mentioned the Sangala a few times, and their leader, the sorcerer Octaxa. Another one with a similar name. Utuxla. No one she'd heard of.

He'd growled out the name *Grodu* several times. Octaxa's man had reported to her father direct. She knew he always liked the former slave gladiator. Turned out he was working for the Yamondons, or Laregozans. Maybe even the Shen? She didn't care, and it didn't matter. Grodu the traitor was high on her death list.

She'd slept fitfully, her ears primed for hoofbeats and boots. But the road remained quiet. More concerning was the change in the weather. That last evening, she saw storm clouds mustering over the silvered waters of the lake. They had to move before that rain soaked him again. His fever was better, the wound healing. But a cold deluge would reverse all that.

The fourth morning spit rain. She could hardly see the lakeshore, and the dark columns of clouds were nearer, threatening torrents and storm.

She woke him, mind made up. He looked pale, but his eyes were clearer.

"How do you feel?"

"Like shit." He grinned at her.

"Can you ride?"

"Not sure."

"Well, you're going to have to. Else we'll drown." She tilted her head in the direction of the lake.

"That's not good," he said.

"Come. I'll help you up, get you seated on that horse. We

need to stay ahead of the rain."

He wiped damp spots from his face. "Seems like it's already found us."

She nodded. "If we ride hard enough, we'll keep ahead. You up for that?"

"Not much choice, have I?"

"None."

She helped him find his feet. He almost stumbled twice, and cried out as the wound spasmed. Worse was getting him in the saddle, especially since the rain was falling harder each moment.

She managed, and led the horses back onto the road. Once there, she urged the mounts pick up pace, keeping an eye on him as they maintained a steady canter. An hour later they'd cleared the rains, a dark line filling the horizon behind. By afternoon, they were under blue skies, the air warmer. Encouraging. She felt better. He'd done well. Hadn't fallen or complained, though she could see he was in pain.

They rested in the sun for an hour and resumed in higher spirits, getting a good few miles covered before dark. That night she saw torchlight nearer the mountain's hem, a dark ridge flanking their right, four or five miles distant.

"Garrison camps," he told her. "Dalcians, I'll bet. More and more arriving on the Yanturi's orders."

"That means there'll be fewer of them in Dalcia." She grinned, but he didn't appreciate the joke.

"I'm slowing you down."

"Nonsense, we kept an even pace all day."

"Even so, I've changed my mind."

She flashed him an angry glance. "What are you talking about?"

"The Borderlands."

"What about them?"

"We're well south of Lake Stezel. We must be getting close to the Borzo River. Beyond that lie the Borderlands. Rough country hedged between the Borzo and Rozaco rivers."

"So? We'll cross both rivers and keep moving south."

"You will, yes. I'll stay put in the Borderlands."

"Evidently, you've lost your wits again." She wiped her mouth, annoyed with his nonsense.

"No. Arraleen. *Damn you*, girl. Listen to me."

She stared at him angrily, but nodded.

"I *will* slow you down. This wound will take time to heal properly, if it ever does. And it might get worse. One of us must avenge our family and honor. I'm starting to think that might have to be you. I know people in the Borderlands. Like Nuosta, they've scant love for the Yanturi or Omala. Unlike him, they're bandits with steel and caves to hide out in."

"Fine, we'll seek them out. Unite as many as we can, and plan the fight back."

"No. They will shelter me, until I can find a way to get back north without being detected. I'm going to kill the Yanturi, and that Sangala scum. I need you to take the game further. Go north, the long way. Take your time. Find Grodu and Ran Genza, and anyone else involved. And kill them all."

"We're staying together.

"My mind's made up."

"We'll talk about it later," she said, cursing beneath her breath. This stubbornness of his was jarring her nerves. "And we have to reach the Borderlands first, before that rain, so we can cross the river."

"True enough," he said. "But I need you to accept what I'm telling you. Grodu was in league with the Yamondons. Shen was involved too. I don't know how, but that little shit messenger their man sent arrived at the villa with Grodu."

"Gujun the Slayer? I'll gut him too."

"This has to be King Ulani's work. Put him on your list."

"That will prove harder." She grinned. "But I'll take Ulani, and slowly. Now stop fretting and get some rest, Father—you need it. We'll leave at dawn and seek your fucking bandit friends."

Next morning, he was stronger, seemed almost recovered. She'd washed his wound in fresh stream water and added another rip of her shirt for bandage.

They rode apace for most that day, daring the road, as the clouds were mustering and bulging behind. The rains would catch them up tonight, no avoiding that. And they'd be colder this far south. They'd had to detour through woods twice that afternoon, as rising smoke columns revealed more mercenary camps off to their right. By evening, they'd reined in on a high ridge and spotted the thin gray line of a river.

"Where do we cross?" she asked him, seeing no bridge.

"There's a ford. Tricky after dark, but we should manage if we're quick."

She gazed back. "We'd best get down there, before those storm clouds swallow us."

They reached the ford. The river was high, but the horses waded across without issue. She was proud of her father. He looked stronger, determined. Close to the south bank were reeds that avoided the worst of the wind. They huddled together for warmth that night, while reedy night birds piped shrill in the black. The thunder rolled north of the river, but mercifully the rains stayed on those hills, until dawn.

When the first gray light allowed, Arraleen walked to the crossing area and gazed back north, taking stock.

A misty morning. The dark ridge they'd left yesterday was occluded by rain. She saw lightning up there, heard the distant booms. The rains were mustering, gathering pace. They wouldn't be able to ride back to Omala for a month, whatever they'd planned. To the south, the road ran straight for a mile, before vanishing into hills. The mountains flanked the right, but those peaks looked smaller. She saw snow glinting on the furthest. The sight filled her with wonder, having never encountered it before.

He saw where she was looking and nodded. "We're near Dalcia. That's a cold country, especially in the coastal regions to the south. Desolate and dry. The Emerald Mountains break into foothills a few miles north of the Rozaco, and Gray River valleys—the Gray's the wide stream that separates Yamondo from Dalcia. A treacherous marsh festers in the region between rivers and foothills. This road greets the Rozaco twenty miles from here."

"Another ford?"

"A ferry. It's manned, for the river is wide and currents strong. Beyond the river, the road continues down to Dal City. You'll need to avoid that."

We will avoid it, Father . . . we. She shook her head, not ready to argue with him again. Instead, she changed the subject.

"Where are these friendly bandits you know?"

He pointed southeast. "In those hills, a few miles, no more. The high caves award fine views of both rivers and the ocean out east. A good vantage point, and hard to attack unnoticed. We'll need to leave the road in a mile or so. Cut across country. Hope to avoid the rains. It's heath and moor with little shelter. Going to be chilly, girl."

"I believe you."

It was more than chilly. The wind was bitter and biting. Her face and ears grew numb with its sting. She thought of the warm Vendeli sunshine. The cats basking idle, her lush home and gardens, and a hot scented bath. All gone. Burned to ashes.

Fuck you, Yanturi. All of you, bastards. Your time is coming.

Two hours later, they guided the horses over a flat-topped hill, the wind whistling in their ears. The first patter of cold rain found them, just as he pointed to a shadow of trees thrust between two larger hills.

"The caves are in there," he told her.

She laughed. "That's fortunate, because we're about to

get drenched."

Half hour later they were soaked to the bone, but he seemed fine and even looked excited. She was edgy, remembering how things had turned out at Nuosta's village.

They entered the dark canopy of pines. She was surprised how much colder it was than yesterday. *Raw.* They hadn't gone far when she reined in sharp, sensing movement. An arrow thudded into a pine trunk to her right. Another struck a tree in front. And a third skidded into the mulch near where they sat their horses.

She reached back for her bow, grabbing a shaft. Her father called out a name.

Silence.

The arrows stopped coming. She looked at him, but he shook his head.

"Give it a moment," he said.

She nodded, but kept an arrow nocked on string.

Several minutes passed, before a crashing announced heavy-shot boots approaching through the trees. Arraleen pulled a face at the clumsiness.

Someone laughed. A man appeared between tall pines. Stocky, red-faced, and smiling, though the grin was almost invisible under the mass of ruddy beard and whiskers. He was clad in steel rings and wet fur, a double-headed ax hung from one side of his belt, and a stout-looking sword on the other.

Her father motioned her to relax. "Master Trendale," he greeted the grinning man. "It's good to see you, old friend."

The tough-looking beard laughed. "As it is you, High Califez.

An honor! And who is this magnificent lady? What a stunner."

This one's full of shit. Arraleen narrowed her gaze and pulled back on the bow.

"Easy . . ." her father said.

Trendale laughed at her expression. "Let me guess, your daughter? The fabulously famous Arraleen Caze."

She felt her cheeks flush. "And who are you to know about me?"

"We've all heard about you, Dreamslayer. They sing bawdy songs about you in the Reech taverns. The corsairs down there like dangerous women."

"He talks too much," she hissed at her father.

"We need your help, Trendale," Tulomon Caze said, ignoring her.

"You'd best dismount and follow me," Trendale told them both while grinning at her. "The caves are warm and dry, tis but a few hundred yards away. But you know that, Spymaster." He switched his easy grin to her father, then back to her. "You can put the bow away, *killer cat.*"

Keep smiling, fat man. I'll shove this arrow up your arse if you don't shut up soon. Arraleen ignored the bandit and glared at her father, who nodded. Reluctantly, she stowed the weapon and shaft and slid off her horse, before assisting him off his. Trendale watched amiably as they guided the beasts toward him.

"How many rogues do you have hiding in the bracken hereabouts," she asked the burly Dalcian as they joined him.

"A few," he told her. "No more than a dozen." He winked, and she wanted to kick him in the balls. She restrained herself. They needed this man's help, though she'd sooner trust a serpent in the grass. Call it a hunch, but she didn't much like this bandit. Something felt wrong here.

"Come, good friends," Trendale told them. "We've fresh deer meat and good Reech ale to drive away the rainy chills." He glanced at her father and noticed him limping. "Is it bad?"

"It was," Arraleen told the bandit chief.

"We have herbs, and my woman, Orla, is skilled in their uses."

"As is my daughter here," her father said.

The trees parted, revealing a crack in the rocks ahead. A deep dark cavern. They entered after tying the horses to the post left for the purpose.

She stooped on entry, but was able to stand after a few strides. There were lanterns wedged in rock shelves. She felt the hearty blaze of a fire ahead and saw the red flames flickering on the lantern-lit cave walls. There were carvings on those walls. Odd-looking and foreign. She wondered what kind of men had lived here long ago.

Trendale urged them to settle. "Come. Sit by the fire, we've chairs and rugs—we live well here."

It seemed so. Arraleen was amazed at the luxury. Ornate lanterns, some painted with gold leaf. Thick rugs, with all manner of pattern and tread. And richly embroidered tapestries hanging from the cave walls. There were barrels of ale and stacked smaller casks of stronger liquor. She saw carcasses hanging from hooks thrust in the stone, and the smell of fresh meat had her nostrils tingling.

By the fire were three hunched figures. Two women and a man. They stared at her and her father as they approached.

"We've some exalted company for supper," Trendale told them.

After they'd dried off, Arraleen and her father were led to wicker chairs, which Trendale proudly explained he'd acquired while raiding a tavern near Dal City.

He was full of himself, this bandit chief. Still . . . they were warm and dry. She was grateful for that much. Her earlier apprehension faded as the fire flickered warm.

They feasted on deer and onions, their thirst replenished by strong ale. The bitter taste was strange to her lips, but not unpleasant. Trendale and his people let them be. He said there was plenty of time to catch up later that evening. He had to go out and meet some of his men who'd been on the coast, watching for traders stopping at the various coves. Wrecking was another of his enterprises.

She sipped her drink and relaxed best she could.

The curt Orla fussed over her father's wound, despite Arraleen saying it was improving. After that she left them be. Both women seemed on edge with Arraleen and mostly kept their distance. The lone bandit left with them appeared to be asleep, nodding by the fire. Her father looked tired, particularly after finishing his ale. She suggested he sleep as well.

A couple of hours passed slowly, the fire crackling, her father snoring beside her hunched in the creaking chair. But, though tired and her mind sluggish from heat and ale, Arraleen was restless. The edginess had returned. Something *was* wrong here. Her father might know this bandit chief well, but Trendale had hardly seemed surprised at their arrival, despite his pretense.

He finally reappeared as the light faded outside the caves. Tulomon Caze was awake and staring at the fire. Arraleen played with a knife, weaving it deftly between her fingers, still anxious, but also bored.

Trendale grinned at her. "I trust you're well rested, you pair?" Her father thanked him, and she nodded. He took the third chair and rubbed his hands together. "Getting colder out there," he said, his sharp blue eyes on them both.

Arraleen heard voices outside the cave. The accents weren't Dalcian, but Vendeli. She glared at Trendale and gripped her dagger. *What's this?*

He smiled and shook his head. "It is good to see your father, Dreamslayer. And to meet such a renowned lady. Unfortunately, others arrived here first and made me an offer I simply can't refuse."

I knew it. Arraleen stood slowly, eyes intent on the Dalcian. Her father swore and struggled to rise. Trendale coughed awkwardly.

She spat in his bandit face and jumped forward, lunging at him with the knife. He'd anticipated her move and threw his chair at her knees. Her father shouted, as shadows rushed into the cavern. Arraleen jabbed at Trendale's eyes, but he avoided her knife, still smiling. A skilled fighter, it appeared.

Someone grabbed her father and pushed him to the ground. She turned, snarling, the knife slicing air. An iron-hard hand slammed up under her chin and lifted, hoisting her off her feet. She broke loose, rolled, and jumped to her toes. There she squatted, hissing in a crouch, but a boot struck her mouth, splitting the upper lip, and knocking her on her back.

Someone stamped hard on her belly, and a dark face loomed over her.

"Good. You've done well, Master Trendale. I'll see you're compensated and the Yanturi's pardon arrives, as promised. We could use your rogues up in Omala." The voice belonged to Olgasha the Sangala, who stood grinning down at her.

"You." She choked back bile.

"The delightful Arraleen Caze. It's excellent to see you, hale and strong. We want you kicking nicely at the scaffold in Omala Palace. Before that special day, we'll have some fun with you."

"Fuck you." It was hard to speak with the blood in her mouth.

"I recall you saying that to me before. And to think you've had good breeding. Best I wash your mouth clean, hey? Hold the bitch," he said to the shadows standing beside him.

She was pinned, while Olgasha, laughing, lifted his leopard-skin kilt and soaked her swollen face as he eased the contents of his bladder. Once done, he kicked her ribs hard and stepped away.

"Hog-tie them well, especially her. We leave at dawn."

Arraleen's face stung with pain and fury. After more kicks and punches, she was overcome and beaten until she faded into black.

CHAPTER 8|THE BROWN LANDS

Gujun's eyes opened as cold water splashed his face. He blinked, and noticed it was morning. A dreary gray sky hung over him, and three tough-looking, very large men were staring at him, much like a hunter surveying his feeble kill. Or a fisherman, a disappointing catch.

He vaguely recognized the nearest face from last night. His vision was blurry, and eyes were swollen. And he was thirsty. He made a noise with his mouth.

"Little fellow's trying to speak." The familiar face smiled, wrinkling his ebony skin, curved scars on both cheeks. The other two had scars as well, but theirs were less impressive.

Gujun chuckled, and one of the men glowered at him. The leader scratched his head.

"You are a strange little fellow. We'll give you some water so you can speak properly and tell us why you were spying on our camp."

"Must be a Vendeli scout," the one on the right said. That one despised him for some reason. That wasn't important. Water was.

The one that hadn't spoken shoved a gourd in his face. Gujun lifted a shaky hand and sipped the warm liquid. Brackish and sour, but it worked. He sipped again, draining the gourd.

"Steady," the leader said. "You want to keep it in your belly."

Gujun nodded and belched. He felt his stomach spasm, but he kept the water down. He smiled up at the three.

"Thank you," he croaked. They looked at him curiously. Slowly his memory returned, as the haze of pain and thirst faded. "What's a Tarak?" he asked the leader.

The man stared back at him, his hard face expressionless. "Where are you from, Outsider?"

"Shen."

"He's got to be the one they mentioned. The killer on the loose," the hostile one said.

The leader sniffed the air. "Are you the little assassin my new friend Captain Cama spoke about?"

Gujun shrugged.

"I'll take that for a yes."

"So? Kill me, and be about your business." Gujun feigned a yawn.

The two warriors looked startled, but the leader laughed.

"We might do that, yes," he said. "But I'm curious about you.

That charming Laregozan fellow said there was a fugitive killer from the east. Cama suspected he was working for the Vendeli, and asked for us to put an end to the pest should we apprehend him."

Gujun said nothing.

"Do you work for the Vendeli?"

"I don't work for anyone. I contract out."

"Who's paying you?"

"No one. I'm retired."

"Pah. He's a funny little fellow, isn't he?" the leader said to the other two.

"Slit his throat and be done, Tarak," the sour-faced one said. "We need to move. Cross the Brown Lands before the bastard nomads arrive."

"You fret too much, Olgara." The leader was still smiling. He seemed genuinely amused by Gujun. That was new. People either hated or feared him. Lately one or two had liked him. Nobody laughed at him.

Gujun looked hard at the leader. "You should do as that one says." Gujun nodded at Olgara, currently glaring back at him. "I don't like people laughing at me."

"Well, that's a pity," the leader said. "And we do have to get moving. Olgara's right. This desert fringe area is notorious for nomadic tribesmen and horse thieves. We Yamondons are fearless and invincible, but a hundred of the turds might cause my six a problem."

Only six, good to know. "So . . . tell me. What's a Tarak. A captain, of sorts?"

"This is what we're going to do," the leader said, ignoring his question again. "We'll water and feed you, keep you alive. You will accompany us back to Cantacari. Our Tarakai will want to interview you. Spy or not, you shouldn't be creeping about out here."

"I've scant interest in journeying with you," Gujun said. "I know little about your country, and don't really give a shit."

The leader struck his face and Gujun smiled.

"The little fool's wrong in the head, Tarak," said the one who'd offered him water.

The leader shook his head. "I don't think so. This tough little bugger has a tale to tell, and we should hear it. With that in mind, I'm going to give him another chance." He turned to Gujun.

"Are you spying for Tulomon Caze?"

Gujun laughed again, but before the leader hit him, he held up his hands. "I'm sorry, but that's a touch ironic, isn't it?"

"Why?"

"Because both that Laregozan hound, Cama, and Big Grodu asked me to kill Tulomon Caze."

"You know Grodu?" The leader's expression turned serious. Gone were the easy smiles and joking manner.

"He's my friend," Gujun said. "Or, at least wants to be."

Olgara stood angrily and reached for a knife at his belt. "He's a fucking liar."

"Leave it," the leader said. Olgara glared at him, but nodded. The Tarak turned to Gujun. "How come you know Grodu? He works for the Sangala in Kulshana."

"We both know that he works for your king," Gujun replied.

"And the Sangala are dead. Or if any live, it's because I haven't killed them yet. I don't like those ghoulish bastards."

The leader's face softened. His dark eyes were curious, but no longer angry. Olgara shook his head but sat back down again, his expression resigned.

"A Tarak commands two hundred men," the leader told him. "A Tarakai, two thousand. Or a Tark, as we call that number. A Tark is similar to the regiments those northern armies have. There are ten Taraks to every Tark. Three Tarks comprise the king's Elite Guard. We're the Royal Third, led by the hero, Dolusa Tarakai."

"Thanks," Gujun said wryly. *I'd write that down if I knew how.*

"Agashi here is Dolusa's cousin," the one with the gourd said. Gujun remembered the name from last night. Agashi the Tarak. These big Yamondons were strange people.

"Distant cousin." The leader, Agashi, smiled. "Else, I might have been promoted to Second Tarakai by now."

"Does the Second Tarakai command half a Tark?" Gujun asked them, deeming it a practical question.

"No? *What's he talking about?*" Agashi looked at his men, who shrugged.

"Grodu is fond of your king," Gujun said softly. The sky had pinkened, and a warm wind blew from a distant ridge.

"He has cause to be," Agashi said. "That warrior owes Ulani everything."

"In return, he surrendered his freedom to work for Caze, as a double spy."

Agashi grinned. "You really do know Grodu."

"Two things about me, big man. You don't laugh at me, and I don't lie. Understand that, and we'll get on."

Agashi nodded slowly, as though chewing that over. "Tell me your name, fierce one."

"Gujun of Pol Shen. Some call me the Slayer."

"Hmm." Agashi shared a wry glance with his men. "Dreamslayer and Slayer. Two sides of a spinning coin. Odd coincidence. Dolusa will be most curious about you. He was in Laregoza a couple of months back, and I seem to recall a mention of your name."

The one with the gourd rose silently. "Sun's rising, we need to move."

Agashi nodded. "Can you ride, Gujun the Slayer?"

Gujun nodded.

"Excellent! You can sit on the pack pony and warm our supplies. We'll talk more this evening."

"Sounds like a plan," Gujun said, and the one with the gourd laughed out loud.

That one punched his shoulder. "You're a strange fellow, Little Brother. But I like you." He grinned and went to fetch the pack pony.

Thanks. Gujun coughed and recovered his balance, as he watched them breaking camp. *Not sure I feel the same way, Big Man. But thanks.*

The terrain got rougher throughout that morning, as Agashi's troop rode their dappled stallions across a maze of tufted grasses, loose shale, and mud. All around were strange-looking towers of rock. Gujun was fascinated by the landscape. The rocks ranged from red and gold, sometimes even dark blue. Carved by weather or gods—he knew not which—into castles, and dragons, and beasts, and smoky demons. *Our world is magical.* He needed to stay alive to see more of it. The thought gave him purpose.

By afternoon they'd reached a wide basin, the strange rock formations slipping behind. It was hot, and a fierce wind whipped dust in his eyes. The six riders guided their beasts in a line. Gujun rode the spare pack horse behind them, his mind and body tired, but no longer hurting. And his eyes were clear.

The cheerful one who'd given him water rode in front. His name was Rogashi, and he seemed a decent sort. But of course, they were all devils. The world might be beautiful, but its people weren't. Except maybe Kanny. And he dared not get soft dwelling on her charms. To trust was to die. Still, these Yamondons made for reasonable company. Gujun was short of options currently, so happy to partake in their journey. At least for the time being.

They crossed that wide basin by dusk and camped the night under bright stars. The moon had risen full, like a blood orange in the west. Shrill birds were calling from far away.

"How long before we reach your country?" Gujun asked Rogashi, as the Tarak and his men discussed the day's progress over a scant fire. He felt better, stronger, and much recovered. And strangely, he was enjoying himself.

Rogashi grinned at him. "A week's steady ride through the Brown Lands to the borders. After that another week's ride south to Cantacari."

"The Brown Lands?"

"This half desert region you're liking so much. Technically, we're in Permio, but this area's disputed by the Permians, the Vendeli, and ourselves. Even Golt sometimes. The Brown Lands are mostly empty, though the caravans have to cross through here from those northern cities at the far side of the Great Sand."

"Permio has cities? I'd heard it was just desert and goat shaggers."

"It's *mostly* desert and goat shaggers. In the far north, there are three great cities. The occupants are even worse than the desert folk."

I need to go there. Gujun was fascinated. He wished he could see a map.

"The Permians are like the Vendeli?"

"Fuck, no." Rogashi stared at him as though he'd lost his wits. "They're filthy throat cutters and camel thieves. But compared to the Ven . . ."

Gujun let that pass.

"Why are you six out here?" he asked eventually. It was Agashi who answered, having joined them.

"Our king seeks trade in the east. The Vendeli commanded those strange waters, as we do the western oceans. Ulani means to change that. With Caze neutered or dead. And the power of the Sangala conjurers broken, Vendel is more vulnerable than it's been for years. Their young ruler is a vain fool, apparently. His court full of fawning turds who have no notion of how to fight a war. Tulomon Caze is different. That man's a battle genius and has caused us trouble for decades."

Gujun nodded. It made sense. "So Cama has promised you trade rights at Largos and Soloza—and not the Vendeli, who Genza supports."

"He needs our help with his little revolution." Agashi tore into his jerky, worrying the dry meat with a tooth. "It's why my men and I volunteered for this foray into the dreary countryside. We help the Laregozans overthrow their tyrant in the north, in exchange for free tariffs and passage to your eastern land, and beyond. Shen will soon bask in Yamondon treasures, my new friend."

"But you need Caze dead first."

"Grodu was tasked with that by the king, after Caze fell out of favor with his master. Caze is devious, and knows many people. Ulani expects him to slip the Yanturi's nets and hide out in Dalcia. He has contacts way down there. Tarakai Dolusa thinks Grodu will make for Dalcia too. Cama told me that he'd already departed for Kulshana, ignoring Genza's orders to stay in Largos."

Gujun nodded slowly. "Say that I decided to kill this renegade spy master. How much gold would your king pay me?"

"More rubies and gold than you could carry."

"I can carry a lot." Gujun pictured the villa in Soloza. Maybe he should have listened to Grodu. The powers were shifting and these Yamondons looked to be gaining ground. With their help he could return to Laregoza, live out his dream. Perhaps even Lin Gu would lose interest in his head if enough Yamondon treasure came his way. *No.* Gu was an honorable man. The assassins would keep coming. Which was good, because else he'd lose his edge.

"What are you thinking, Slayer?" Agashi's keen eyes probed his.

"That the world is very big," Gujun said.

"It's small, when your reach is long enough."

The next days were a haze of leaden skies and constant wind. They passed one struggling stream and filled the water gourds, while allowing the mounts have their fill of the muddy water. Rogashi explained that camels were better for this part of the journey, but the ungainly beasts were hard to acquire since the Permians usually stole them from the markets or caravans.

"What's a camel?" Gujun had asked.

"Horrible bad-tempered horse-like beast, with a giant baked turd on its back," had been the answer.

Gujun decided the pack horse suited him fine.

On the fifth day, the terrain changed. Ahead rose a reddish wall of rock. Above it, Gujun saw birds circling high.

"Vultures," Rogashi said. "Something dead out there."

An hour later they reined in at a gruesome sight. The storm of birds above had revealed more of the ugly things, hopping and feasting on decaying flesh. Some fifty or more bodies were strewn across a camp, all filled with arrows.

Agashi signaled and they rode closer. There were horses'

hoof marks in the clay, and the unshod cloven tread of other beasts, perhaps the camels Rogashi had mentioned. The animals must have been stolen by the raiders. Gujun frowned when he saw women and the odd child among the corpses. What reckless folk would lead their families out here?

Rogashi saw where he was looking and nodded. "Merchant caravan. See the wagons?" He pointed off to a rise at the base of the ridge. Over there Gujun saw strange-looking carts abandoned in the wind, their red and yellow cloth sides flapping and contents spilled out on the dirt. The wagons were painted in gaudy colors and daubed with reddish satins.

"Down from Syrranos, I'd guess," Rogashi said.

"Where's that?"

"Miles from here. One of the coastal cities I mentioned. Far beyond the Crystal Mountains and Copper Desert. A month's journey, maybe more."

Gujun shook his head. "Why come here? Risk death?" It didn't make sense.

"Because Yamondo is rich, Little Shen Brother." Rogashi grinned at him. "And those Permian merchants like their gold. They trade goods they've stolen from Kaelin and Raleen and the other northlands beyond the ocean up there. A life on the road is dangerous, but profitable."

"A large caravan," Agashi said, as he rode back to join them. "We counted twenty wagons a mile back. Nomads had a good time here it seems. Couldn't even be bothered collecting their arrows."

"Where have they gone?" Gujun asked.

"Hopefully back north. Or west into the sand to gorge on their booty. But we need to move, in case there are more around. Like those devil birds, and flies, the nomads tend to cluster in large groups."

"I think I'd enjoy killing some of these nomads," Gujun said, staring at the body of a young girl with her dress torn, legs akimbo and throat cut.

"You might get your wish before this day is over," Agashi told him grimly.

They left the caravan mess behind and guided their beasts up the steep ridge, leading to a fine vista awarding panoramic views south.

Gujun shielded his eyes from the glare and stared from his pony, seeing a vague green haze in the distance.

"Yamondo," Rogashi told him proudly. "The green marks the path of the Yagano River. That wide stream forms a marshy boundary between our country, Permio, and Golt."

"Golt?"

"You don't need to know about Golt."

Gujun remembered something. "Grodu comes from Golt."

"Best thing he did was leave that place," Rogashi said, and he spoke no more on the matter.

They were halfway down the far side of the ridge when an arrow struck one of the six in his thigh.

"Nomads!" Agashi yelled, raising his hand. The wounded rider slumped forward but kept his seat as more arrows zinged past Gujun's ears. He heard the thunder of hoofs on stone, and turned in his saddle, seeing twenty or more robe-swathed riders—a few firing bows, but most hefting long spears.

Riding beside him, Rogashi pulled his horn bow free and nocked an arrow. He turned and loosed in one fluid movement. Gujun saw a nomad tumble from his horse.

"I couldn't have done that much better myself," he muttered, impressed.

"More ahead!" he heard Agashi shout, as fresh arrows spat down at them from the ridge to the right.

"Here, climb over, Little Brother," Rogashi told him. "That pack nag's too slow." The Yamondon slowed his horse, allowing Gujun to jump across from the pony onto his destrier. He kicked his heels and spurred the beast faster, catching up with the other five heading for a narrow gulley of rock.

"Bad place for an ambush," Gujun yelled in Rogashi's ear as they funneled into the canyon.

Predictably, more arrows came from above as they cantered through the canyon, weaving their horses from side to side. They were excellent riders, as well as fine shots. Gujun had his Jians and knives, but both the Chiang spear and his bow had been left behind with the struggling pack horse. Too bad.

As they reached the end of the canyon, a small group of robed riders appeared and blocked them off. A larger knot was closing on them from behind. And more still on the ridge above.

"What do you think, lads?" Agashi yelled.

"Let's take 'em!" his men roared as one.

Gujun slid his Jians free, and his knees gripped Rogashi's

horse. The six Yamondon mounts thundered toward the milling riders at the canyon end. Algashi shot one through the eye. Someone else skewered a second.

Then they were on them and Gujun got his wish. Wedged in a press of horse and rider, he sliced and jabbed, lunged and twisted.

A tribesman with a spear thrust at Rogashi's leg, biting through leather and flesh. That stab would have severed the limb, had Gujun not intervened. His left Jian trapped the spear, while the right stung the nomad's face, and he dropped away.

Steel clashed and men screamed. Horses snorted and pushed. Gujun killed three more. Then they were through with open ground ahead. The nomads poured arrows after them, but the Yamondons got away without further hurt.

Algashi ordered a stop when they'd pulled far enough in front to ease back. Rogashi was grinning, despite his calf bleeding into his left boot.

"I owe you a leg, Little Brother," he said, and Gujun grinned back.

"Will they follow?" Gujun asked Agashi, as he checked horses and men. The one who'd been shot was smiling fiercely, the shaft still protruding from his thigh.

"Unlikely," Agashi replied, as he helped the wounded man from his horse. Gujun watched the rocks behind. He turned, seeing Agashi twist and pull the arrow from his man. The fellow grinned as the shaft came free. After that he blacked out. They were tough bastards, these Yamondons.

They rode until dusk, then camped in a dry riverbed, as fruit bats shimmered in the moonlight.

"We're nearing the river," Rogashi told him. "Can you sense it in the air?"

"No." Gujun couldn't smell anything but the same fly-stinking shit that had lingered around his nose since leaving Laregoza.

"Yamondo." Rogashi grinned. "She's close."

"You talk about your land as though it's a woman."

"She is—and the greatest one living."

Gujun let that go. Strange folk indeed.

"You saved my life, Little Brother," Rogashi told him. "From this day forward, Gujun the mighty Shen Slayer, you are my friend."

Gujun barked back a laugh.

Rogashi looked pained. "Now you insult me. What is funny?"

"You're the third person who's called me that in a month. I'm Gujun the *Slayer*. I don't have friends."

"You do now." Rogashi slapped his back, a sledgehammer bow that left him choking.

The nomads left them alone that night. Gujun suspected the cowards had been surprised by the savagery of their intended prey. Better they stick to the caravans and merchants. He vowed if he ever returned to these parts, he'd kill every nomad and tribesman he encountered.

By the following afternoon, even Gujun's nose detected a change in the atmosphere. He smelled water an hour before seeing it. It was almost evening when they arrived at the muddy reedy banks of a broad steamy river.

Agashi grinned at him. "The Yagano. We'll cross in the morning and ride south. Welcome to Yamondo, Slayer."

"Thank you, but how do we cross that?" The river was almost half a mile in width.

"We sit on our horses and they carry us over."

"Snakes?"

"Lots." Rogashi grinned. "Crocodiles too. And leeches. And nasty stinging flies."

"You people are mad."

"That's why you fit in so well, my friend."

"Don't call me that."

"All right, Little Brother. Sleep well."

CHAPTER 9| THE GLADIATOR

Arraleen struggled in vain as the horses trotted along a ridge, the sun glinting through trees and stabbing her eyes. Her lip was swollen badly and she half choked in pain. Ropes were lashed to her wrists and ankles, and her bruised body was straddled over the pony.

Worse was the smell. And the outrage visited upon her by their captor. How many of them rode with Olgasha? No way of knowing. But that villain Trendale had sold them to the Sangala. She should have trusted her senses. Seething, she worked her fierce mind as best she could, as the jolting and thuds sent spasms of pain through her head.

Where was her father? Somewhere in front, she assumed. Olgasha had gone that way. The ropes had no give. She still had her tiny thumb dagger in the secret sleeve fold. But how to reach it?

Tonight. She'd try tonight.

Any night, and every night. She only needed the one chance. It was a long ride back to Omala.

Free herself and her father. Kill the Sangala and his Dalcian dog. *No problem.* She spat blood in the dirt passing beneath her eyes. She forced her mind to relax, absorbing the pain and discomfort. She needed her strength for later.

An hour passed, perhaps two. Hard to tell when trussed like a sack of grain over a swaying saddle. She'd almost dozed at the monotony when a harsh cry brought her back. Another shout. And a third, and someone's death cry following. They were being attacked. But by whom?

Damn this.

The pony jolted to a halt as the column ahead faltered. She saw a black arrow scud into a tree. Another struck soil, and more riders were screaming.

Father! What if he was killed in the crossfire?

She wriggled and twisted. More shouting. More whistling arrows and death screams. The sounds of fighting faded off. She was at the back of the column, abandoned for the moment.

On impulse, she wormed her lean body forward, until her head hung over the pony. She kept working her elbows and knees, and at last her upper body slid under the animal's belly. The beast stayed put despite stamping its feet. The fighting had resumed somewhere deeper in the woods.

Upside down, she flexed her wrist and wriggled, until the tiny thumb dagger dropped into her palm. She squeezed with swollen fingers, gripped the knife handle tenuously, and sliced up. The rope tore, but not enough. She sliced again, nearly dropping the knife as the pony jolted in panic.

"Hold still, fuck you."

She sliced hard at the rope, cutting through but nicking the animal's skin. The pony snorted and shook its body, throwing her off to the side, the ropes binding her painfully and almost breaking her right wrist in the fall.

She cursed in pain and wriggled, sliced again. Her left hand came free and still gripped the knife. She worked quickly, freeing the hurt wrist and cutting the lashes at her ankles. Finally, she painfully dropped into the soil and rolled free of the kicking pony. She rubbed her bruises and cursed again.

Father . . .

Arraleen ran for the cover of brush, the sound of fighting off to her left. She scanned the track through the woods. They hadn't reached the road. Maybe other bandits had wanted Trendale's catch? It didn't matter. She had to find and save her father.

There were bodies a few yards up the track. Three men, all Vendeli. She smiled when she saw that the third had her scimitars strapped to his belts. She stole back out onto the track, being careful not to get noticed. She tore her swords from the corpse's belt and spat on his dead face. Arraleen helped herself to daggers and a short spear from the three.

Once sufficiently armed, she crept back into the undergrowth and started crawling over toward the noise. Men fighting desperately, it faded to the sounds of scuffles. She froze when she heard a long-agonized scream. An execution. Or punishment. After that, the sound of hoofs thundered into the distance. Then nothing. She was alone in the woods. They'd taken her father. But where, and who were they?

She returned to the track, walking briskly, the swords strapped to her side and spear held ready with both hands. More corpses. She grabbed a bow and scooped up some arrows.

Agarra, Mighty Huntress, guide me.

She felt better, in control again. Her mouth stung with rage and pain. The wrist had swollen already. But at least the day was looking up.

She'd counted twenty corpses by the time she reached the road. All the slain were Vendeli. The raiders had known where to strike. Seemed like Trendale wasn't that worried about the Yanturi's pardon. And where was that bastard Olgasha? She wanted him alive. No sign. The snake had escaped and left his men to die. Small matter. She'd deal with him soon enough.

"Father, your plan's shit," she muttered, trotting along the road looking for signs. She found the hoof marks where they'd left the woods. Twenty, perhaps thirty riders. *Heading south?* She shook her head in confusion. Why south? Scant rewards down there.

"South it is," Arraleen said irritably, as she started hobbling down the lane, bow nocked with arrow in left hand, spear gripped in right. She reached the crest of a small hill and saw their horses in the distance. A mile or so. No more. She'd never catch them without a horse. But she'd walk all night until she reached their camp. They'd stop at dusk with no need to hurry, their party just begun.

She was fortunate, because half a mile later a stray horse wandered toward her down the road. One of the Vendeli mounts had escaped the ambush.

"Game on," Arraleen snarled as she vaulted onto the horse's back, cursing her sore wrist and wiping blood from her seeping upper lip.

She rode apace for an hour, keeping the Dalcians in view but staying far enough back to avoid getting spotted. She was right. They camped by a river at dusk, scarce twenty yards from the road. She'd wait until nightfall, grab some rest first. She was bone weary, and hurting bad. Her body need attention, and her lip would pucker. She'd find needle and thread in that camp, and stitch it once she'd freed him.

First, she had to find where he was trussed up. Sick or not, he'd be waiting his chance to evade capture. He'd also assume she'd escape and come after him.

Stay strong, Father. I will free you.

She closed her eyes and dozed for a time. Somewhere an owl spoke, and she blinked, seeing the full moon riding the trees above. She shivered. *Agarra hunts beneath the night skies.* Time she did the same. Arraleen rubbed her swollen arm and stole toward the campfires. She crouched low in some furze and scanned their movement.

She counted twenty-two bandits. But there would be guards. Men like Trendale took nothing for granted. She could see the bandit chief chewing on a shin bone, laughing in his beard with another two hunched by the fire. A miserable bundle squatted uncomfortably to the right. She scowled seeing her father move his head. His face was covered in blood. She barely contained her rage, as she stood and nocked silent arrow to string.

Trendale was laughing. She aimed and waited, and a cloud stole the moon. *Agarra, help, I need more light to guide my arrow.* She mouthed the silent prayer and eased back on the string, the men having vanished as darkness settled in the camp. The faggots flickered and she glimpsed Trendale's face. He wasn't laughing. She heard the owl again, closer this time.

Damn these clouds. They were racing above, too damn dark to shoot. Her only option was getting closer. She started moving, but froze when a sudden stab of lightning lit up the wood. For the briefest second, she imagined she saw a man leaning on a staff, his face intense and hair the deepest red she'd ever seen. Thunder rolled and he vanished back into gloom.

She shook her head, moved forward. The fire was abandoned, the flames barely embers. "Where are they?" she hissed under her breath.

She sensed movement off to her right. The tossed knife glinted. She ducked low as the blade struck a tree. Running at crouch, she caught up with the lookout. He turned, swiping with steel. She tripped his legs with the bow and stabbed the arrow into his eye, smothering his mouth to stifle the scream.

She moved forward. The camp looked empty. Where had they gone? And who the fuck was that stranger with the fiery hair?

A shout to her right, followed by a stifled scream and thud. Someone else was hunting. Who? *Agarra, help me, damn you!* What was happening here?

Angry, and intent, Arraleen raced into the camp, just as fighting and shouts broke out further away from the road. The faggots had been kicked out, and she saw the shadows of men clambering onto horses.

For a second, she glimpsed Trendale staring back at her. He raised a hand in greeting, and vanished into the trees. She set arrow to nock, but the sound of hoofs thudded off deeper into the woods. She had missed her chance.

Cursing both the goddess and herself, she ran, searching and seeking. Trendale had fled, but men were still fighting close by. Perhaps the bandits had quarreled amongst themselves about who would keep her father's bounty. Where was he? Trendale must still have him. But why hadn't he come for her too?

She saw moving shadows framed by a large oak. A big man was wielding a spear, hacking left and right and jabbing. Three attackers were cornering him.

On impulse she rushed that way, dropping the bow and tossing the spear into the nearest one's back. The Dalcian pitched forward, his face thudding into dirt.

The big shadow pinned the second attacker through his chest

with the spear as she leaped at the third, her spear jabbing. The Dalcian blocked with a heavy sword. She deflected the blade, and slid her spear tip along its length, slicing through his fingers.

He yelled and let go, and she jabbed him in the throat.

Someone laughed. The shadow warrior had vanished. Instead, she was surrounded by grinning Dalcians. One held a net and started spinning.

She dived low, avoiding the cast net, rolling and wrenching a scimitar free, slicing the legs out from the first attacker.

The net whooshed over her head. She kicked out, taking one man in the groin, but was forced back by a second. A knife jabbed at her throat, the attacker grabbing her from behind. She twisted, slammed her elbow back into his face, and spun about, the scimitar cutting air.

It was no good. A dozen Dalcians had her hemmed. The one with the net was grinning without teeth. "This bitch will fetch a fine price in the markets," he said.

"Where's my father?" she spat at them.

"On his way to the Reech." The net carrier laughed.

"Where?" she hissed.

"Eagle Kelgar's lair. He's a feared Reecher and got word of your plight, my dear. Trendale's happy to comply." He laughed, and was about to say more when the shadow reappeared, crashing into his back. He was a huge warrior wielding a heavy sword and spear.

The net carrier lurched forward and stumbled, as his head rolled free from the neck. The shadow killer rammed the spear into the next man and twisted the blade, pulling it free before stabbing a third.

She sliced into the back of another, killing the next as he turned her way.

The big warrior had dropped his spear and held the heavy curved sword with both hands, slicing, hacking, and battering any flesh in reach.

She panted, swore. Swiped and sliced. Cut and stabbed, until nothing moved except the big fighter who stood staring at her from the gloom of trees.

The moon appeared and she caught a glimpse of his face. It was Grodu, her father's man in the east. The traitor who'd betrayed them.

"You." She walked toward him, her scimitar dripping blood.

He waited, resting on his tulwar.

"Defend yourself," she told him, her sword hot and slippery in her fingers.

"Kill me, and you'll never see your father again." The voice was deep, sonorous.

"You betrayed us. This is all your fault." She jabbed at him with the scimitar. He didn't move, sensing her strike was a bluff.

"It's a matter of perspective," he said. "You, girl, wouldn't understand."

You bet I fucking wouldn't. "Try me."

"Maybe if you stow that blade."

"Not before I stick it up your arse."

"Again. You won't save him without my help."

"Your help?" She laughed bitterly. "I thought that twisted cunt Olgasha was bad news. *You—*"

"Are your ally, for the moment, at least."

She hissed back at him, but he folded his massive arms over the sword hilt.

"All right, talk." She rested the scimitar. The sky was paling off east. Dawn soon. She needed to get going once she'd killed this bastard.

"I know where they're taking him."

"The Reech. I've already heard."

"The Reech is a big area, Dreamslayer. Even you wouldn't last long alone in that place."

"It will take tougher bastards than you to stop me."

He chuckled and wiped blood from his face. "Trendale works for Eagle Kelgar the Corsair, has done for years. Kelgar is one of the most notorious among the corsairs. There are dozens of rival camps on the Reech, Kelgar's crew and Torax Stone Eyes among them."

"So?"

"I know Kelgar, and his lair's location. On an ice island just off the mainland. Grim place. You see, my real master has dealings with him from time to time. Needs must. The corsairs are practical folk. Not fussy who they work with. Both Eagle Kelgar and Stone Eyes know everything that happens south of the Rozaco, and most above too."

"I'll find him, I don't need a traitor's help."

He scowled. "I work for Ulani III. The greatest king in the world. Your father meant little to me, and it was him who placed me in the fighting pits, under the old Yanturi's orders."

"You're the Sangala's scum."

He looked angry hearing that. "Octaxa freed me because he and your father saw my worth. And I was helpful to both of them. But more so to my king."

"Tell me how to find this corsair, and I'll kill you quickly."

"We work together, else I kill you instead."

"You're too fat and slow."

"Try me." He flashed her a grin. "But know first that your father is lost to you forever. I suspect Kelgar will sell him on to Olgasha at a higher price."

"Where's the Sangala hiding?"

"Gone, but not far, I'd warrant. Sangala don't take well for being made fools. He won't want to return north without your father, or at least his head. I expect we'll encounter Olgasha again soon. Or worse, his sorcery."

Arraleen nodded slowly. "You've been stalking us for a while, Creeper."

"Since the caves. I'm familiar with Trendale too, you see."

"Say I agree . . . what do you get out of this?"

"I get to serve my king, by bringing him your father as a . . . *guest*, or hostage. But alive, on that you have my word."

"The word of a traitor."

"The word of a gladiator, and winner of thirty-five contests. Tulomon Caze is out of options, lady. Your father will die horribly. Either in the Reech, or under Olgasha's hot knife. Or worse still, on the Yanturi's velvet pleasure scaffold. I've seen what they do to prisoners there."

"And more likely worse yet in Yamondo."

"*No.* Ulani has always admired your father as a worthy adversary and cunning player. Both of you will be treated with the respect you deserve. I know my king, and he wants Vendeli neutered. That means your father removed from the game."

"In other words, dead."

Grodu stowed his sword and held his huge hands out wide.

"What choice have you, Dreamslayer? It's almost light, we've horses nearby. I know Dalcia. I know their strange ways. Help me find your father and rescue him. After that we can decide whether we still want to kill each other."

She stared at him as the sky paled through the trees.

"Agreed?" He flashed her that evil grin.

"You help me find and rescue my father. Then I'll kill you. *Agreed*, it is."

He laughed. "Excellent. Best we find some horses, Arraleen Caze."

"First, I need to search these bastards for some needle and thread."

He watched indifferently, as she pored over the corpses' purses and pouches, taking whatever she deemed useful. Odd copper coins, a wafer, token, or talisman. An occasional small knife. You could never have enough knives in this world. She found what she needed and seated herself on a stump, working the needle through her upper lip. The hip flask of alcohol was a bonus.

He watched her in silence until she'd tied off the end. Her

mouth throbbed badly but the pain made her focus. Last up, she poured the flask's contents over and into her mouth, washing the blood and crust away. It was strong and burned and made her smile.

She stared at him, her head buzzing nicely. "You ready, traitor?"

He turned away and she joined him in searching for a stray Dalcian horse.

An hour later, Arraleen Caze rode apace behind her massive enemy, her mind angry and full of questions. Her body was numb from the strong drink and weariness. The country was open and easy. No sign of the Dalcians. That night, as they camped in reeds near a stream, she considered her options. Easy to stab his kidneys while he slept and let him bleed out. Tempting, but she'd wait. He was right. She knew nothing of these lands. This Borderlands region was dreary, but Dalcia was rumored far worse.

He'd told her they'd arrive at the Rozaco River next day. As she sat by the meager fire chewing stolen meat, she watched him roll in his blanket and snore. He was either brave or stupid, knowing she was there watching. *I'm the one who's stupid.* Never mind, she'd work it out once this bastard got her to him safely.

Next morning, he rose grinning and yawned at her.

"You been sitting up brooding all night?"

"Why wait till Dalcia?" she asked. "We can attack them before they cross the river."

"We don't know how many there are. And their number will

grow. Kelgar has men manning the stations on the river. Trading camps that favor him, as opposed to Torax and the others. It's all about who pays the most in Dalcia."

"I counted twenty-two, and we killed more than half that."

"That still leaves ten with Trendale. And more will join him at the river when they learn about Caze. Trust me, the only way we can succeed here is at Kelgar's lair, when they're drunk in their cups. Corsairs like drinking more than anything, save perhaps wenching, and murdering, and sailing their skinny ships."

"How long before we get there?"

"Two-week ride, maybe longer."

"Two fucking weeks . . . are you joking, man?"

"Unless we're delayed."

"*Shit*. Well, that's plenty of time to decide how to kill you, I suppose."

Grodu raised a brow. "Keep the attitude, girl. It won't help your father none, stabbing me in the dark."

"But it will make me feel a lot better."

By afternoon they reached a wide green plain, leading to the lazy curve of a large river that glinted in the late hazy sunshine. To the right were marshes, the last of the foothills fallen far behind them. Her wrist still troubled her, and her mouth throbbed painfully. But she ignored both.

"My father mentioned a ferry," she said, seated on her horse, a hand shielding her eyes as she looked for signs of Trendale's riders. Probably crossed over by now.

"Several, and all manned by Kelgar's people. Or Torax, which is just as bad."

Arraleen wondered how her father would have handled that. He'd seemed confident they'd get over. Perhaps he'd dealt with these Reechers before. She gave him a level stare. "So how do we cross?"

"We steer west, skirting the marshes until the Rozaco narrows to a stream. That's near the Yamondon border and close to the Yagon River source. A remote region. I know a place we can cross unseen and without issue. It's forest for miles once we enter Dalcia. Beyond that a few villages, and the heathlands that hem the Razor River. That fast-running stream separates the Reech from the rest of Dalcia."

She nodded indifferently, not seeing any other option. A mile before reaching the Rozaco he veered off to the right, cutting through the green sward of long grass. She followed, guiding her horse at a steady canter.

That second night they camped in reeds again at the edge of the marshes. Arraleen decided she needed answers, and that meant feigning civility. She even offered a rare smile.

"Why are you so fond of King Ulani? I've heard my father say you're from Golt, wherever that lies."

"Northeast," he said, crunching on jerky. "Bordering Yamondo and Permio, and the blue sea far beyond."

"*Well?* How come you ended up in Omala, a slave?"

"I allowed myself to get captured during a skirmish," he told her. "The king needed eyes inside Vendel. Someone he could trust who would get close to the High Califez and his people. I didn't know about the Sangala back then. Not that that would have dissuaded me. And I owed my king."

"But he's not your king, is he? Why so loyal to a foreign ruler when you betray another good man who always thought well of you?"

"I respected your father too, as a great mind and master schemer. But King Ulani saved my life when I was a boy."

"I'm listening."

"He's a fine hunter, the king. And in his younger days, he rode far with his people. On one such foray, he crossed into Golt and stalked the great cats of our southern forests. I'd been fetching water for my village when a lion attacked me. The king rode down and killed the lion, and I was saved. I was twelve years old and half-starved from our meager life in that border jungle village, my family devastated by blight and sickness."

Arraleen raised a brow. "How heroic." *Am I supposed to feel sorrow for you now?*

He ignored her comment. "Ulani took me in as an orphan child and treated me as well as any of his seventy-two children. I became a warrior at fifteen and rode with the hunt. By twenty-one I was one of his best, and most trusted. Unlike his blood children, I had no ambition but to please my hero, the king.

"He sent me scouting in enemy lands. First in Dalcia, and beyond. Finally, in Vendel. It was my idea to get captured. I had a reasonable notion how I'd impress your father in the fighting pits. But Octaxa got there first."

She let that sink in. "What do you know of this land we're entering?"

"Dalcia?"

"The Reech, or is it one country?"

"Technically, yes. The Reech is a part of Dalcia. But it has its own rules—or lack of any—and is the home of every villain and scourge you could imagine. Dalcia is a hard land with cruel people. The Reech is far worse. A terrible place of wind and ice and frozen rain. The corsairs operate both sides of the Graze. That's the name for the southern shore where the icebergs drift."

"I can't imagine such a place."

"We'll need winter clothes. There are villages before the Razor River. One of them should provide us with what we need. You should get some sleep. You look rough. Go on, allow that lip and hand to heal."

How considerate. She smiled at him. "If I sleep, you might stab me instead."

"I might, but I'm enjoying your company. So it's unlikely."

"Do your worst, Lion Man." She flashed him a challenging grin and turned on her side. After a time, she sat up and saw him still watching her in the sparkle of firelight.

"Why are you staring at me?" she asked, blinking back sleep.

"I'm thinking about our options."

"You don't have any. Long term. But since we're both awake, here's another question. I saw an odd-looking man in Trendale's camp when that sudden lightning struck."

"So? One of his guards, maybe even me on my way there?"

"No. He was unlike anyone I'd seen before. He had flaming bright-red hair. He stared right at me and vanished into the darkness. And I mean vanished. A djinn, I thought him."

Grodu said nothing for a long time. Finally, he stared at her and smiled. "Life is strange. My little Shen friend mentioned a man with bright-red hair. A demon warrior, he called him, back there in Shen. An *Aikashi.*"

"A *what?*" She suppressed a shiver. The word had power, and she felt uneasy without knowing why.

"I don't know, maybe you're right. One of the djinni perhaps?"

"You're saying my instinct was right? The man wasn't real?"

"I'm saying there are things in this life we will never understand, Dreamslayer."

Another thought struck her. "This Shen friend of yours. What's he called?"

"Funny you should ask about him. *Gujun.* People call him the *Slayer.*"

CHAPTER 10 |THE KING'S OFFER

Cantacari was a giant hill of dazzling lights, capped by a huge golden dome, which blazed in the evening sun. Gujun's face was soaked with sweat. The heat was oppressive. Gone were the dry winds and arid brown terrain. Yamondo was lush and rich and emerald green.

The crossing and the week's ride from the Yagano River had passed without event. Although wide, the Yagano was shallow, and he'd seen no snakes. During the ride south, he'd taken stock of the deep hills and velvet-green folds of valley—cut by clean, well-constructed roads—and the jungle forests sweeping down from the mountains in the east, like a vast shimmering hem of curtain.

A place like no other, and strange to his eyes. More remarkable still were the great thundering beasts that marched the roads near the city. These gray-horned, long-snouted monsters were called elephants, Rogashi informed him. He'd learned much from the garrulous Yamondon, and by the time they reached the king's city, he felt he had a good idea about the way the people here lived their lives, and what they valued and honored.

Ten miles outside the city, Agashi had ordered a halt as they crested a wide ridge. He'd beckoned Gujun dismount and join him. He'd done so and the Tarak had slapped his back.

"See you, little killer. Is that not the finest sight your eyes have ever seen?"

"It is splendid," Gujun agreed. "Though I prefer the gardens of Ta Shen."

Agashi raised a brow. "Don't say that to Ulani."

"The king will see me?"

"I am certain of it."

Gujun had shrugged, thinking about his options.

They'd arrived at the Third's barracks just outside the city. A bed was provided for him. He slept on the floor, not being overly familiar with beds. Those sheets could hide things like serpents and scorpions. Why break a habit of a lifetime?

Next morning Agashi was summoned to the city to meet his Tarakai. He returned an hour later with an older man who he introduced to Gujun as Dolusa, the Third's Tarakai. A handsome, tough-looking warrior, who bore similar scars to Agashi.

"I've heard your name before," Dolusa told him. "The king

awaits you. He is most interested in your Shen news from the east."

They'd ridden into the city soon after: the Tarakai Dolusa, his Tarak Agashi, and Gujun the Slayer wedged between them. He felt comfortable, and liked these big smiling warriors who seemed to let so little upset them.

The gates were gilded and he saw ornate lanterns everywhere resting on tall poles. The streets wound up in tight steep circles, and there were palms and date trees and fountains, and chiming miniature waterfalls. It was a beautiful city, but odd to his eyes. The narrow streets were empty, rising in concentric curves until they greeted the huge palace with columns of palms, fanning the high golden dome.

A thin smiling man greeted them at the palace gates and introduced himself as Jelagi Gur. Gujun didn't like the look of him much, as something about his manner reminded him of Chulan. The steward led them through a labyrinth of airy rooms and light-flooded corridors, until they reached a stairway winding up to a high verandah.

"The king will receive you in the summer rooms," the smiling Jelagi Gur told him.

Gujun looked at Agashi, who shook his head.

"Just you," Dolusa told him.

Gujun shrugged and made for the stairs. He let his hands brush the wide golden rails as he climbed. This palace was grander than Empress Rasnei's had been in Pol Shen. Even more imposing than the pleasure gardens palace in his favorite city, Ta Shen. He reached the top and was rewarded by a stunning view of Cantacari and the surrounding steamy lands, reaching out for miles below. Far off to the west he glimpsed a faint blue glimmer through the haze. That must be the western ocean. It gave him a sense of his bearings.

A door opened to his right. A huge warrior stood there, his tattooed arms and massive hands resting on a tulwar, the blade curving to six inches broad before tapering narrower at the tip. He was badly scarred and reminded Gujun of the Northmen he'd encountered. He was just as large, though his skin was almost black instead of their pale blotchy demeanor. He had their savage look, the latent violence lurking in the back of his eyes.

"You're expected." The warrior glanced at the doors.

Gujun nodded and walked past the sentry without a second look. The doors opened to another section of the huge verandah. There were fountains and rich foliage here too. He saw hummingbirds flitting and darting, urgent flashes of green and red and sparkling blue.

He gazed about, seeing no one. To his right was a small pond where the flash of fish shimmered beneath shiny water. He walked over, gazing down.

The tiny tingle of bells sounded close by. A pretty, deeply tanned girl in a low-cut olive tunic appeared through the foliage and beckoned him follow. She wore tiny bells on her wrists, and the brief tunic showed off her sturdy legs and arms.

He complied happily and watched her swaying in front of him as she glided sylphlike through mosaic paths toward the sound of more water tingling.

"I like the view here," Gujun said to the girl, but she never turned his way or uttered a sound.

Finally, she stopped by a gazebo where lively blue birds capered and hopped. Beneath its golden canopy were a large round table and four chairs. She pointed at the chairs and nodded. He thanked her, and she shook her head nervously before vanishing back into the fronds.

A slave, perhaps? Shame. But he hadn't heard mention of any slaves here. Gujun soon forgot about the girl as he gazed around, taking in the many sights. Birds singing and water tingling in harmony, fused perfectly with the soft background of intricate piped music that even a Shen Empress would appreciate. He saw no sign of the pipers through the foliage. Beyond the endless gardens steamed the smoky haze of city and countryside. The air around clung sweet, tingling his nostrils with hints of honeysuckle and cinnamon. He glimpsed the green wrap of a mountain's shoulder off to the west. Gujun smiled. It was as though you could see the entire world from this high place.

He entered the gazebo and gazed around.

"Do you like my gardens?" The voice was rich and deep. Commanding.

Gujun turned slowly, fingers on his hidden dagger.

A man stood smiling at the edge of the frond path. He was perhaps fifty, his hair and beard flecked with gray. He bore the same scars as the Tarakai and Agashi, but his were stained dark red and curved up from either side of his mouth to the outer edge of his brows. A ferocious-looking warrior, he appeared. As big as Agashi. The brown eyes clever and curious. He wore a short golden robe and sandals. A broad leather belt supported two heavy-looking curved swords.

Gujun dipped his head. "You are the king."

"And you must be the illustrious assassin, Gujun the Slayer."

"I am he, yes."

"Excellent. Please, be seated."

"I prefer standing, Your Highness."

"Indulge me."

Gujun shrugged and pulled up a chair. The king smiled and took the one facing him. He leaned forward and stared hard at Gujun.

"I want to study your face," he said.

Gujun said nothing as the king probed his eyes. Finally, he nodded. "I see truth in you. A hard man with cynical eyes, who trusts no one and spares few. Tough and durable, tenacious and clever. A survivor. Am I not right?"

Gujun nodded. *That does sound like me.*

"Hmm . . . what do you see when you look at me?" the king asked him.

Was this a trap? He had better be careful here. Gujun masked his surprise with a smile. "A warrior," he said eventually. "And a shrewd battle master. Reader of men, and hunter of prey. A much-loved ruler whose warriors are proud to die for."

The king chuckled. "Tarak Agashi taught you well in our ways."

"He told me a little, Highness. Rogashi was more helpful. That one talks too much."

"I hear you saved his life."

"The leg, perhaps."

"Good. I'm fond of young Rogashi, despite his quirks. And his notable Tarak, Agashi, too. Fine warriors. I know all my Tark Guard by their names. Can you guess how many there are?"

Gujun thought for a moment. "Three Tarks. Each led by a Tarakai, commanding ten Taraks—each leading troops of warriors."

"Well done. You've described my personal guard—the Royal Tarkaizi. There are also the regulars posted around the country, and conscripts. My armies number twenty-five thousand strong."

Gujun raised a brow. "A good number, Highness."

"Are you hungry? I've heard you Shen don't eat very much."

"I haven't eaten much lately."

"We'll remedy that, and you'll share a flask of wine with me. I've much to ask you."

Gujun nodded, and the girl reappeared from nowhere and filled two goblets with crystal clear liquid. He glanced at her briefly.

The king caught his glance. "One of my adopted children. Sixteen, and a blessing. She works hard, does Galisha. Raleenian," the king added, as Gujun gazed at the glass.

"I don't know where that is."

"Raleen lies north of the desert lands. It's one of the Crystal Kingdoms, or was long ago. Founded by Kael the Wanderer, a survivor from Gol. These days it's tortured by civil wars between the proud Dukes of Atarios and the robber barons of Kador and Starkhold."

"You've been there, Highness?"

"I have indeed, and the cold lands beyond. In my youth, I journeyed far."

"Grodu spoke highly of you."

"It's because of Grodu that I wanted to see you personally. Of course, I'm curious about your country, but I could have gotten that from Dolusa or Agashi. But Grodu said you were a good man—unlike the stories I've heard, branding you the worst kind of villain."

"Grodu exaggerates. I'm a killer. Nothing more, or less."

"Of course you are. And he approached you about the Vendeli spymaster, Tulomon Caze?"

"He did, when I met him in Cardalis. Wanted me to help him find him."

"You met Caze in Laregoza, briefly, I'm told?"

"I did."

"Your opinion?"

"Arrogant, like most of his kind. Cool manner. Can't say I liked the man, but he wasn't as bad as the Sangala who accompanied him."

The king's shrewd eyes studied him again. "Tulomon Caze is a careful man. A thinker. It's why he's still alive, and on the loose. And that's a problem for me."

"I was told Grodu left to deal with him."

"Rashly, I fear, and without my permission."

Gujun blinked. "I thought it was on your orders."

"Grodu is like a son to me, Gujun the Slayer. Truth is, I love him more than most my blood children. But he's headstrong and proud, believes himself invincible. You know he allowed the Vendeli to capture and enslave him, just so he could spy on them? I never asked him to do that."

"You're worried about Grodu."

"I am."

"He's probably the most efficient fighter I've encountered."

"Even so, I fear he's out of his depth this time. Tulomon Caze will know he's been betrayed, and by Grodu—as he sees it. The Yanturi has sent people after Caze, my sources in his court have told me. Including a Sangala conjuror. One of the few who didn't fare east, or die in your realm. Olgasha was away in the far south when the Yanturi ordered the Sangala journey east and immerse themselves in the affairs of Ran Genza and his enemies. He's a skilled necromancer and a very dangerous man. Like Caze, I'd prefer him out of the game. Unlike him, I want Olgasha dead."

"Why not the spymaster?"

"Because I admire him, and I'm interested in clever people. What makes them function. You, killer, included, and I might have an offer you'd be keen to hear."

Gujun nodded. *Here we go . . . the crux moment when I must choose.*

Ulani smiled as though reading his thoughts. "Tulomon Caze has been a worthy opponent for decades. Without their disgraced High Califez, we would have broken the Vendel hold in the east years ago. Caze knew how to use the Dalcians to his advantage. Unlike most in Omala City, he was willing to trade and barter with the worst of that despicable race."

"Then why is he on the run?"

"He failed in your country. The Yanturi is not fond of failure. I've never gleaned exactly what they were planning there, but the Sangala would have made things worse. I'm sure you know more about that business, having met him and Octaxa that time. And Grodu met your Shen master, did he not? On Ran Genza's orders."

"Octaxa's, I believe. Though Genza most likely knew about it too. They both believed Grodu to be their man. And Magister Chulan wasn't my master. But that was where I first encountered your big man from Golt. Chulan promised the Vendeli a fortune in gold if they helped him bring down Empress Rasnei and plunder her garden city, Ta Shen. But things got cloudy last summer."

The king smiled. "So the bird messages Grodu sent informed me. And you played an important part in that conflict, so I hear. You can tell me about that later. For now, know this. Tulomon Caze will survive unless Olgasha gets to him. And by that, I mean he'll be hiding out in Dalcia where he has contacts aplenty. Grodu will seek him out but could be caught in his own nets. Caze will recover, lick his wounds, and plan vengeance. My spies informed me that the Yanturi confiscated his house and murdered his family. All save the wayward son. *And . . .* worse, that bitch girl."

"The Dreamslayer?" Gujun was curious. Nobody seemed to like her much.

"Aye, *her.* What do you know about Caze's troublesome daughter?"

"Nothing. Maybe a little. Grodu mentioned her once or twice. Bad news, I gather. He called her the Dreamslayer, and thought it funny, a connection to me perhaps. That name stuck in my memory."

King Ulani nodded. "She's got to be helping him too, and that means Grodu has two enemies smart enough to outwit him, as he hunts for Caze. Olgasha wants Caze dismembered in Omala City Palace. His trophy. Once he knows Grodu's in the mix, he'll be sure to take him out. And as for Arraleen Caze . . . someone needs to kill that awful woman."

"You admire the father, but not his child?"

"Like you, she's a killer. Unlike you, she's spoiled and overproud and treacherous as snakes in long grass. Like Olgasha, I want Arraleen Caze dead. That cat woman has killed too many of my people."

Cat woman? Was there something else he should know about her?

"What do you want from me, King?"

Ulani awarded him a measured glance. "Journey south to Dalcia. Find Grodu, and help him capture Tulomon Caze. If that means dealing with his daughter, and the Sangala, so be it. The big lout stands a chance with you down there. I need Caze here in Cantacari, neutered and talkative. I'd like to discuss business with him, before I have him killed."

Gujun almost smiled. *So, you are going to kill him. Eventually . . .* The thought restored his customary jaded opinion of the world.

He gazed down at his hands resting on the table. "Why should I do this thing you ask? A perilous journey? I told Grodu I'm retired."

The king's eyes narrowed. "You're on shaky ground, killer. Do have any idea what I can do to you, were you to displease me?"

Gujun shrugged. "I don't think you're the kind of ruler who

likes nervous men. Besides, all men die. It doesn't matter how."

The king smiled. "True. And I like you, Gujun the Slayer. I see why Grodu was impressed. He said you were unappreciated by your own people. Perhaps you'll consider working for someone who values your help, for a change? See, I'm asking . . . nicely." He showed those magnificent teeth again.

Gujun took a breath. "What if I still say no?"

The king waved a hand. "You saved Rogashi. I've a foolish daughter who moons over that boy. And Tarak Agashi's one of my finest warriors, and he spoke highly of you. You can leave Yamondo with my blessings, and always call us your friend. No strings. But think about it carefully, Slayer. You'll never get a better offer, and men like you don't retire well."

Gujun stared into the king's eyes, matching his gaze for seconds, before politely dropping his own. This ruler had real power and was a man to admire. The Yamondons he'd met were as fierce and proud as the Northmen, but smarter and less miserable. Nor were they ugly like those scruffy oafs. A handsome race. He could do far worse than serve this king.

"If I say yes, what can I expect in return?"

"The usual recompense. Gold and coin. Servants and land. Plus, anything else you'd care for. Perhaps . . . Galisha." He smiled.

Gujun thought about the girl in the tunic, but Kanny's dark laughing eyes flashed at him.

"Well?" The king stared hard at his eyes.

He swallowed hard. "Grodu informed me that you want to aid the Laregozans in overthrowing Genza, or at least keeping him at bay. Gain a foothold in that land's ports enabling trade expansion. You want to squeeze the Vendeli ships out."

"And you can help me with that by telling me about Shen, and its cities. And Genza's people too. How vulnerable he is. Agashi informed me this Cama rebel in Laregoza's no fool. But I cannot back a losing side. I would know more about the east lands."

"I could watch things over there for you. I like Laregoza, have my eye on a place near Soloza. A villa. Genza owns it. But for how long . . ."

"It's good to make plans." The king rubbed his huge hands together. "You never know, you could get lucky. Help me out down there and we shall see what happens. Ran Genza is rumored a scorpion who deals with and bleeds whoever he can. The Vendeli are equally devious, and the two make good allies. Eventually someone will stab or poison that Cardalan despot. Grodu told me he couldn't see Genza lasting much longer than his brothers. From what I hear, the Cardalan Republic is full of fools."

"The Cards are ugly folk. Coarse and stupid, like the Northmen. Maybe not that ugly. But also like them, good fighters. I'll give them that. Though, I've heard Ran Genza prefers drinking to fighting."

"Hmm . . . the Northmen. You don't like them? I'll have you know there was a Northman seated in your chair scarce three months ago."

Gujun shrugged, not seeing the relevance.

"A good fighter, Valgarn. I liked him. And the woman he was with was a gem. Wonderful girl. I often ponder on what happened to those two."

He clapped his hands suddenly, and the girl Galisha appeared with two steamy plates of shrimp and some strange-looking vegetables.

"We'll eat, and speak more afterward," the king told him.

The food was delicious, and Gujun hadn't realized how hungry he was. The wine was affecting his head, so he carefully placed the glass aside. The king drained three goblets of the heady stuff and snapped his fingers for another.

"Questions?" he asked Gujun, after wiping his mouth with a silk cloth and belching heroically.

"Where is Dalcia, and where should I look for Grodu, the others?"

The king smiled. "I decided Rogashi should accompany you. He's a good sailor and has a merchant friend who owns a vessel on the coast."

"I don't like boats."

"A stout dhow will take you both to Reechers Bay. From there, you'll drop into Dalcia and learn all you can. One thing to remember. Don't go near the Reech."

"When do I leave?"

"In the morning. Rogashi will meet you with horses at the west gate. From there, you'll ride for Scaltee and board ship. Enjoy the voyage!"

"What if I'd said no?"

"I knew you wouldn't." The king smiled and supped his wine, requesting yet another.

Gujun smiled too, and decided to drain his glass and follow with a second.

"And watch out for that evil kitten, Arraleen Caze," the king told him.

"The Dreamslayer. I shall indeed," Gujun said.

END OF PART ONE

PART TWO|HUNTERS AND PREY

CHAPTER 11|DALCIA

Arraleen stood at the edge of the forest, watching the lights flicker in the nearby huts. To call this a village was generous. A week's ride skirting the marshes and crossing the Rozaco near its source had led them to the disputed border regions.

She'd seen another river off to the right, sparkling in the rare afternoon sun. Grodu had told her that was the Gray River, and vast Yamondo lay beyond. She'd seen lights that evening. He'd said those were from one of the border forts edging Reechers Bay, where the Yamondons kept garrisons to keep eyes on Dalcian Corsairs and far-raiding northern pirates who sometimes infested the area.

They'd entered Dalcia the following day and were immediately swallowed by a dense wood. That had taken five days to cross—sometimes they'd had to lead the horses on foot. The forest was ancient and tangled, and she wondered how he knew his way.

They emerged that evening, the village lights glinting ahead.

"We ride in and help ourselves?" she asked him, scratching the scab on her lip. It was healing well, and her wrist seldom troubled her.

"No need," he told her. "I know the head man. He's in Ulani's pay. Best we wait here awhile to make sure no one sees us leaving the woods."

She curled her lip in distaste. "Another spy."

"We're in Dalcia. No one can be trusted. But Olbray fears Yamondon wrath more than bandits, or even Reech Corsairs. He will help us."

"I can see why you fit in so well down here."

He awarded her a sharp glance, but said nothing. They waited another half an hour, though she didn't know why.

Finally, he seemed satisfied. She watched him click his tongue, guiding the horse forward. She followed behind, bidding her beast walk. They approached the buildings and entered the stockade, and she saw a single figure standing at the gates, with a lantern held high.

"Master Grodu, what a surprise! And who's this lovely lady?"

Arraleen glared at the smiling man. She didn't like him. Reminded her of Trendale, but these people all looked similar. His face was florid in the lantern light. Round and grizzled with whiskers, the pale eyes puffing and red, as though he often drank too much. He struck her as oily, and she imagined he'd seen them waiting in the forest. Perhaps Grodu had carved a sign in the trees that these people could follow. She'd had to sleep a little each night, her dagger gripped in her fingers. He could have met someone.

The portly smiler introduced himself as Olbray the Keeper, with a slight bow of the head. "You'll need ale and food," he chatted, still grinning. "And I'll have a boy tend to your horses. There's beds available in the inn."

"Inn?" Arraleen couldn't make out a proper house, let alone a hostelry.

"At the far end of the village," Grodu told her.

They dismounted and led their horses behind Olbray, who strolled toward more lights casting glow on a lane. The huts she'd spotted turned out to be a storage area and cattle stations. She could hear the beasts shuffling and blowing close by.

It was colder here than it had been in the forest. She felt her nose run and wiped it in disgust. She'd seldom experienced cold in Vendel. Most her work for her father had involved killing Yamondons in the jungle forests flanking the Emerald Mountains, a stifling sweaty business. But never cold. This chill was new to her. She didn't care for it.

The shapes of hovels and low thatched crofts loomed close. At the far end she saw more lanterns, and what looked to be the inn. Not inspiring, the damaged door creaking and banging in the night wind.

Olbray whistled, and a skinny toothless boy appeared from the gloom. He gaped at her and nervously took the horses' reins.

"Look after them," she said sharply as the boy led the horses into the shadow of stables beyond.

They entered the inn. *No one here.* A single candle flickered on a long table. She saw a keg and three mugs filled with ale.

"So, you were expecting us," she said.

Olbray rubbed his gray whiskers. "We watch the woods from dusk to dawn. Pays to be cautious, since there are bandits from time to time. Your big friend here knew that and was being polite by waiting. His patience allowed me have my woman prepare some food and welcome for unexpected travelers."

"Grodu is not my friend," Arraleen said, but the man wasn't listening.

He bid them sit at the table and passed across two mugs of ale.

She sniffed hers and made a sour motion with her mouth. "It smells stale," she told him.

Olbray looked troubled for the first time.

"Don't mind her." Grodu laughed, and downed his mug in a single gulp. Olbray poured him another, his eyes watching her.

Yes, keep guessing, red face. Arraleen sipped the brew slowly, wincing at the bitter taste. She hoped the food would be better. Happily, it was, arriving several minutes later. A broad-beamed, no-nonsense-looking woman placed a hot carving of venison and carrots on the table in front of her. She thanked the woman— who she assumed was Olbray's wife—with a rare smile, deeming her better than her husband, who was talking overmuch.

"How fares the king?" Olbray asked Grodu.

"Well, as far as I know." Grodu chewed and spat a chunk of gristle on the table. Arraleen shuddered at his revolting manners. *These people . . .*

"Where have you been, my old friend?" Olbray asked him as Arraleen watched them. "It's gone six months, perhaps even a year? And you were here so often before."

"The Vendeli have been active of late." Grodu cast a careful eye at her before continuing. "I've been kept busy in the east and north. There's been war out there."

"That's to be expected with savage folk." Olbray grinned at Arraleen.

"Are you going to help us?" she asked him. *Or just keep smiling?*

He nodded. "With warm clothes, fresh horses, and a week's dry jerky. How's that sound, lady?"

Arraleen nodded curtly and looked at Grodu. These two were up to something. No sleeping for her tonight.

"You've known this big oaf a long time?" she asked the Dalcian.

Olbray looked shocked at the way she spoke about Grodu. He glanced at the warrior, who shook his head, a slight smile on his lips. "I'd say you get used to her ways, but that would be an exaggeration."

Olbray shrugged, nodded, and turned to her. "Yes, lady. Grodu always comes here when he needs news and assistance in the south. I have connections in Dal City, and the coastal towns, Brassport on Graze and Easthaven. Even some stout fellows on the Reech."

"Olbray knows Kelgar," Grodu said.

"Not really. I've only met the Eagle twice. But I do know

some of his people—through necessity, you understand?"

"We need to find him," Grodu said.

"Eagle Kelgar? A Reech Corsair? Have you lost your wits in the wild lands?"

"We're making for the Reech."

"You can't take this woman there." He looked genuinely shocked. Hard to sham that expression with such a red face.

"He isn't taking me anywhere," Arraleen said. "Kelgar's men stole something from me, and this drunken lout has promised to help me get it back."

Olbray looked uneasy.

"Part of what she said is true," Grodu grunted, avoiding her sideways glance.

"Who are you, fierce Vendeli lady?" Olbray seemed suddenly uncomfortable in her presence. His former bluff manner and veneer congeniality was replaced by a wary edginess.

Arraleen smiled at Grodu. "Go on. Tell him."

"You're better off not knowing," Grodu told Olbray.

Enough games. "How far to the Reech?" she demanded, ignoring their moon faces.

"Day's ride southwest," Olbray told her, finding his smile again. "The river crossings will be watched."

"I know," Grodu said, as though they'd spoken on this before.

"Kelgar will know you're coming long before you reach him."

"Give him something to worry about," Arraleen said. *Before I visit him a whole lot more.*

Olbray sipped his ale uncomfortably. "You know your

business, I suppose."

"Kelgar still on that island?" Grodu asked.

Arraleen stared at him. "What island? You never mentioned an island." Or if he had, she couldn't recall. How the fuck would they get to an island in this shithole freezing country?

Both men looked at her. "Yes, his lair," Grodu said. "I thought I'd told you."

She shook her head.

Olbray continued after glancing at them both. "Aye, same spot. Camp on windward shore."

She held back a laugh. *Windward? This entire land is nothing but wind and shitty rain.*

"There's been trouble between Kelgar and the other corsairs," Olbray added. "Blue Face Xeeg, one of Torax's men, has set up on his own. Xeeg stole some contraband from the Eagle's men last summer. That robber's got bolder of late, and his men include foreigners from lands I've never heard of. Black souls, the lot of 'em. Kelgar's had to recruit more stout fellows from this side of the river."

"Where is his island?" Arraleen demanded. *Point me in the right direction, and tell me who to kill.*

Olbray stared at her. "Off the west coast, barely a mile offshore—but too cold to swim." He laughed, but she didn't see the funny side.

The two discussed other matters for several minutes, Olbray avoiding her stares. Grodu gulped his ale. Arraleen decided it better getting some rest than listening to foolish drunken chatter all night. What she'd learned was sufficient.

They'd have to cross to an island. That meant stealing a boat. *No problem.* He'd row, and she'd watch him. She left them to their banter, and Olbray's wife led her to a chilly low-ceilinged room with a solitary window.

Later that night, Arraleen watched from the window as Grodu snored in the small room across the landing. The gibbous moon rose over the cowsheds and she saw a flicker of light off to the west. Lightning perhaps, but hard to be sure. Grodu and his garrulous contact had spoken long into the night. He'd most likely consumed half a keg of that awful brew. She'd rested her body but kept her eyes open and ears tuned.

She felt irritable. Even more than usual. Her lip itched. Things had gotten out of hand. She'd always guided her life, even as a child. Willful and headstrong, she'd been called. And especially after her mother died so cruelly.

The one person I loved without bitterness.

She'd watched the illness fester. Seen Anyarvana's beautiful face wither and fade. And she screamed at her to stay. Pleaded and begged. Mother! And he'd done nothing. Her hero, her father. *Nothing.* Save weep alongside her. While the gods fucking laughed. Except cold Agarra, who alone of them knew what it was to lose everything. That's why She still hunted the night sky, searching for her stolen soul.

Her mother left them during the rains all those bitter years ago, the sun's warmth departing with her. Arraleen had died that day too, leaving behind an angry young woman who wanted payback from the malign gods for the pain they'd caused her and her family.

Her father had never remarried, but instead doted on the dull-eyed leman who gave him those soppy daughters. Since that time, she'd kept her own counsel, even with her father. But he'd got his way recently, and here she was in this grim place—with an enemy who'd betrayed them and yet claimed he wanted to help her.

And she knew nothing of these people. Olbray and his greasy smiles. Kelgar the Terrible, or whatever they called him. And slippery Trendale, also a smiler. The only Dalcian she'd met with honor was Crastus of Kamor outside her home. She wondered what had happened to him. Most likely executed by the Yanturi, along with the others who'd failed to snare her and her father.

She yawned. *I'm so damned tired.*

The light flashed again. Off in the woods this time. *Closer.* That wasn't lightning, and the clouds were racing past the moon but showed no sign of rain. This was no storm brewing.

Someone's out there.

On impulse, she rolled free of the blankets and strapped her scimitars to her belt. She stole a glance at Grodu, currently sprawled on his face, the big sword pinned underneath his body. Pig ugly, and out cold. She ventured down the rickety stairs and saw the glimmer of light coming from over by the cattle stores. She glimpsed the other light again off in the woods.

Someone was signaling they were here. Olbray to Trendale? Olgasha perhaps? Didn't matter, she needed to leave. She berated herself for allowing Grodu win her over by coming here. He'd probably just wanted ale and food. Driven by his stomach like most men. Let him deal with whoever was out there. She'd continue alone. At least Olbray had given them blankets and a warm cloak. And thick woolen trousers, which she'd slipped into as soon as she could, it being so chilly down here.

She entered the inn taproom and saw the fire had burned low. Outside, the light glinted again. This time she heard hushed voices, the sounds of rushing feet. She needed to get to the stables. She turned, stopping sharp as the inn door creaked open.

Arraleen cursed. She'd been caught out again. Should have trusted her instincts with Olbray.

A large shaggy-looking man stood there, a sword in each hand. He saw her and grinned, then turned his head to speak to someone behind. She reached for her dagger, but a rough hand grabbed her throat from behind.

"That devil threatened me, I had no choice." Olbray's voice sounded edgy, afraid.

She turned, snake swift, stabbing her thumb dagger into the side of his neck. Olbray sunk. "Tell Grodu I'm sorry . . ." he croaked and collapsed.

She stepped back, eyeing the door. Three grinning Dalcians stood with swords and axes held ready. She flicked her knife and held it ready as another figure entered the inn. Tall and dark, a crimson-hooded cloak covered his body. He pushed the hood back and grinned at her.

Olgasha the Sangala smiled. "We have some unfinished

business, Arraleen Caze."

She tossed the dagger. He raised two horned fingers in response. The weapon thudded to the floor at his feet.

"Bring her here," he told the men beside him.

The nearest Dalcian reversed his blade and stepped forward, meaning to knock her unconscious. Olgasha was grinning. His dark eyes held a power that sapped her strength. But she still had her fury. It would suffice.

As the Dalcian made to strike her head, she leaned to her left, and jabbed the thumb dagger up under his chin. She pushed the choking man forward at the next one and turned, making for the door upstairs, her only other option.

"There's no escaping your fate," Olgasha called after her, sounding bored. "Go fetch her."

She reached the landing. Grodu's bulk blocked her.

She glared at him and pushed past. "We've company."

"Olbray?"

"Dead. And so would you be, if I had more time. Olgasha is here."

"The Sangala?" He was groggy with sleep and ale fug.

"All yours, Big Boy. I'm leaving." She left him staring down at the Dalcians as she made for the window. She angrily kicked the glass out, allowing her to crawl through and clamber out onto the roof.

There were men out there with torches. She slid from the thatch and crashed into a rain barrel. She jumped and rolled free, pushing a would-be attacker aside.

Shouts. More men rushing her way. A face loomed close. She butted it, breaking the nose. Another figure emerged and swung an ax at her. She twisted away, freed a scimitar, and danced back, lunging. Behind her in the inn, she heard Grodu roaring in rage, and the sound of clashing steel.

That will teach you to get drunk on the job.

She casually cut down another attacker in the darkness and ran out into the lane. Grodu was shouting hoarsely, and she could hear Olgasha's dark voice too. Three Dalcians blocked her way to the stables. She took the first with a jab in the throat. Slicing sideways, she skewered the second, then stabbed at the eyes of the third until he fell backward, tripping, and she dispatched him with a back slice.

She reached the stables, where another raider lurched toward her, and she ran him through. She walked past him and saw a small shape leaning against the central beam. The stable boy was bleeding badly from his stomach, and weeping softly.

She crouched next to him and examined the gut wound. Bad way to go.

"I'm sorry," she said quietly. "Now be brave and close your eyes." He looked at her in terror. She forced a smile. "I'll chase the pain away, sweetheart. My gift to you, as Dreamslayer." His eyes closed. "Good! You're *free.*"

She sliced the dagger cleanly across his throat. He shuddered and stilled. Best she could do for him.

She stood. Her eyes glazed with fury. The sound of fighting was still coming from the inn. Grodu was selling himself hard.

Good for him. Shame he'd almost got them both killed.

She heard Olgasha shout again and the sounds of fighting ceased. Grodu must be dead. She grabbed the nearest horse and stepped into a stirrup, pushing the horse forward as it clattered out the stable.

"I'll get to your father before you can," she heard Olgasha shout as she urged the horse up the lane. There were two Dalcians at the gates, and she cut them down as though they were ripe corn at harvest.

Sobbing with rage, she reentered the woods and guided the horse as best she could through the tangle and gloom. That bastard Olgasha had used sorcery on her. How had he found them? And why were Dalcians helping him, after they'd betrayed him earlier?

Through his witchery, Olgasha knew where her father was. And Grodu was dead, so she'd have to find Kelgar's lair on her own. *I'll manage.* The Reech was southwest of here. She remembered him mentioning the Razor River. There'd be a bridge or ford. She'd cross that somehow, and face the next problem when it came.

First, she needed to get away from this area, lest Olgasha catch up with her again. She struggled through the dark, dismounting and leading the horse along the edge of a stream. The moon brushed the tops of the trees, awarding enough light for her to keep moving.

She reached a ridge, and an owl called from a tree close by. Something scurried under her feet. A rat? She felt an icy shiver, and sensed someone was watching.

She turned and saw Olgasha's image smiling at her. He became a red snake sliding crisply down the bark of a tree. The snake became a vine sprouting writhing leaves and thorns. She freed a sword and approached the creeping mass. She struck the poisonous coils and they vanished.

The sound of wings came from her right. She blinked and saw the owl settle and ruffle crimson feathers. The bird stared back at her with Olgasha's laughing eyes.

"Are you scared to face me like a man, conjuror?"

"Happy to."

The voice came from behind her. She spun on her boots, the scimitar slicing air. He stood with arms folded in the middle of the stream, the water washing his red cloak and boots. He reached inside the cloth and pulled something out. It looked like a small animal skull glinting in the moonlight. He uttered some words and she felt her throat tighten in pain, as if she'd been stung by a venomous Scale fly.

She choked, and he laughed, the pain vanishing as she gulped in air.

"That's just a taste of what I can do."

He walked toward her, a long finger pointing at her chest. She tried to move but couldn't, her legs stiff and her tongue stuck like wood wedged in her mouth.

"You . . ." She felt weak and giddy. *Must hang on . . .*

His smile deepened. "I'll kill your father slowly, just like those Dalcian dogs are doing to that fool Grodu. You were careless aligning yourself with that blunt tool. I expected better from you, Dreamslayer."

"Those Dalcians will kill you." She choked the words out.

"No. These are Blue Face's men. They don't like Kelgar much, or Trendale, his puppy. When I'm done with you and your father, I'll be visiting master Trendale. So much to do!" He produced a knife from his cloak and walked toward her smiling.

She made to jump back, but couldn't move. She spat at him, and again he laughed.

"Be grateful I've not the time to make you suffer for the trouble you've caused me," he said, as he stabbed the blade toward her eyes.

No!

A trick of the light.

She heard him falter and stumble. He coughed, saw something. She saw where he was looking and glimpsed movement. A bright flash of red. A man leaning on a strange-looking spear. The red-haired stranger vanished, as did Olgasha. Her legs gave way, and she sank to her knees, the dread of sorcery creeping off into the night.

Forgotten, the owl lifted and flew silently up into the canopy, as the moon hid under a veil of cloud. She shook on her knees, rocking and sobbing with rage. She had never known real fear before. Anger and fury and anticipation, but not blood-draining terror like this.

The forest was clean again. Olgasha had gone. The red-haired djinn had saved her. But why? And who was he?

Get a hold of yourself, bitch.

She stood, shakily. Leaning heavily on the sword, cussing and spitting at the soil. Forcing her anger drive off the dread. The odds were stacked high against her. Kelgar the Corsair and Trendale meant to sell her father. Olgasha would persuade them to hand him over, using the same evil he'd tried on her.

She had to get there first. Kill them all. Impossible task, but what else had she been born for? She was the Dreamslayer, and she wasn't done yet. Arraleen Caze forced a savage smile to her lips.

"I'm just getting started," she said to the trees, as she guided the skittish horse back out into the open fields outside the village. She saw the flames rising from where the Dalcians had torched the buildings. Dalcians seemed to enjoy burning things.

She left village and forest behind, urging her mount to pick up pace and canter, leaving the darkness with the night. As dawn rose behind, she reached the muddy banks of a fast-flowing river. At the far bank, low crumbling cliffs watched her like ugly broken teeth. She'd made it to the Reech. Let the killing commence.

CHAPTER 12| THE VOYAGE SOUTH

Gujun watched in wonder as the waves crashed against the ship's hull. He knew nothing of boats or their workings. Rogashi had informed him this was a dhow. Much like the Vendeli craft but better constructed, of course, as it was made by Yamondon fishermen. The fishers of the west coast roamed wide, casting nets out for all manner of catch. Gujun had been fascinated.

He'd also been edgy. Never voyaged on a boat, let alone a large vessel like this one. Two masts, each supporting a sloping boom and ochre triangular sail. Heavy anchor, a rack of oars, and a dozen wiry sailors, who moved gracefully with every creak of timber.

They'd left Cantacari nine days ago. A fast ride to the coast, followed by Rogashi meeting with his friend, the fisher captain, and negotiating coin. The sailors were rough-looking and coarse, and to Gujun seemed irreverent to Rogashi's rank as a noble Baha. Not that he seemed bothered in the least. Moreover, he joked with some as though they were all old friends. Gujun kept his distance from the crew. The odd glances he'd received hadn't been friendly. He didn't want to hurt anyone during the voyage, so he'd focused on the scenery instead.

Since departing harbor that afternoon over a week ago, he'd enjoyed watching the long strip of sandy shore parading their east, broken by the odd smudge of cliffs or hazy fan of velvet nodding palm trees. A pleasing pastime, it had proved. He'd seen strange gray beasts leaping and diving in and out of the waves, and once, a huge creature spouting a jet of water higher than the ship's masts. Amazing.

This world was full of wonders. So much to see, and so little time. Especially for someone in his line of work. You had to enjoy each moment you could. The knife in the dark was always waiting.

If I live long enough, I'll travel widely, he told himself, smiling at the sun.

He was standing on the prow—his favorite perch—when Rogashi appeared beside him, grinning and sipping an ale. Courtesy of the skipper, Dasco, who was a native of Golt like Grodu, and almost as ugly, though considerably smaller. He sported a forked beard, dyed steely blue. A strange custom, but these were superstitious folk. A gold teardrop dazzled from his left ear lobe. The skipper was an unsavory fellow, in Gujun's opinion, but he knew his craft, and the men obeyed his shouts without grumbles.

There were many strays from Golt among the coastal folk. Another thing he'd learned on the voyage. Though, as before, Rogashi stayed clear of talking about that mysterious country. Gujun decided he'd have to visit Golt himself one day. Add that land to the list.

He sniffed the air. "It's colder today." Gujun had noted the sting in the breeze. The wind had picked up and a swell gathered further offshore. He'd felt queasy for a time, but it had soon passed. He'd stayed away from the ale, leaving that to his companion and the fishers, who seemed to thrive off the nut-brown liquid, despite the chop.

"Be a lot colder when we arrive," Rogashi replied, grinning. "You'll appreciate the extra clothes I brought with the pack horse."

"I dare say." Gujun nodded, watching the shore. He was from foggy Pol Shen, thus not bothered by the cold or damp. But these Yamondons were not fond of the climate in Dalcia, which sounded similar to his home in northern Shen—gray, chilly, and wet.

"How long before we arrive in Dalcia?"

"Four, maybe five days."

"That long?"

"Aye. And Dasco wants to stop at Grapoor to sell his catch, and restock. He doesn't normally venture beyond that town. Too many hazards."

"Such as?"

Rogashi gestured dismissively. "Northern pirates. The odd

Permian war galley looking for a fight, or more rowing slaves. Far more likely, Reechers."

"Who?"

"Corsairs from the Reech. That's the westernmost part of Dalcia, and we'll want to avoid it."

Gujun let that go. He had other questions. "So where will Tulomon Caze be hiding?"

"I spoke to Dolusa and the king. Both thought he'd be making for Bleakport or Easthaven on the far south coast. From there, whoever's helping him could bribe a whaling captain to assist his escape overseas. Sailing up to Golt, or across to your lands. Tulomon Caze knows a lot of people in Dalcia."

"Our plan?"

"Dasco will drop us off in Reechers Bay. Dangerous area. We'll have to move fast, make for the woods that fringe the northern region. There are villages near there, and the king has contacts among them. He gave me some names. We'll be able to get horses. Before that, we'll need to manage the first stretch on foot, mostly through the forest. You've a lot of weapons with you. Too much to carry what with our packs, I'm thinking."

"I'll be fine."

"The king wants Caze alive."

"So he told me, but not the daughter. I'm curious about her. This Dreamslayer."

Rogashi chewed his whiskers. "I'm hoping she's somewhere else."

"Tell me about her."

"If I must. Arraleen Caze has been a stone in Yamondo's

sandal for almost a decade. Trained by her father, and others. She's a killer, is the Dreamslayer. Enjoys it, they say. Clever, and colder than a cat. I've heard she keeps jungle panthers and feeds them with her prisoners."

"Sounds lively." Gujun smiled, privately hoping he'd meet this Dreamslayer. They seemed to have a lot in common.

"We're to kill her, if we see her. And quickly. That one has no give. The father's more pragmatic, a survivor."

"Tell me about the Dalcians."

"Coarse and greedy. I don't like them very much."

"You Yamondons don't like anyone."

"Not true. King Ulani has friends in the far north. A tradition from the days of his legendary forbear. Ulani I, first of the magnificent Baha kings. Greatest warrior who ever lived. That first Ulani fought in the Crystal Wars alongside the northern warriors, and even a famous Northman voyager who became his best friend. Barin of Valkador was the only champion who could match him in an arm wrestle. A time of heroes."

"So it seems." Gujun wished he knew more about those ancient times. But he'd have to find a library, and before that learn how to read. There hadn't been many opportunities for either, scraping a living on the midden slopes of outer Pol Shen. Chulan had taught him symbols and signs. And of course, he knew the gang codes. But ancient text? Another challenge he'd like to face one day.

"Our country has always had eyes in the north," Rogashi said.

Gujun looked at him. "Your king said there was a Northman

in Cantacari a few months back."

"Valgarn of Leeth. Both Ulani and the Tarakai liked him. I've heard his mother's a sorceress." He added the last in a quieter voice.

"I know that name." Gujun recalled a meeting by the River Shen. At Ran Calla's camp. He'd been escorting Shen dignitaries across to meet the enemy, as Chulan was scheming to betray his empress by allowing the rabid wolf, Calla, into Shen. There'd been two Northmen brothers in Calla's camp that day. One had mocked him. Gujun had made the lout pay for that. He'd wished he'd done more, but had to use constraint. But at least he'd made Gorn look a fool. The other brother, Valgarn, had seemed brighter.

He smiled at the sunshine. "Life is strange," he said, eventually.

"Aye, Little Brother. It is that. But compared to what?"

They stopped in Grapoor as planned, spending the one night anchored in the harbor. Gujun stayed put on the dhow, preferring the ocean view to the shoddy-looking huts and harbor area. Over there, artful traders and merchants clustered like flies with their silent slaves. And, closer, smiling night girls hovered on the key, tempting sailors with their delights. It was much colder down here. He'd donned thick plaid trousers and a heavy fur tunic, slipping his leathers and mail over the top.

A day's sail later the sky darkened, and the first bulging clouds mustered in the south.

"Winter starts early in Dalcia," Rogashi said, his face glum.

Gujun scratched an ear. "I thought that the further south

you went the hotter it got?"

Rogashi smiled. "You Shen are strange folk."

Gujun let that be.

Later that day, as cold rain washed the decks for the first time during their voyage, Gujun saw distant cliffs. Far stranger was the remarkable sight of two huge, twisted horns, rising hundreds of feet over the farthest bluff. They looked like the tusks of some giant dead creature. Pale in hue. A relic from legend? He'd heard the sailors speak of walruses and other odd beasts down here.

"What is that monstrosity?" he asked Rogashi who'd joined him at the prow again.

"The Hooks."

"A giant animal corpse?"

Rogashi shrugged. "Nobody knows for certain. Rumor speaks of an ancient fortress ruled by a long-dead race. The Aralais—wizards from another time. Sailors avoid that headland. Even Reechers steer clear. There are stories."

Gujun watched as the strange horn towers slipped from sight, as the rain clouds swallowed the distant cliffs.

"I know nothing of this world," he said, as fresh rain pattered against the deck.

"You should journey to the Crystal Kingdoms, Little Brother. There are archives hidden in a dead city up there. A place of ghosts, but knowledge too. The king went there in his youth, honoring his ancestor."

I would if I could read them. "Maybe I'll go there," Gujun said, blinking in the rain as he followed Rogashi under the cover of canvas.

The sky cleared by evening, and skipper Dasco seemed pleased. Gujun saw what he assumed was the southern shore of Reechers Bay. Beyond that were low hills and a forest darkening the horizon.

"We'll anchor before dark and slip away once you're both ashore," Dasco said, rubbing his golden teardrop. His plan was to row them to the beach personally, so he could report that back to Dolusa in Cantacari.

Gujun had enjoyed the voyage but was ready to get moving. Find Tulomon Caze, bring him back to the king. Get paid. Return to Laregoza. As good a plan as any.

They were a mile offshore when a sailor yelled from above.

"Reechers!"

Dasco came running, joining Rogashi and Gujun watching at the prow. The skipper pressed his eyeglass to an eye and cursed.

"Trouble?" Gujun asked him.

"Fucking corsairs, I knew we'd been too lucky. They'll catch us—those cursed skinny ships of theirs are fast as eels."

Gujun raised a brow. "Best I go get my bow."

Rogashi grinned. "As shall I. The exercise will warm our blood."

But Dasco looked alarmed. "You fools, those are Reechers. See the crimson square sail?"

Gujun watched as the dark shape of a ship glided through the silvery water, cutting toward them with impressive speed. A lean vessel, much smaller than Dasco's dhow. It bore a single dark-red sail. As it clipped nearer, he saw figures standing with weapons held high. Judging by the speed, they had ten minutes, no more.

"Will they board?"

"If they can," Rogashi said, returning with his weapons, the horn bow in hand, tulwar and knives strapped to belt. Gujun went below and armed himself. On his return, he saw the ship was close enough to risk an arrow.

He could make out pale faces swaddled in fur, the odd one wrapped in a helmet. Some of those with horns protruding. He didn't see any archers.

The raiders were trying to cut them off from the shore. Dasco, on the helm, yelled at his sailors who worked the sail and oars furiously. On a whim, Gujun nocked arrow to bow.

"It's too far," Rogashi said beside him.

For answer, he smiled and pulled, leaning as far back as he could and counting silently, his legs bracing and absorbing the dhow's rhythm.

Now. He let fly, and watched the dart trap sunlight, before dropping amidst the deck of the corsair's ship. He heard a yell, saw the men over there milling around.

"That was a legendary shot, Little Brother." Rogashi slapped his back. "My turn."

Gujun and Rogashi fired several more shafts, before the lean vessel caught up with them, skimming alongside, the oars pulled back as the craft raked against Casco's dhow.

Men lurched as the dhow's oars were snapped and broken. Gujun saw the Reechers yelling as they dragged a wooden plank out, spanning the watery gap. The first raider ran across. A burly fur-wrapped warrior, horns jutting from his iron helm. Gujun's arrow pierced his left eye, and he dropped without a sound, disappearing in the churning water below.

The next Reecher made it to the dhow's deck, and three others behind. Within moments there were twenty or more well-armed ruddy-faced fighters. All like the first one garbed in fur and iron. Most carried short-bladed swords and axes, the odd brightly painted round shield. They set about attacking Dasco's crew with apparent relish.

Gujun and Rogashi met the Reechers in a blaze of sparks and steel. Gujun smiled as he skewered a man, while Rogashi's tulwar felled another beside him.

Dasco was yelling in fury, seeing his men die. No warrior, he wielded the scimitar Gujun had given him as best he could, felling a Reecher and wounding another. More were coming, and they wouldn't last long without his help.

Gujun ducked and weaved. Rogashi and the others were separated from him as he got cornered at the prow. There were six of them, pressing down. Bearded grinning puckered faces, the skin red and raw from years of wind, sea, and ice.

"And I had always thought the Northmen ugly," Gujun said, walking forward.

"Who's this foreign bastard," the nearest and biggest spat at him, his accent thick. "I'll feed your liver to the sharks." He leaped forward, slicing down with his blade.

Gujun danced to his left and jabbed across, stabbing the Reecher in his side. He crumpled but the other five were on him, snarling and cursing, as they clustered close with their short blades, clearly not used to enemies who fought back.

Gujun stabbed one through the heart with one Jian, and sliced off a second's hand with the other. The other three pressed close. He dropped the swords and grabbed a knife in each fist. Stabbing at eyes, slicing at throats. Cutting. Killing. He heard Rogashi's Baha battle roar. He stepped forward and dispatched the last one. Done here, he went to see how the Yamondons fared.

"Welcome to Dalcia." Rogashi grinned as Gujun joined him and watched Dasco kick the last corpse overboard. The Reechers cursed at them from the ship, but the gangway had fallen off, as Dasco's tillerman steered their dhow clear.

Half the Reechers were dead, and all of those who'd come across. Gujun had slit the last one's throat, before reclaiming his bow and shooting some more on the raiders' deck. That dissuaded them from following, and their ship keeled and chopped off into the gloom.

Dasco had lost five men. He was angry, and slightly wounded, but mostly amazed that they were still alive.

"You're on your own," he told Gujun and Rogashi an hour later, as he rowed them to shore. His men watched with bows from the dhow. As Gujun suspected, the corsairs had lost the appetite for attacking again. "I'll report back that you've landed," Dasco said, as he worked the oars, leaving them standing on the cold pebble beach. "Stay alive."

"You too, old friend," Rogashi shouted back. Gujun watched the small craft bob back and forth, until Dasco safely reached the dhow and clambered aboard, his sailors winching up the skiff.

Twenty minutes later, the dhow had vanished into misty cloud. Gujun hoped they'd get home safely.

They stayed hidden in the thickets hemming the beach until dusk.

"We'll make for the woods as planned," Rogashi said, and they picked up their weapons and started trotting toward the dark line of trees to the south.

"I enjoyed that voyage," Gujun told Rogashi as they jogged into the cover of trees.

"That's good, Little Brother. Because from now on, things get difficult."

CHAPTER 13| BEYOND THE RIVER

Arraleen saw the flicker of campfire through the trees. She tied her horse's reins to a branch and crept closer, the cold wind whipping her face. Three days out from the river, these were the first men she'd encountered. And she needed answers, so one had best prove useful.

She'd crossed at a ford and proceeded best she could through the rocky wet terrain. This country was cursed by ugliness and the worst kind of weather. A dismal realm of gray rocks, boggy brown grasses, and slatey skies. The bitter winds and constant rain showers were her only companions. She'd felt cold since leaving the village. Even the meager fires she'd risked at night were scant comfort to her aching bones. Her nose ran and fingers tingled. And the wrist she'd hurt in the Borderlands ached with the nagging chill.

What a horrible place. On the bright side, her lip had healed, and the fury caged inside helped keep her focused and moving.

And now some answers. She smiled, crouching closer.

She counted five around the campfire. A good blaze, she'd enjoy warming her hands over that soon. She took stock, moved around in a circle, crawling on elbows, the scimitars gripped in her hands above the ground to stop any noise. She clenched a knife between her teeth.

No sentry. She returned to her original spot and spat the dagger out, stowing it with the others in her belt.

They were laughing at some bawdy joke one of them was telling. Big, hairy, swaddled in wool and fur, uncouth-looking oafs. White hairy faces, cheeks reddened by grog. They had thick-bladed swords glinting at their sides. She saw spears resting idly against a trunk. One of the men had a sack of wine and passed it among his friends. It was late, and they appeared drunk enough not to care.

She stood, the crescent moon rising behind her, framed by trees. They laughed at the joke, and one kicked his comrade in the knee. Another cursed and shoved his neighbor. They were happy. She smiled. Time to change that.

She walked forward briskly, the scimitars in each hand. The one facing her swore and stood, clumsily reaching for his sword.

Arraleen ran at him, her scimitar slicing out and severing

his throat. A second man swore and leaped at her. She ran him through with the other blade.

The third tried to stand but she kicked him in the face, cracking his nose.

"Devil bitch!" Number four had his sword leveled at her, as the last one reached for a spear, grabbing one from the tree and knocking the others over.

Arraleen took the man snarling at her through the throat with a lunge. She kicked him back, tossed a sword down, and scooped a knife from her belt. The one with the spear made to throw the weapon. *Too slow.* She flicked her good wrist. He dropped, her dagger in an eye.

Almost done. She turned to the wounded one, smiled, and crouched over him.

"Who are you?" he coughed up at her. The breath stank, and his thick reddish beard was grimy with stale food and other filth. There were scars and pockmarks on his cheeks.

Arraleen turned her face away at the stale aroma. "Gods, you're ugly," she muttered. He struggled, tried to stand, but her fingers shot out and gripped his neck, jerking his head back.

"You're going to be helpful, *yes?*"

"Fuck you."

"Hmm, trust me. You're going to want to do better than that." She smiled at his hateful eyes and grabbed his hand, jabbing the knife under a fingernail and twisting sharp. He gasped as the nail came off.

She grinned at him. "You still have nine. After that it's the toes. I'm in no rush."

He slyly reached for his sword with his good hand, desperate to get at her. She slapped that away and jabbed under another finger, twisting the blade. He swore and spat at her.

She changed tack and poked the knife under his eye, stabbing just enough to prick the soft flesh. "Maybe you'd prefer not to see what pieces I remove?"

He sobbed in rage, but nodded eventually.

"Excellent. Tell me where Trendale is, and I'll let you live."

"Don't know the name."

"Wrong answer." She took a third fingernail.

"Works for Kelgar."

"Yes, I know that. Best of three, or it's an entire finger this time. Where are they?"

"Kelgar's lair. Island offshore. West of here."

"How far?"

"Two days' ride."

"You work for this Kelgar too?"

"We're free men." He looked at his dead comrades and shook his head. "Who are you, devil bitch?"

She smiled. "They're free, but you're not, until I'm done with you. Who do you serve? The other corsair chief? The Sangala, Olgasha? Don't tell me you haven't seen him around. A sorcerer in a red cloak. He must have passed near here."

"We were free Reechers minding our own business," he pleaded.

Arraleen sighed. "Perhaps you were, but I'm growing bored with your answers. Where's Trendale? Where's the fucking

Sangala? You must have seen them, and the men with them. Both were large companies crossing his land. Tell me quickly, or I'll take both your eyes. I'm losing patience."

"Trendale will be with Kelgar by now. That devil in the cloak was working with Blue Face's men. They smell coin and both want to get Kelgar's prisoner, so they're heading for his lair too."

So you do know about Father. "How do I get to the island?"

"Aside Kelgar's docks, there are canoes further up, at a jetty. A man called Porg hires them out at a price."

"Good, that works." She stood and stowed her knife and walked to the fire, warming her hands for a moment.

"What about me?" he croaked across to her.

She turned, flashed him a grin. "What does an honest man like you do for work around here?"

"We were traders, furs and jewelry."

"Jewelry? Not very successful by your look." She stared at one of the bodies and frowned, noticing something for the first time. She kneeled and retrieved a metal object from the corpse's belt. Like a clam shell, but made of steel with a clasp and thumb nut on one side. She fiddled with the nut and the trap sprung open.

Arraleen frowned. "What is this, for game?"

"Yes."

"You're lying." She examined the steel trap and pressed it together. The perfect size to fit a small mouth, a young woman's or child perhaps? She searched the other bodies and found more tools and clues, which left her in no doubt.

"You were slavers."

"Please, no . . ." He saw her eyes, and she smiled at the fear in his face. "Traders and whalers, just passing through."

"I don't think so."

"I can prove—"

The scimitar sliced open his throat. He gurgled, thrashed. She watched with dispassion as the slaver choked and wriggled, until his eyes glazed over.

May Agarra take your soul, slaver.

She searched the bodies again, found some coin, dry meat, and wine. She fetched her horse and gave him water, while allowing her tired body take its ease by the crackling blaze. She slept for a time, the horse cropping grass and the seeping corpses her only companions.

Next morning the sun shone. A good sign. She'd left the woods before noon and traveled across an open country of stone-cropped hills and bleak windy ridges. She saw signs of movement. Tracks showing hoofs and some boot scuffs. A few days old. That must be Trendale's party. But where was Olgasha?

She rode apace most of that day. There were times when she needed to dismount and lead the beast over rocky terrain. No trees out here, and the wind a constant nagging sigh in her ears. She'd need to risk a fire again tonight, else she'd freeze.

After dark she found a hollow hidden in a fold of rock, allowing good views a few dozen feet above. She stayed warm as she could with a few faggots crackling. She heard wolves calling to each other. Aside that, nothing except the wretched wind.

Next morning sleety rain darkened her mood again. She

guided the horse along that ridge as the wind picked up and damp snowflakes swirled into her eyes, half blinding her. The blizzard passed and she moved on, the skies clearing quickly above.

By afternoon, she cleared the last of the hills and was rewarded by a good view of the countryside ahead. From that snowcapped ridge, she saw the land to the east falling sharply away into a dreary, wet-looking plain comprising brown brush and heathlands, broken by the occasional stream running through. Beyond the heath, the gray wash of water revealed the west coast shrouded by clouds. She saw no roads or sign of people moving. Olgasha was at large somewhere, maybe even watching her.

She shivered. Berated herself. Wasn't useful thinking about such things. She studied the coastline until she descried what might be a track. A thin jagged line cutting through the brown haze. Beyond that she saw something that resembled a hut or small building. The jetty, it had to be. She waited as the clouds shifted west, and she smiled as a rocky island came into view a mile or so beyond the jetty. The destination was in sight.

She descended the ridge and led the horse through a scrubby area, scanning and searching until she saw signs of the brush being disturbed. A track appeared and she mounted, her eyes missing nothing as she rode at a trot toward the coast.

By dusk she'd reached the area of the jetty. She dismounted and watered her horse, allowing him to crop the dead grasses. Having tied his bridle to a thorn break, she squelched through a brackish bog, the icy black water soaking into her boots and slowing her progress. She saw the huts and the strut of wooden jetty beyond. Past those, the rocky walls of the island rose gray and steep, seeming almost in arm's reach.

She approached the huts, making sure no one was around. Three low roofs were built over stone hovels. The furthest had a trail of smoke rising from its middle, hardly visible, as the wind scattered it almost immediately.

Arraleen approached the croft and other buildings. She could see no one, and the wind was freezing her ears. She needed shelter else she get hyperthermia. That meant the croft. There'd be warm food in there too, she hoped.

She returned for the horse, tying him off at a stone ring by the croft wall, closer than she'd liked, but the wind's ceaseless buffeting drowned out all other sounds.

She entered the croft and froze. Smoke clogged her nostrils. She had to stoop beneath the rickety door. Her eyes adjusted to the gloom. She saw a man's body strewn across the filthy bulrushes covering the floor, blood seeping from a wound at his side.

Recent. She kneeled beside the prone figure and placed an ear to his mouth. *Still alive.* She rolled him over and he groaned, opening a swollen eye.

A gut wound—he wouldn't last long and must have already lain here for some time. She saw a cask in the corner and poured cloudy ale into a wooden cup left for the purpose. She drank some herself and then placed it to the dying man's mouth.

He spluttered, blinked. Saw her and choked with fear.

"It's all right, I'll help you." She smiled until the panic left his eyes.

"It hurts . . ."

"I'll stop that. Allow you to rest. Drink up, good man. Are you Porg?" He nodded.

"Good. So, Porg. Tell me who did this to you."

She held the cup to his mouth. He dribbled and slurped, but some went in. He choked and she shook him gently. She lifted his shoulders until he groaned with pain, then she lowered him again.

"Can you speak clearly?"

"More ale."

She poured more into his mouth, washing the blood away with her hands. She smiled at him, wiping his brow. "I will avenge you, Porg. That I promise."

He shook his head. "You . . . *can't* fight him."

"*Who?* And why not?"

"Sorcerer. He . . . his men . . ."

"Doesn't matter, relax. I'll kill them all—you have my word. But first, I'll need to get across to that island."

"They took my canoes."

"Is there another place nearby with boats?"

He shook his head, and she gave him more ale. "My store . . ." He coughed. "They wouldn't have taken that one. Just finished carving it out. Needs caulking, but will float. There are paddles . . ."

"I'll find them." She smiled. "When did this sorcerer and his men leave?"

He tried to answer but groaned as fresh agony assaulted him.

"It's all right," she said. "You've been most helpful to me, and I'm grateful. Rest assured, I will avenge you and your kin, if there are others out there."

"You . . . can't . . . you should run . . ."

"Oh, but I can, Porg! You see, I'm the Dreamslayer." She let him sip the ale until his eyes half closed. His ragged breath was unsteady. "Sleep well, Porg. May Agarra bless your journey across," she told him, and placed the dagger against his heart. He closed his eyes and she stabbed down, hard and clean.

She dragged Porg's body outside and returned, searching for food in his hovel. She found broth in a cauldron, congealed and stale. She worked the fire until it crackled healthily, then added more kindling and logs, creating a blaze. She found a trivet and hook and hung the cauldron over the fire. Next, she found blankets over in the corner where his cot had been. She stripped naked and wrapped herself in wool, allowing her feet warm by the blaze. Her teeth rattled and she shivered, fearing she'd caught a chill.

She needed rest. Tomorrow would prove a busy day. Her enemies were on that island, and her father a prisoner, or worse. No, he was alive. Too valuable for them to hurt.

She didn't want to sleep in case Olgasha returned, or his wickedness found her. But the heat and her weariness won, and after she'd finished the eel stew, she curled up and collapsed in exhaustion in front of the fire.

Arraleen's dreams were vivid. Her mind wandered dark roads as her body sweated and trembled, fever shaking her. They were coming for her. Dark faces in red robes. Black oily smoking daggers glinting in their gloved hands. She saw Olgasha, tallest among them, and her father stripped and beaten, tied to a pole as they whipped him senseless.

She'd screamed, but her dream voice had been choked as black blood filled her mouth. Olgasha had smiled as he ripped out her father's heart with a bird claw gripped in his bloodstained fingers.

It's your turn, Dreamslayer . . .

He'd called across to her, and the shadows beside him had risen to grab her. She'd tried to run, but found that her legs wouldn't move, or support her weight. He'd kneeled in front of her, the crooked knife hovering over her eyes.

She'd tried to speak again, but this time hot maggots spilled from her mouth.

He laughed. *You are already dead.*

She choked into blackness, and distant deep cold.

I am lost . . .

Nothing is lost.

The voice was a surge of warm wind rising inside her. She saw a face. Handsome, the eyes a strange brown, flecked with gold. His long hair sparkled like firelight in sunshine. He was smiling as he stood over her, reaching down with an offered hand.

Who are you, djinni? She felt the pain and fear and shadow of Olgasha vanish, like mist in morning heat, replaced by the warm comfort of protection.

Someone who has scant love for the Sangala.

The voice was all around her, but his face was fading,

harder to define.

Your name?

That's not important. I'm no longer in your realm, but from where I am, I can see so much more. Olgasha is expecting you.

Then kill him for me!

She'd screamed the word out silently and rolled free of the cot, the jolt opening her eyes. *I'm failing.* She was shivering badly, her face and body shiny with sweat. *This won't do, Arraleen Caze. I can't be sick. I won't . . .*

She shook herself into motion, wrapped the blankets around her, found some dry meat, and crunched down hard. Next, she heated water and drank deeply, until her belly felt warm again. After that she wrapped and rolled tight in the filthy blanket, sobbing in frustration before finally relenting and sleeping for several hours.

Waking alarmed, daylight stabbed her eyes through cracks in the door and wind hammered her ears. She stood naked but warm. Her body felt stronger, her mind clear. The danger had passed. She was strong again. But those dreams?

They were nothing. I was feverish.

Time for action. She dressed quickly and strapped the swords to her belt. Outside, the horse still cropped grass by the post tether where she'd left him. A gray morning. Perhaps even afternoon? She wandered about and looked inside the huts until she found a small dugout covered with furs. A hollow tree limb, no more than seven feet in length, a hole scooped out where she could kneel. Further inspection revealed a short, sturdy-looking wooden paddle. Not pretty, but it would work.

A broader search revealed a bow half hidden by cloth, the gut string lying coiled close by. This she tested, stringing the bow and pulling back hard. A hunter's weapon, but it would do. She searched about and found a bundle of arrows. She smiled, as the gods were back on her side again. Maybe the fiery-haired djinn had left them for her? Or Agarra had chosen to answer her prayers.

She freed the horse. "You'll have to fare for yourself," she told him as she patted his neck, grateful for his help and companionship. She'd always preferred animals to people. Next, she struggled with the heavy canoe, sliding it down to the jetty where icy water lapped and surged, soaking her boots again.

She got positioned in the canoe carefully, placing bow and arrow bundle inside and adjusting her other weapons, while getting as comfortable as she could in the unstable craft. After practice, she found she could balance with her knees braced against the scooped wood, enabling her to use the paddle and thrust herself free of the jetty.

The waves buffeted her and almost rolled her twice, but she managed to work the paddle deftly until she'd cleared the shore current and made progress toward the island. It wasn't as far as she'd feared. Perhaps half a mile, no more.

Arraleen was soaked by salty splashes and spray by the time she dragged the canoe up the stony beach of the island. She lay panting in exhaustion from her efforts. Next was a climb, and those cliffs looked steep. There had to be a track close by.

She hid the canoe under a fold of rock, gathered her bow and sack of shafts, and went searching the beach. A mile along were boats bobbing, anchored a few feet offshore. A closer inspection revealed a campfire and the sign of boots and scuffs. A track led up between a cleft in the rocks. This she followed and trotted up, her body warming nicely with the exertion.

She reached a high place where the sea sparkled far below. She could still make out the boats bobbing in the distance, and nearer, the channel she'd crossed with Porg's croft, huts, and the jetty beyond. Far away, she could see the distant line of ridge where she'd slept the night before.

She turned and ventured on up until she crested the hill crown and saw the rest of the island spreading like a bird's talons beneath her. The most northerly spur sparkled with firelight. There was a camp over there, with a stockade and circular cluster of buildings, the trail of smoke rising and shifting in the wind. She spied white birds soaring and dipping, and more ships bobbing in the steely water beyond.

Kelgar's lair.

Arraleen unslung the bow from her shoulder and placed an arrow on the nock, setting it aside. Next, she adjusted her swords and checked the knives. She flexed her fingers and allowed her breath to slow. A few miles trot, through brush and heather. The steep climb down, followed by the cover of the shrubby trees to the camp. She'd wait for dusk and plan her move.

Before that, she'd get closer and discover what she could.

Arraleen smiled. "Hold on, Father—I'm coming to get you."

CHAPTER 14| THE HEALER

Gujun stood on the hill, the cold wind whipping his hair. A mile south, the ashen ruins of a village or homestead still burned in places. A raid. It had to be. But by whom?

Two days in the forest had led them to southern slopes, opening on windy heathland and a river in the distance. They'd seen no one and their progress had been good, mostly trotting through the deer paths in the woods, and sheltering from the worst of the chill.

Rogashi held up the spy-glass Dasco had lent him, despite concerns that the sailors would need it more should they be chased by Reechers or pirates again. His fisher friend had insisted he take it with him.

"A few days, no more." Rogashi passed the glass to Gujun. He pressed it to an eye and saw smoke rising in several places. A stockade, and a few loose horses grazing on grass. That solved one problem. They'd make good speed south once they'd caught those nags.

"No one in sight." Satisfied, Gujun passed the glass back.

"We'll go see and grab three of those animals," Rogashi said, his eyes troubled, his customary easy manner replaced by edgy anger.

They trotted down the windy slope and continued through stiff brush and heath, skirting the occasional bog. The wind was brutal. Gujun was grateful for the warmer gear, especially the hood on the woolen cloak he wore.

They approached the smoking ruins warily. Gujun saw crows scatter and lift, their harsh voices calling across to the two men walking below. Gujun stopped, seeing a body sprawled outside the tangled crumple of a half-burned building. He tapped Rogashi's shoulder. His companion's face was grim.

"Your contact lived here?"

"One of them."

"Best we go investigate."

They walked closer, Rogashi leaning on his spear and Gujun gripping the bow, his Jians resting ready across his back. More bodies appeared as they reached the broken gates to the stockade. Gujun counted fifteen badly burned corpses, among them women and one small child. One of the women had tried to fight back, her face locked in a death scowl of defiance.

"Your Reecher friends did this?"

"Don't think so," Rogashi said, his voice raw with anger. "They stick to their ships mostly. The people near the river are poor. These folks certainly were."

"Then who?"

They walked through the ash and burning carcasses of buildings. At the end of the pitted lane was a larger building that resembled an inn, or hostelry. A meeting place for the villagers perhaps.

Rogashi made for the building. The roof had collapsed, and more corpses lay scattered around the base, all of them showing signs of a violent end.

Rogashi cursed when he saw a figure resting against a wall, his eyes missing and both arms bent back and broken. He'd been tied to a stick and tortured badly.

"The elder?"

"Aye, Olbray. A stout soul." He shook his head, his dark eyes vicious with rage. "These can't have been random pillagers. Why this wanton slaughter? These were no common raiders."

Gujun studied the corpse curiously. "This was done to him after he was dead. See that neck wound? Suggests a different weapon, used earlier. A small knife perhaps?" Rogashi had turned away. Gujun scratched his chin. "Why would anyone do that?"

Rogashi cursed. "It's evil, Little Brother. Witchery. Someone has left us a message."

Gujun nodded. "Perhaps." *And I'll be glad to respond to that when we catch up with whoever did this.* He turned his head upon hearing a soft sound close by. He tapped Rogashi's arm.

"Someone's alive."

They skirted the ash pile and saw a small, hunched figure at the back of the inn—a woman buried beneath a heavy shawl, her weeping frail and feeble.

Rogashi ran and crouched beside her, as Gujun watched for any movement elsewhere. The woman screamed as she saw the big warrior leaning over her. Rogashi said something, calming her, and stooped down to whisper in her ear. She stared at him and returned to her sobbing.

The Yamondon questioned her for some time, waiting patiently for every response. Finally, he stood, resting a reassuring palm on her shoulder, and stared off into the ruins, as though lost in his troubles.

"Is she hurt?" Gujun said, joining him.

"Her body's hale, but the soul's shredded." Rogashi shook his head. "She hid, and somehow they missed her. Name's Misala. She was Olbray's wife. A good woman and a fine cook. I always liked her better than him."

Gujun wondered how many times Rogashi had been here. He seemed to know these people well. His outrage spoke of more than casual acquaintance. The Baha was a warrior born. Warriors saw death every day. There was something personal here. *Rogashi's right. It's a message.* That made him wonder about the dealings between the Yamondons and Vendeli in this hostile impoverished country. More to learn.

"What can we do for her?" he asked.

"She wants to be left alone. Mourn her kin and see to

her husband."

"She'll die, and badly. Other bandits, or wolves."

"She's Dalcian." Rogashi stared hard at him, until Gujun shrugged.

"What did she tell you?"

"That Grodu was here. A woman too."

"Obviously Grodu wouldn't have done this."

"Seems the perpetrators were following him. She blames his stopping here with the woman. She said Grodu killed some of them but was overcome, and they dragged him away." Rogashi shook his head. "Grodu's dead, Little Brother."

"I'll believe that when I see it," Gujun said, his eyes narrowing to flints. "Does she know where they took him?"

"Over to that circle of trees. See the rise?"

Gujun nodded. He saw a small clump of birch trees capping a hill, half a mile to the west. More worrying were the black birds hovering above.

"I think we're done here," Gujun said, his jaw set firm.

"Wait. There's more." Rogashi's face was hard. Gujun had never seen him so angry.

Gujun had a bad feeling. "You know who did this?"

"I think so. She described the leader, and he wasn't Dalcian."

"Vendeli?"

"Yes, but worse. A Sangala chief."

Fuck. "I thought them all dead."

"Not this one. She said she heard the men with him were Reechers in his pay. On loan from Blue Face Xeeg—he's one of the better known Reech Corsairs."

"So this Sangala was after Grodu and tracked him to her village. Seems excessive."

"More likely chasing Tulomon Caze, and Grodu showed up. Bad timing."

"You said she mentioned a woman with Grodu."

"Aye, so. I can't work that part out. I mean, *why?* She described the woman in detail. It can only be one person."

"Your Dreamslayer."

He nodded. "Arraleen Caze herself. But with Grodu? That doesn't make sense. She would blame him for her father's plight as much as the Sangala."

"We need to find Grodu."

"We do. And after that, cross the river and make west."

"You think the Sangala has Caze too?"

"If his daughter was with Grodu, she's either dead or escaped. And knowing her, in hot pursuit. The Sangala or a Reecher corsair must have captured Caze. Our answers lie across the Razor River."

"Come help me get those horses," Gujun said, and Rogashi nodded. He returned to speak with the woman, who shook her head fiercely and waved him away.

An hour later, Gujun watched as the big birds drifted and swooped low. He climbed the hill, the dark pines sighing in the stiffening breeze. His cloak whirled around his shoulders, and

Rogashi's hood was pulled down low as he sprinted up the rise ahead. They'd secured three mounts, saddle gear, and some food and water they'd sourced in the wreckage. They'd tied the beasts off at the bottom of the hill and climbed.

Cresting the crown, it wasn't long before they found a large prone figure slumped against a stump. Grodu appeared asleep. Rogashi rushed up to him, and Gujun followed close behind, his eyes on the hill and the rugged lands beyond, looking for clues or any sign of movement. No one around. The Sangala, or whoever did this, was miles away.

"He's still breathing," Rogashi said, as he knelt beside the former gladiator. "Lost a lot of blood." On closer inspection, Grodu had been stabbed several times, and the index finger was missing on his right hand.

"Why didn't they finish the job?" Gujun stared down at his friend, the rage swelling inside.

Grodu opened an eye and smiled up at him. "Because they were careless."

"I knew you'd survive." Gujun grinned. "You're indestructible."

"I *was* dead, or good as. He saved me."

Gujun looked at Rogashi, who shrugged, puzzled.

"Who saved you?" Gujun smiled. His friend was in bad shape, and most likely delirious. He must be half-starved, and had lost a lot of blood. Rogashi held a gourd to his lips, and he drank slowly.

"The healer from Rundali," he said eventually, making no sense.

"Rundali?" Rogashi looked at Gujun.

"A country near Shen." Gujun pictured a face he'd known. Intense brown-gold eyes and fiery red hair. That Rundali had been his enemy, but he'd disappeared after the fall of Ta Shen and the death of the woman he'd loved—Empress Rasnei. Despite them being foes, he'd always admired the man.

"Tell me about this healer," Gujun said. "You are badly wounded and should be dead, or bled dry. Instead, you appear in good humor."

"I'm hungry and sore. And pissed right off," Grodu said. "But you're right. Dead, I should be. I fucked up, lads, and almost paid in full."

"The healer?"

"Forget that, Little Brother," Rogashi said. "We need to catch up with those who did this."

Grodu looked at both of them. He drank more water and cursed. "I don't think I can walk far presently."

"We'll take you back to the village," Rogashi said. "Misala will look after you. Take her mind off—"

"More likely she'll finish me off, and I can't say I blame her."

"She's Dalcian," Rogashi said. "They're practical folk, as you know more than most. We'll explain that, once you've recovered, you'll join us and avenge her kin."

"Which I shall."

"You'll need to mend first," Gujun said. "That means rest, sleep, and food."

"I'll catch you up." He stared at them, his eyes full of shame. "I got drunk with Olbray. The bastards surprised us. She must have slipped their net. Olgasha took the rest, including me."

"A Sangala?" Gujun asked.

Grodu spat. "Yes, and a bad one even by their standards. Aided by fucking Reech Corsairs. They brought me here after I'd killed as many as I could. That devil cut me, and started planning more fun. But it got strange after that."

"The Rundali ..." Gujun said, and Rogashi looked at him in irritation. "You need to hear this," he told the Yamondon.

"The *healer*, yes," Grodu mumbled. "I ... don't recall how he came. It was dreamlike, but of course I was dying. Olgasha's hot knives were tearing at my flesh. But I saw his face, the stranger. The red hair. He carried skinny swords like yours, Slayer. Olgasha recognized him and seemed afraid."

"Here, drink. You're fading." Gujun held the gourd to his mouth.

Grodu sipped and coughed up blood. "It's all right, just hiccups."

Gujun raised a brow, and Rogashi laughed. "Go on," Gujun said.

"After that, the pain sent my mind down dark roads," Grodu told them. "I must have drifted off. The Sangala and his men had gone. The Rundali was kneeling beside me, chanting words in a strange language. I felt the pain leave, like water seeping from my veins.

"Finally, he stood and smiled. Told me to wait here. That I would recover, and help was coming. I'd thought him a dream, but here you are. I remember asking him why he'd helped me. He'd said he owed a debt to the Sangala and would aid those who dared challenge their evil, as he'd cause to hate them more than most."

"A vengeful spirit." Rogashi looked alarmed. "A djinn roused by that Sangala's sorcery."

"No. A man," Gujun said. "But an unusual one with special talents." Rogashi stared at him, but Gujun shook his head. There were more pressing matters to resolve. "Why was Caze's daughter with you? Was she helping the Sangala?"

For answer, Grodu twisted his neck painfully, as though looking for her. "Did she . . ."

"Gone," Gujun said.

Grodu smiled. "That's good," he said.

"How can that be good?" Rogashi asked. "He's not right in the head, Little Brother. We're talking about the fucking Dreamslayer. That woman's hated in Yamondo more than anyone, save perhaps the Yanturi himself. Or the Sangala. I think his mind's gone."

"Yours will be gone, Rogashi, if you don't shut up," Grodu growled. Rogashi shook his head. Grodu stared at Gujun. "I liked her," he said. "I'd met her once or twice with her father, but never spent much time. She's efficient. But there's more to her than that."

"She's an enemy," Gujun said.

"True, but also an ally. They have her father."

"Olgasha?"

"No. But he's heading that way. Trendale the bandit captured Tulomon Caze and is taking him to Eagle Kelgar's lair. I knew Trendale's reputation but didn't realize he worked for that bastard."

"Kelgar's one of the Reech Corsairs," Rogashi added. "Rumored the worst. His camp's on an island just off the west coast. Calls it his lair. Across the Razor River. Couple of days' ride from here."

Gujun smiled. "And Arraleen Caze is heading that way too."

"And Olgasha," Grodu added, coughing. "He wants Caze badly, as he captured him before. Arraleen told me that Trendale betrayed the Sangala who'd paid him to help. And rival Dalcian bandits took him, when Olgasha's party was waylaid. Olgasha got away and found some of Kelgar's enemies to help him get her back."

"So we have two rival corsair gangs after Caze?" Gujun mused, sensing an opportunity.

Grodu grunted. "Looks like it will be crowded when you get to Kelgar's lair."

"We'd best leave," Rogashi said. "Check on Misala. Get you warm and fed, Old Grumps. Come, Little Brother. Let's carry him down."

"Fuck off," Grodu said. "Just because you're a Baha and a distant cousin of Tarakai Dolusa—and maybe even related to the king—doesn't mean you're my nursemaid, Gash. I remember when you were a squally little brat."

Rogashi glared down at his wounded friend. "What should we do with you then?"

"Leave me here. I'm enjoying the view."

Rogashi mouthed a curse. "You've no food, and those buzzards look interested. Doubtless the wolves will be too."

Grodu squinted. "You have food?"

Gujun nodded, producing a small parcel of wrapped jerky.

"Good. That will work."

"You're not thinking right," Rogashi said.

Grodu grinned up at Rogashi. "Get you riding west, boyo. That way, you'll cross the Razor before nightfall. Don't fret about me."

"You might die."

"Everyone dies," Grodu said, winking at Gujun. "Ain't that so, Slayer?"

"We'll leave you the spare horse we brought and the supplies," Gujun said. "If it's only two days' ride, we won't need much portage. Just our weapons, water, and some dry meat. That way you can join us when you're strong enough."

Grodu grinned up at him. "I shall," he said. "Save some Reechers for me to kill."

They left him with the water and jerky and returned to the horses at the bottom of the hill.

"He'll die up there," Rogashi said. "His head's damaged, and those wounds will get infected."

"That is possible," Gujun said as he vaulted into the saddle. "But I'd sooner not place a wager on it."

"Me neither." Rogashi grinned for the first time that day. "Ya! Let's go find the Razor River, Little Brother."

CHAPTER 15|NIGHT WORK

Arraleen crouched in the shrubby brush twenty yards from the buildings. The smoke rose and twisted, as the buffeting wind carried it away. She was cold and half soaked by the heavy squall that had caught her descending the ridge. The clouds and weather shifted constantly on this cursed rock.

She'd made good progress in the gloom, reaching the camp area and lying low until dusk. She made the most of that dying light, skirting the lair and counting the guards. Only three, and they looked lazy as slugs. But neither Trendale nor his master would be expecting company.

She wondered what Olgasha was up to. Why she hadn't heard

from him yet. She put that out of her mind. Fix one problem, move on to the next. Find her father, and get the fuck out. If Olgasha arrives, worry about him then. Complications cause mistakes. Her enemies could afford those, Arraleen couldn't.

Her scouting had provided a clear access plan. A stockade, log jammed with heavy stakes they must have barged over from the mainland. Kelgar's lair looked organized. Three big fires roared outside the buildings, awarding light. She'd seen a stable area. Docks for their ships were at the far side, where the water lashed stone.

Four squat buildings surrounded a larger one that could accommodate over a hundred men. She hoped there weren't that many. A sturdy wooden gate barred the entrance through the brush. She could see two of the guards grinning as they cheated at dice. The other one was by the water, manning the second, smaller gate. That way lay her exit plan.

The main gate wasn't an option. The area approaching had been scrubbed clean. Even those idle sods would see her coming. Same with the water gate. That meant a climb. The stakes were pointed at the tip, and over ten feet high. Not a problem. She'd climbed higher, and often over stone and bricks.

An owl called out as the wind dropped. Seaward, a dark line of cloud barreled close. More squally rain on the way. That would hamper her climb.

Time to move.

She checked her swords were swaddled by the cloth she'd found in Porg's store to prevent them from clanking. She slung the bow across her shoulders and tied the arrow sack to her belt.

She chose her two favorite daggers and trotted off to a bank of brush that allowed her to creep closer to the wall.

The two men were cussing and laughing, already drunk by their oafish manner. She was tempted to run over and gut them, but one was bound to make a squawk and ruin her chances of keeping hidden. She needed this clean and fast. In and out. Plenty of time to clear any loose ends later.

She crept over to the pine stakes, her eyes on the guards. Satisfied she was clear, she reached up and wedged a knife into the joint between two stakes and pulled herself up, swinging her other blade over her head, and jabbing that into the cracks above. A tricky process for your average warrior, but no sweat for her. She'd done this blindfolded, climbing high over hot bubbling cauldrons during her final training test in Omala oubliette. Her father watching, his eyes filled with pride. She'd pulled the blindfold off and flashed him a grin from the top. Happier days.

Focus, Arraleen.

Hand over hand, she proceeded quickly, until she slid her lithe body clear of the sharp points, taking care not to catch her legs or trap her clothes. She'd left the cloak behind, as it would have hindered her movement. She wouldn't freeze if she kept busy. She'd get another once she'd freed him.

She gazed down and through the gap between buildings. No dogs. That was good. Besides the guards, she saw no one. Hopefully all were as drunk as them, if not more so, and sleeping by the fires inside that big structure.

She dropped, stone swift. Landing, light and balanced. She

smiled, the adrenaline kicking in. This was her favorite kind of work. She made for the nearest building and crept along its side. A huge fire crackled to her right. Beyond that she saw the glint of silvery waves washing ashore. Seconds later, that view had gone, as the rain arrived and heavy clouds raced above.

She checked the first building, inching open the door. A warehouse or store. She saw containers and jugs. Large urns and other random objects. No one here. She moved on to the next. Same. And the third, the one closest to the water. This shed contained skinny boats, and racks filled with spears, axes, and harpoons. The odd round shield. No bows, which surprised her. Reechers didn't seem to like bows. Again, she silently thanked Agarra for the one she'd found in Porg's boat store.

That left the main building. They were in there, her father too. She adjusted the bow on her shoulder and slipped her scimitars free, the steel glinting in the firelight. She made briskly for the entrance.

A man slumped against the door as he fumbled with his drawstrings. He dropped silent, as her sword sliced open his gullet. She inched the door open, adjusting her eyes to the reddish glow. She heard laughing, other voices. Still no dogs.

She slipped inside, keeping to the shadows rimming the long square hall. She crouched low, making sure her swords were hidden from the glow. To her left were three long tables where thirty or more men sat, chewing meat and cussing. More were over at the far end by the fire, and judging by their richer furs and garb, those must be the leaders.

She inched her way closer. Mouse silent, hugging the shadows and stopping whenever someone looked her way. She cleared the long tables, as the ale-sodden men shouted and belched and jostled each other. They were well into their cups, but any spare glance could ruin things for her.

It took her fifteen minutes, but she got close as she dared to the chieftain's table. She saw six men, their hard eyes sober, despite cheeks florid with drink. Three surrounded a huge burly man, with a thick red beard and curly locks. One of his eyes glinted in the firelight. A cast, she assumed. The other men were listening to him in deference.

Eagle Kelgar. It had to be. The fifth man turned her way, and she cursed silently, seeing Trendale laugh at something Kelgar had said. The bandit called across cheerfully to the men at the long tables, and a few shouted back. They were in good spirits. It was when she saw the sixth man on that table that she almost hissed out loud.

Her father sat hunched and defeated, a flagon of ale clenched in his hands. He appeared none the worse considering, his eyes dreamy and half closed. Cast Eye shoved him once and said something, which made his companions roar with laughter. She had to force herself to stay put.

She waited. The crew at the long tables drank and joked and swore. They laughed and clapped, while hurling meat bones at each other. One big fellow stood on a table and dropped his kecks. His companions roared approval, as he held a fiery brand to his buttocks and farted noisily, shooting more flames across the table. Arraleen pictured an arrow disappearing up his fat pink arse. She turned away, ignoring the fools.

The chiefs with her father were steeped in close talk, Kelgar Cast Eye wagging his finger. She saw her father glance around, his eyes wary. He was playing them. She smiled, and froze when his gaze locked on hers.

He nodded faintly and turned away, pretending to drift off. *The signal.*

The Reechers on the long tables were to her right, their leaders ahead. This would take precision and speed. Arraleen Caze excelled at both.

Smiling, she stood, scimitars swinging out in a scissor dance. She walked up, and a face turned her way. The one next to Trendale. He made to shout, but her sword sliced into his neck. Trendale yelled and jumped aside.

The other two bunched in front of the leader. Kelgar roared and reached for the ax resting at his side. She jumped onto the table as the hall erupted with angry shouts. A man grabbed her boot but she stamped down hard, breaking his fingers. She kicked Kelgar in his face with the other boot as he tried to stand. He slumped back, and she slammed a heel into the man on his right who'd been trying to trip her.

Her father was sliding to the end of the table. Trendale reached for him, but Arraleen's kick knocked him backward. The benches were crashing behind her as the confused rabble struggled to glean what was happening in the shadowy dark.

She stowed a sword and grabbed her father's arm, pushing

him toward the far door to the left of the fire. She saw Trendale running for the other door, meaning to cut off their escape that way, five or six of his men close behind.

One of Kelgar's top men lunged at her with a thick-bladed short sword. She blocked, slid her scimitar over his blade, and jabbed down into his belly. He toppled, gurgling.

Eagle Kelgar jumped onto the dead man's body, roaring and spitting, his ax swinging hard for her neck.

Arraleen ducked as she pushed her father toward the door. Kelgar crashed forward and swung again, as his men leaped up behind him, surrounding her with angry steel.

The ax swung out again. She dropped to her knees, cutting sideways and up with the scimitar, stabbing into the flesh under his left arm and pushing deep.

He glared at her, half hoisted the ax, but stopped as he choked. The men behind him froze.

Kelgar's glass eye glittered as the other glared at her in hatred. She smiled, tugged the blade free, and swung, slicing hard across, severing the shaggy head from his shoulders and sending it rolling into the flames.

Silence.

Kelgar's men stood gaping in disbelief. She caught her father's eye as he leaned by the doorway. He nodded. Timing was everything. She took a wild dive toward him as the hall erupted into thunderous noise again.

"Can you run?" she asked as she almost crashed into him.

"Yes, I'll try."

She pushed the door open and stabbed the man peering in from outside. They ran through, and Kelgar's vengeful corsairs followed hot behind. The boats were close, and she'd already planned which one to grab.

She pushed her father forward. Together they ran for the dock, stopping when laughter cut off their escape. A tall figure appeared wrapped in a deep red cloak. Olgasha showed his perfect teeth.

"Arraleen Caze, we meet again, as was expected. Kind of you to return my prize."

"Fuck you." She pushed her father aside as more men appeared from the docks, jumping clear of the boats that had just arrived.

Olgasha signaled to cut them off, but Arraleen and her father ran back into the stockade, making the most of the confusion, as Eagle Kelgar's men emerged like swarming hornets and crashed into Olgasha's party.

She heard Olgasha shouting to ignore them and catch the quarry, but the corsairs were rival gangs and soon fell about tearing at each other with swords, spears, and axes. She smiled cruelly at the miscalculation on the Sangala's part.

She saw Trendale with his men watching and fleeing out the gate when they saw Olgasha had arrived with the other Reechers.

Your turn soon, Trendale.

She soon forgot the bandit as she nudged her father on

through the stockade, the sound of fighting rising behind.

A corsair jumped out at her from behind a water barrel. She stabbed him in the eyes and ran on, but her father tripped and fell beside her. Another two saw them and came running. Arraleen stood over her father, her legs straddled wide, as she dealt with the first attacker and tossed a knife at the second.

"You all right?" she asked her father in a hoarse whisper.

"Alive," he muttered miserably as she helped him up.

She pushed him forward again and stooped to reclaim her dagger from the dying man's back. He begged her for mercy. She left him bleeding.

They reached the land gate, where she saw the two guards sprawled with their throats cut wide. Served them right for being sluggards. Clearly Trendale the bandit was cutting his losses. She could see torchlight off to the left. There must be more boats that way, and he was steering toward them, not wanting to get close to Olgasha. Fortunately for both Trendale and herself, the Sangala and his hired team of corsairs were still preoccupied with the last of Kelgar's wasp-crazy gang.

They cleared the stockade and reached the cover of brush wood.

"Keep moving," she hissed in her father's ear, as he staggered forward.

"Where?"

"Other side, I've a canoe stowed. You'll have to take your chance crossing to the mainland in that, while I find another way off this fucking rock."

He glared back at her, too exhausted and weak to argue.

"We'll keep to these woods and brush," she told him, pushing him on, the sound of shouting and screams, steel biting and ringing getter closer. "Once through, we'll make for the hill. Stay ahead of Olgasha."

"What about Trendale?"

"Fuck him. If he appears, he's dead. Otherwise, irrelevant."

The rain found them again, as they stumbled and half crawled through the maze of bushes and wind-torn thorns. They'd almost cleared the last break when he collapsed to his knees, his face red and eyes wild.

"Are you hurt?"

"Just tired. Need a rest, girl. Been a rough few days."

She cursed, but nodded. Olgasha was closing in, she could feel that unquiet she'd experienced before. Her father's wild look told her he felt it too.

"Hold to courage," she said and crouched low beside him, pulling his cloak over his head to shield him from the worst of the rain.

"Leave me here," he said, after he'd done with panting and getting his breath back. "I'm done, Arraleen."

"Shut up, Father. You're just winded."

"Bitch," he muttered and half chuckled. "I trained you too well."

"Soon as you can, we make for that hill and start climbing. I'll support you. Once at the top, we can rest again. But we have to get up there, else that bastard warlock finds us creeping in the woods."

"He'll find us for sure if you stay with me. It's my time, Arraleen. Escape safely, and I'll die happy knowing you'll avenge me. You know I'm right. *Go!*"

She was about to respond, when she saw a shadow racing off to her right. Seconds later there were more. Olgasha was almost upon them. The fighting broke out again, and close by, a man screamed.

"Come on," she hissed in his ear. "Last chance."

The clash of steel was close, but it trailed off as fresh shouts sounded further away. She thought she heard Trendale's voice amongst them, and seconds later, Olgasha. Hopefully he'd concentrate on the treacherous bandit first, deeming she and her father had nowhere to go.

Painfully slow, they reached the edge of the woods, the craggy slopes rising yards ahead. He stared mournfully up at the hillside.

"One foot at a time," she told him.

"Damn you." He hobbled forward.

The sounds of fighting drifted up as they got higher, their pace painfully slow. Eventually they reached a ridge and she dared allow him rest.

He slumped against a wet rock, as she gazed down through the gloom at the trees. Clouds raced above, and the distant sea smeared gray with the odd glimmer of sheen. She heard distant shouts. No one close. Olgasha must have caught up with Trendale. She smiled at the thought.

"We can't escape this island," he said, wiping sweat from his brow.

She cuffed his shoulder. "Why are you being so damn negative? Not like you, *Spymaster*."

"Because I'm finished, Arraleen. I see it now. Had plenty time to think. Trendale's treachery changed things. Survive this time and it will only happen later. And again. It will never stop until one of them gets me. But with you free, we win in the end. Take your time. Kill them all—it's what I trained you for."

"I'm putting you in that canoe and pushing you out to sea. After that, it's up to you to paddle and float. The thing's tricky, but you'll manage. I'll find another boat while they keep busy murdering each other, hopefully before sun up. Once I'm ashore, I'll come find you. Use the bird call, and stay well hidden in the reeds by the shore."

"I don't have the strength to paddle."

"Shut up, Father. I'm done with your excuses. We'd best get moving again."

He looked at her for a moment and nodded. "All right, have it your way, Dreamslayer. But you had better stay alive, or I'm going to be so damned angry."

She ignored his barb. Together they climbed up, her allowing him pause every so often to catch his breath. She could tell he was struggling, his voice ragged and face pale. Not like him to quit. She suspected he was on the edge of fever induced by body stress. He hadn't been well since they'd left Vendel. The ordeal, injuries, and travail had worn him thin. Then the capture, and now this hectic escape in the freezing rain and winds. But once off this island, she could find a place for them to hide out, and nurse him back to health. After that. *Revenge.*

They reached the top of the hill and gazed down. The wind surged through her ears, and she could see nothing moving down there. It would be dawn in an hour or two. She walked the ridge until she found the track where she'd climbed the day before.

Together they descended, almost as slowly as they'd climbed, with him stumbling and tripping and her having to catch him. The canoe was where she'd left it. She pulled the dugout from the hide and dragged it across to the beach. He stared at her.

"Get in, and I'll push you out." She passed him the paddle. "All you have to do is stay afloat long enough for the tide to carry you over there."

He smiled at her. "Arraleen, I'm proud of you, girl." He was about to say something else when the arrow struck his shoulder, spinning him around.

She heard shouts. Saw men running along the beach toward them, carrying spears and bows. A second arrow struck the canoe. She heard a familiar voice. Trendale had slipped Olgasha's net and was planning on stealing his prize again.

"Arraleen, run!" Tulomon Caze gasped as he gripped his shoulder and lurched forward.

"I'm staying put," she said, freeing her scimitars.

CHAPTER 16| DEALERS IN DEATH

Gujun stood over the graying corpse, the wind slamming the makeshift door shut behind him. Rogashi was outside rummaging through the stores. He appeared, and Gujun nodded.

"Seems like they've all been here. Grodu's Sangala, the Dalcians. And the woman. There are mixed boot prints everywhere."

"She must have taken a boat from the store," he said, looking down at the dead man. "Something's been dragged down to the water."

"She was here after them," Gujun said. He examined the corpse, the different wounds. "That Sangala most likely carved these out of spite. Someone else, probably her, finished him off.

An act of mercy helping him on his way."

Rogashi shook his head. "Arraleen Caze wouldn't waste time on a poor old fool like this."

"Unless he was still able to speak and told her about the boat. Any more crafts available?"

"No. We're out of luck. Olgasha and his new Dalcian friends must have taken them all, save the one hidden in the store."

Gujun nodded. To be expected. "Best we search elsewhere. Since they're all on that island, we need to get over there."

Rogashi rubbed an eye. "Nothing north but the wild headland. And Hooks—they won't have camps up there. Nothing but rabbits and wind and . . . *rumors*. Best we ride the shore south, see if there are boats down there. Kelgar must have a dock somewhere."

"Agreed." *And doubtless men guarding them.*

They left the drafty croft and stood staring at the island, its hills covered in mist.

"We could try swimming there," Rogashi suggested.

Gujun looked at him. "No, we won't."

"You've scant sense of adventure, Little Brother."

"It's why I'm alive. Come on, let's get riding. Else, Caze is dead by the time we get to him."

It had taken a day and a night to cross the Reech. After fording the Razor River, they'd ridden through woods and heath, crested some hills, and seen the distant ocean. They'd camped without a fire for a few hours and moved on by dawn, reaching the marshy region where the croft and hovels lay. Rogashi had spotted them with Casco's glass the day before.

They guided their mounts along the beach track for an hour as the gray morning emerged, the rain brushing the ridges of the island flanking their left. It was fully light when Gujun spotted the ships resting in the lee of a hook of sand. As they rode closer, eyes sharp, he saw a jetty and three huts. The island's shore was closer here. Perhaps only a couple of hundred yards, but the current appeared stronger. A hard row to get across.

They reined in, watching for movement.

Rogashi handed him the glass. "What do you think?"

Gujun pressed it to his eye. "We need a sail to get across that chop. That means one of those crafts, unless something smaller's at hand."

"Let's go see."

They rode as close as they dared and dismounted, tying the horses to a thatch of gorse. The two stole closer, dropping to their bellies, as the view opened ahead revealing a flat level area, the three huts, and a group of heavily armed individuals lounging around. Gujun counted a dozen, perhaps thirteen men. There were three others on the dock looking out at the island, as though expecting someone. Maybe Caze himself, under heavy guard.

"You thinking what I'm thinking?" Rogashi asked him.

Gujun grinned at the big Yamondon. "We rush 'em." They returned to the horses and vaulted into the saddles.

"Ya!" Gujun said, as Rogashi clicked his tongue spurring his mount forward. They were halfway to the dock area before the first man saw them and yelled a warning.

Gujun's arrow took the shouter in the throat. He saw one of the three on the dock calling across and shot again, watching with satisfaction as the man pitched headfirst into the eddying water.

The others were rushing to the huts, grabbing spears from a stack resting against the nearest one. Gujun shot another two, and Rogashi three more. That left six, and the two rushing across from the dock.

They reached the shelter of the huts as the nearest Reechers came running at them with spears. Gujun shot one through the eye and tossed his bow aside. He leaned back and slid his Jians free, scissor-slicing as he crashed the horse amongst them.

To his right, Rogashi roared his Yamondon battle cry and struck out with his tulwar, hewing heads and cleaving bone. In seconds, they were through the press, the two survivors running for cover behind the huts.

"I'll deal with those, you get the two on the dock," Rogashi yelled at him.

"We need one alive."

"Two's better."

"On it."

The two men on the dock had seen how their comrades had fared and were racing back for the nearest craft, yelling at someone over there.

Gujun spurred his horse and crashed onto the worn planks of the dock. He sheathed a Jian and struck the mare with a gloved hand, urging her after the runners. He rode down the first, who screamed, and the horse trampled his bones. The last one had almost reached the nearest craft. Gujun saw two fellows on the small deck, one cranking a crossbow.

He bemoaned himself for casting the bow aside. An error.

The bolt cranked and loosed. Gujun leaped from the horse's back, landing poised on the dock planks, his Jian swinging and twisting out into the runner's back.

He shoved him off the jetty and weaved lithely. A second bolt skidded over the planks, while a third struck a stanchion. The other man was cutting the mooring ropes to allow the craft drift away, as his companion cranked another bolt.

Gujun reached the end of the dock, scooped a dagger from his belt, and hurled it across. The crossbowman collapsed with the dagger in his chest.

Gujun vaulted onto the deck. The last one had severed the ropes and was grabbing an oar. Gujun's kick sent him sprawling. A second one in the ribs kept him down, and the stamp on the back of his neck rendered him harmless for the moment.

Gujun seized an oar and jabbed it into the dock, pulling the craft over. The other two ships appeared empty. A relief, considering he'd forgotten about those.

I'm losing my edge, he thought, angry with himself.

He tied the boat off again as best he could with the shredded ropes. A quick glance at the prone Reecher told him he'd stay put for a while. Gujun jumped back onto the jetty where the horse was wandering skittish, as the water crashed and frothed muddy-white below.

"Easy, girl." Gujun caught up with the animal and grabbed the reins, steadying the mare. He heard a shout and saw Rogashi arrive, leading his horse onto the dock, an unconscious Reecher sprawled over the saddle.

"Think those boats will take our horses?" Rogashi asked, as he led his mare across to where Gujun steadied his animal.

"I'm hoping so," Gujun said. He looked at the slumped body sprawled over the saddle. "That fellow doesn't look overly useful."

"Neither does your one on the boat," Rogashi said, as he glanced that way.

"He'll wake up in a moment."

Rogashi grinned. "As will this one." It took half an hour before one of them could talk. Gujun set them to work, helping Rogashi get the horses onboard, while he prodded the Reechers with steel for incentive. A precarious business, but it worked eventually. The beasts were nervous, but Rogashi's cool words seemed to calm them. Gujun smiled, watching. Even horses appreciated the big Yamondon's charms.

Rogashi held the animals as Gujun studied the Reechers, his knife pressed against the nearest.

"Blue Face is coming," Rogashi's prisoner said. The other just nodded his head. Gujun must have damaged his jaw with the stamp. Too bad. But his arms and legs were working, so he could ready the boat while his friend jabbered.

"Xeeg Blue Face himself?" Rogashi raised a brow at Gujun, who shrugged.

"A strange name."

"Well known for atrocities in these parts. Torax's head thug, until he decided he wanted all the gold for himself and broke away from his boss. He's rumored half mad. And like his former chief, Xeeg's no friend of Kelgar. But these Reechers are all rabid dogs ..."

Gujun glanced at the pitiful pair as Rogashi kicked the nearest.

"Olgasha must have tempted Blue Face with Caze. Am I not right? Answer, unless you want another kick?" Rogashi glared at the Reechers crouched bleeding on the deck, Gujun's dagger pressed behind the talker's ear.

"If you want to keep this ear, you'd better answer my big Yamondon friend."

"Fuck you."

Gujun shook his head. These Reech Corsairs weren't that bright. *Must be the climate.* He sliced, and the ear came off. The man spat at him, so he pressed the blade against an eye. That did the trick.

"The Vendeli devil has promised us Tulomon Caze. He's over there fetching him, while Kelgar's farts are too drunk to piss straight. Blue Face will sell him to the Yamondons."

"I doubt Olgasha will let that happen," Rogashi said, smiling. "Your leader's been duped, poor fellow. Olgasha will use your gang to deal with Kelgar's lot, while he kidnaps Caze. It's in both your interests to sail us over and help us catch up with your boss's new Sangala friend."

Gujun switched the blade from one eye to the other, causing the man to blink and twitch. "How many of your men does Olgasha have with him?"

"A score are with the Vendeli on the island. Aside from us,

the main crew are coming with Blue Face."

"Where's Blue Face now?"

"On his way," the other man croaked a response. "Who are you people?"

So you can speak after all?

Gujun stowed the knife. "Get us to that island quickly, and you won't need to worry about that."

"Meaning you'll kill us."

Gujun stared coolly at the wretch. "*Meaning,* cast off and set sail. Else we start removing more pieces from both of you."

"He's from the east. They're twisted over there," Rogashi told the two. "But I'll stop him from doing his worst, if you're useful. Who knows, you could help us on the island. There could be gold and rewards. We've nothing personal against you. The Vendeli warlock's the real enemy here."

They both nodded at once. "We'll help."

I thought you would. Gujun watched as the two prisoners stood shakily. His prisoner untied the sail as the other one worked the tiller, while Rogashi cut the ropes again and cast off with an oar, having tied the horses' reins to the mast.

The current was very strong, but the Reechers proved canny in handling their craft. Halfway across, one of the horses kicked, but Rogashi calmed the beast. As they neared the island's dark slopes, Gujun saw a shingle beach and a couple of huts with another dock jutting out.

"Your people leave any guards there?" he asked the one on the tiller.

"A few, most likely. Stayed around after doing so for Kelgar's men."

"Where do you corsairs keep your raiding ships?" Rogashi asked. Gujun had wondered the same thing.

"Off the south shore," the one on the tiller said. "Another island. Xeeg's Lair. A converted iceberg. He's sailing this way, but he had blood business with Torax in Bleakport to attend to first. Kelgar has ships on the far side of this island. Where he raids from."

"Since you're being helpful, you might want to persuade anyone waiting that we're not here," Gujun said. "We don't want your friends getting excited. So easy does it. No warning shouts and you get to keep your tongues." He'd almost said *ears*, but . . . too late for one of them.

The two nodded, and twenty minutes later the craft eased alongside the island's dock. A man called out angrily from close by. Gujun and Rogashi were crouched below the clinker sides, Gujun with the dead man's crossbow cranked ready, having salvaged the weapon alongside a few stray bolts. He also had a knife pressed against the ankle of the tillerman. Rogashi's tulwar pricked the other's leg.

The shore man shouted again.

"One of you two say something to shut him up," Rogashi hissed, jabbing his man with the edge of his blade.

"Blue Face is over there," that one called out. "Said the Vendeli's not to be trusted."

The other corsair tied off, as the craft slammed against the dock.

"Why are you here?" the one on the dock demanded.

Gujun rolled to his knees, saw the corsair walking toward them, and shot him with the crossbow.

Rogashi pushed one of the prisoners forward as Gujun cornered the tillerman.

"Thanks," he told him. "You've been very helpful. Now help us with the horses."

The pair obliged begrudgingly, and the horses made it across to the dock. Unfortunately, during the process, Gujun's mare lashed out and kicked one of the Reechers into the water. He disappeared almost immediately, the current whipping him away.

"Best you go help your friend, old son." Rogashi shoved the other one off the deck. He, too, vanished in the dark churning water.

Two more corsairs appeared onshore, saw them with the horses, and rushed forward. Gujun shot them both. He placed boot in stirrup and hoisted his body up. Rogashi followed suit, clicking his tongue and steadying his animal. Gujun glimpsed the two swimming frantically, as their bodies bobbed like logs in a flood.

"What are their chances?" Gujun asked Rogashi as they rode free of the dock.

"Not good," Rogashi replied. "Current will take 'em out until the cold finishes them."

"Shame," Gujun replied. "They tried so hard."

They rode along the beach until Gujun spotted a track leading up through a cleft in the cliffs. They guided the horses up the shale slope until it steepened. They had to dismount and struggle leading them on foot.

Morning cast a pale light on the shingle below. At the hilltop, they stopped and sheltered from the relentless wind. The skies had cleared and it looked to be a bright day, the first Gujun had experienced since leaving Yamondon waters.

The two looked around. They were hidden by rocks and had tied the horses to a dead thorn. These grazed on brown grass as Gujun stood with folded arms, his eyes shielded from the sun. Rogashi held the glass to an eye and scanned from left to right.

"I see the camp. That must be Kelgar's lair." He pointed northeast and passed the spy-glass over.

"Lots of smoke," Gujun said, passing the glass back. "I saw ships and buildings, but the haze hides most of it."

"Fires? Or Olgasha attacking?" Rogashi looked at him. "Perhaps the Dreamslayer's up to something?"

"Best get over there and see. How far do you estimate?"

"Two, maybe three miles. We won't get close with these nags."

Gujun nodded. He turned and walked back to the horses, but on instinct paced over to the other side of the rock screening them. From there, he could see the cleft they'd climbed and the strand of pale beach below. The boat bobbed on the dock, but he saw no one down there.

He turned away as Rogashi untied the horses. He was about to join him, when a flash of light caught his eye. "Over here," he called across.

Rogashi led the horses over. "What is it?"

"A light a few miles north up the beach. A flash. Look, there it is again."

"Steel on steel," Rogashi said, and put the glass to his eye again. He shook his head. "Too far to tell, and the rocks are hiding half the beach. But that's got to be people fighting."

They stood and watched for several moments as the flashes came and went.

"Best we go see," Gujun said.

"We'll not guide the horses along that ridge."

"We either go back down and ride the beach, or we run the crest."

They chose the second option. Rogashi found a sturdier thorn break for the animals. Half hour later they crouched low, scanning. Ahead, another track cut down through stunted trees. They ran to the ridge and saw it lead down through heath toward the distant camp, which Gujun suspected was under attack judging by the flames and worsening smoke.

"If that's Olgasha attacking Kelgar's people, who's fighting down there on the beach?" Gujun hoped the Reechers were killing each other. Less to mop up.

Rogashi shook his head. "No idea." The two of them turned and trotted down the track toward the leeward side of the island. They'd almost reached the strand when Gujun gripped his companion's arm.

"See that?"

"I do." They dropped closer and crept to a ridge twenty feet higher than the beach. Gujun saw five bodies lying scattered like toys on the sand. No sign of the attacker, but a tiny boat lay abandoned half washed by the rollers. Someone arriving, or trying to escape?

"That's got to be the canoe she took from the dead man's boat store," Rogashi said.

"You think she killed this lot?"

"Makes sense."

"Does it?" He scratched an ear thoughtfully. "Those are fresh corpses by their look. No carrion in sight. This was recent, perhaps early this morning, and her tracks on the mainland showed she left with that canoe some time ago. She'd be at the camp by now."

"You think she found Caze and was heading back? And they attacked her?"

Gujun nodded. "If so, she's still around, and that means Tulomon Caze is too."

"Olgasha could have followed her here."

I hope so. Gujun looked at his companion. "Let's find out, shall we?"

"Be careful, Little Brother. She's something else, is Arraleen Caze."

So you keep telling me, Bro.

They jumped down and ran across to the bodies. All Reechers, and killed by a sword. One had an empty sack of arrows tied to his belt. That one's eyes were missing. And closer inspection revealed that his genitals were too.

"This poor fellow must have pissed her off," Rogashi said.

"But where is she hiding?" Gujun wondered out loud.

"Behind you."

Gujun laughed, hearing the voice. *Nicely played.* He turned very slowly. A striking young woman, with windswept black hair and sharp jet eyes, was staring hard at his face. She had a bow nocked and ready, and a cold smile on her face.

Arraleen watched their faces, reading the reactions. The big Yamondon looked alarmed, but not afraid. The pale-faced little one appeared half amused. Smug even.

"Toss those swords on the sand," she said.

They complied slowly, the little one folding his arms and feigning a yawn.

"You're an arrogant little shit," she told him.

He smiled back at her, but said nothing.

"We're not your enemies today, Dreamslayer," the Yamondon said. A Baha by his look. Perhaps related to the king himself. Proud, vain, and handsome. She'd have got a ton of gold for his head, had she brought it back to the Yanturi in previous times.

"Kneel on the stones, so I can slay you quickly."

Neither moved.

She pulled back on the bowstring.

"Where's your father?" the little one asked.

"I'm asking the questions. Get on your knees, else I shoot you."

"You can't kill that Sangala and all the Reechers, and expect to save your father too," the cool-eyed pale one said. "We could help you. As my big friend says, we are not your enemies today."

"I don't need your help, shithead. Kneel!"

They remained put.

"As you wish." She made to loose, but stopped when the small one stepped forward.

"They call me the Slayer."

She eased back on the bow. "The Shen renegade? Grodu's contact in the east? I don't much care. *Kneel.*"

"We both know that's not going to happen." He stepped toward her and smiled again. She was intrigued, her eyes on him and flicking across to the Baha, who stood wary and ready behind.

"You came here to kill my father and claim gold for his head. Probably did a deal with this Baha scum."

"Grodu sends his regards," the Yamondon said, as the Shen still smiled at her.

"Grodu betrayed us." She spat in the sand. "He's the reason my father's wanted in Vendel."

"We can help," Gujun the Slayer said.

"Bollocks."

"I'll help cut off Olgasha's," he replied.

She didn't care for this Shen. He was tricky, but interesting. She raised a brow. "All right . . . since I'm curious. Speak."

"Way I see, it's common sense," the Shen said. "We can keep up these pleasantries on this windy beach until Olgasha, or Eagle Kelgar, or Xeeg fucking Blue Face, all show up for the party." He arched a brow. "*Or* . . . we can help you kill them."

"Why would you do that?"

"Because my big Yamondon friend here wants to speak with

234

your father, and he has an offer from his king that might interest him. And you."

Arraleen choked back a laugh. "Lies. What about you, Shen? Why are you here?"

"Two reasons. Grodu was my friend. I don't have many of those. And . . . I've met Sangala before and don't care for their company. You could honor me by letting me kill this Olgasha fellow. Once you've removed his bollocks."

"Olgasha is a sorcerer." Arraleen chewed her lip and watched their faces for long moments. This might be her only choice. The wind had picked up again and time was pressing. Her father lay bleeding badly in the cave she'd found. He wouldn't last long without help.

The arrow in his shoulder needed drawing out. That meant hot water, and herbs. Therefore, the mainland. These men were her enemies. But so was everyone else on this island. She decided there was little option. Get them to help him escape across. After that, kill them both while he recovered somewhere safe.

"Well?" The Shen was staring at her, as though reading her thoughts.

"Trendale's men." She pointed her bow at the corpses. "That archer shot my father in the shoulder. Tulomon Caze needs help, else he'll not last."

"Trendale the bandit? Is he one of these fellows?" The Yamondon looked at the dead strewn across the beach.

"Nope. That slippery fox escaped with half his men. And I was just getting warmed up."

The Shen's eyes hardened. "Which way?"

"It was barely light, I don't know."

"If they went south, they'd have clashed with Blue Face's crew," the Shen muttered to his companion. "Must be north, or they circled back to Kelgar's lair."

"Olgasha burned it down," she told him.

"We have horses tied up on that ridge," he replied. "Rogashi here will bring them down to the beach, while I help you move your father."

She stared at them. *I hate this.*

The Shen killer flashed her a grin. "It's either that or die here with him."

She glared back at him. "Perhaps I prefer that option to working with enemies."

"I doubt that." He smiled. "You're a survivor, I know your type."

"You know nothing about me, Gujun the *Slayer*. Save what that lying Yamondon's told you. And Grodu."

"We Yamondons don't lie." Rogashi appeared offended.

Arraleen laughed at his pained expression. She noted the fists clenching and unclenching at his sides. *This one's a hothead.*

"As you've guessed, I'm Baha," he told her. "And I swear on my family's honor that we two will not hurt your father. And we will assist you, if you'll let us."

"Unfortunately, you're all out of time."

A rich voice interrupted them. Arraleen cursed and pulled back on the bowstring as Olgasha emerged from the rocks. A group of corsairs following behind. The Sangala held out both his hands, and the bow hummed hot in her fingers and started burning them.

She dropped the weapon and reached for her swords.

CHAPTER 17|THE STRANGER

Gujun counted twenty men behind the tall Sangala. Corsairs carrying spears and swords, a few hefted round shields on their backs. He saw no bowmen among them. Again, he was grateful that they didn't appear to like bows. That gave the three of them a chance, though not a good one, admittedly.

The corsairs were confident. Their hard pale eyes switched between Rogashi and himself, and across to the woman. The Sangala's dark gaze was fixed on her alone. He clearly deemed himself a wolf among sheep. There lay his weakness. *I've met your kind before, sorcerer.*

Gujun chuckled. All eyes turned his way. He caught the

woman's face. She looked angry, but curious. Almost impressed by his attitude. He winked at her, and she glared back.

The Sangala rounded on him. "What is funny, Shen?"

"Life."

"Yours is over, my friend." The Sangala took a step toward him and raised his hand.

"You dare turn your back on me?" Arraleen Caze said.

Olgasha clicked his tongue. "Kill these two," he told the corsairs. "I'll deal with the girl and find her father. He must be in bad shape, or he'd be here."

The corsairs circled Gujun and Rogashi, who stayed put, covering each other's backs. He caught Rogashi's eye and grinned. "They're fat and lazy," he said, staring at them, and goading the anger in their eyes.

"I think so too," Rogashi replied, and crouched with tulwar ready.

"Kill them," Olgasha said irritably, as he turned and walked briskly toward the woman who, like Gujun and his friend, hadn't moved. She stood with feet braced and lips curled down in loathing. Her eyes were blazing magnificently. *No fear.* Pure fury and hatred. A snake's cold stare. First impressions, he admired the girl.

The men surrounding them seemed edgy. Hesitant. Gujun feigned boredom and scratched an ear.

"You tasted a touch of my power before," Olgasha said to the woman. "That was nothing. But this is going to hurt." He chanted something, and Gujun saw him carve a sign in the air. Arraleen Caze cried out and covered her face, the sword dropping to the sand. "Burns, doesn't it?" The Sangala laughed, as he raised both hands and chanted. She screamed, scratched at her eyes, and dropped to her knees.

Blue Face's corsairs were distracted by the noise. Their hesitation gave Gujun all the time he needed. He leaped toward the nearest, slicing his Jian through the man's throat, before twisting and skewering the next. To his right, Rogashi stepped forward and bludgeoned the third with his tulwar, cleaving him from shoulder to groin. He twisted and tugged the heavy blade out, and swung again.

The girl had stopped screaming, as, distracted by their attack on his men, Olgasha turned to use his sorcery on them. Spears jabbed at Gujun's face. Rogashi hewed the hands off one fellow. Gujun danced and stabbed across, a Jian in each hand. Cutting and killing.

He could hear the Sangala chanting behind him. *He's working on me . . .* The sudden pain struck his eyes like venom. He squinted, saw Rogashi clutch at his throat and drop the tulwar.

A corsair jammed at the Yamondon with his spear. Gujun, half blinded by pain, jumped in close and stabbed the attacker under his arm. But it was no good. They were surrounded again, and the pain behind his eyes was almost unbearable.

Gujun staggered, fighting the agony.

Too bad, but everyone dies.

He'd have preferred an honest fight to sorcery. Too bad . . .

You shouldn't have turned your back on me.

Her rage held the searing agony at bay. It seemed like her face was on fire, her vision blurred and stomach lurching. But the fear she felt made her so fucking angry. How dare he?

No one turns their back on me.

He was enjoying himself, this Sangala. The corsair scum were closing on the two men as his sorcery blinded them, as it had her. He was almost done, and it would be her turn again. But sometimes you could be too confident of winning.

Her head throbbing and eyes streaming with tears, Arraleen Caze fumbled for a dagger and ran up behind the Sangala. She tripped on the pebbles. He turned and smiled down at her. She jabbed up, stabbing the knife into his calf.

He cursed and kicked her face, knocking her back. She saw him tug the blade free, and lick the blood from the steel. He grinned at her.

"You'll pay for that, bitch." He stood over her, reaching down and grabbing her hair, wrenching her head back to expose her neck.

She slammed a back fist against him, but he knocked it aside. She spat in his face. He spat back and struck the side of her head, knocking her prone, and kicking her hard in the ribs. Finally, he crouched with the knife and grinned, his dark face smeared with blood.

"I'm going to take your eyes first, Dreamslayer. Such pretty eyes . . ."

The searing pain vanished. He saw Rogashi stumble as a corsair caught him with a sword. Gujun danced across and stabbed the man through the throat.

"You hurt?"

Rogashi coughed, though his neck was bleeding badly. "Flesh wound."

The corsairs had backed off again. Nine left. He could tell they wanted to live and were dismayed at losing half their companions. Their leader, Xeeg, wouldn't be pleased when he arrived. The Sangala was leaning over the woman, a knife held close to her face.

Gujun shouted a warning, but a flash of light startled him and he heard one of the corsairs cry out in fear.

Beside him, Rogashi gasped. "What the . . ."

A stranger stood on the beach. A smallish man, Gujun's build. An ornate, ruby-studded Jian gripped in either hand. He appeared faint, as though somewhere else, and this was but his reflection.

The Rundali.

Gujun felt a flood of emotion. He knew this man, if man he still was.

Gujun vaguely noticed the swords slipping through his numb fingers as he watched the apparition approach where the Sangala stood by the girl. Olgasha had forgotten her and was staring at the stranger, his hands held out in warning, the fore and index fingers making the Sangala horn sign.

Gujun's legs trembled. *Rundali. Can it be you? I must already be dead . . .*

He felt the glisten of a tear dampen his face. The memories

came rushing back like a hot searing blade in the soul. He saw Empress Rasnei's dying face as her red-haired lover crouched over her, moments after he, Gujun the Slayer, had killed the man who'd stabbed her—the Shen Magister, Chulan. The Sangala had been there, and had played a part in that outrage. As had he. And now the Rundali had returned to avenge that atrocity.

As though bewitched, Gujun watched, his mouth moving but no words leaving the lips.

The avenger's long red hair seemed to drift in the wind, smoky and vague like the face. Hard to define. *It's only part of you.* Gujun wanted to call across, but his mouth was frozen. He heard Rogashi chanting in fear beside him.

The corsairs had fled the beach. He hadn't noticed them leaving.

He saw Olgasha stumble, holding his hands high as though warding off an attacker from above. He was shouting. The desperate yells turned into a scream. Gujun saw Arraleen Caze roll to her knees and grab the dagger. He watched, frozen, as she stabbed it into the Sangala's kidneys, first one then the other.

Olgasha sobbed as he slumped forward. She stood, shoved her fingers into his nostrils, and wrenched his head back, before slicing the knife hard across his throat. He quivered and kicked, and eventually lay still.

Gujun hardly noticed. He stood stark and witless, trapped inside someone else's dream. The Rundali smiled across at him and raised a Jian in salute. Gujun felt his hand lift in response. The stranger faded, disappearing like wood smoke caught by a sudden gale.

Gujun dropped to his knees, as Rogashi stood blinking like a man stricken dumb by sudden lightning.

"Vian!" Gujun called out the name on his lips. But the Rundali had gone. No trace of his shadow remained.

Arraleen sobbed as fear, pain, and confusion fused with rage. She stabbed at Olgasha's corpse, over and over, until she slumped to her knees exhausted. The two men were watching her in silence. Even the Shen appeared stunned by what he'd witnessed.

The Stanger had come. The red-haired ghost-warrior who'd saved her in the woods. He'd returned, as he said he would. But who was he? And how could she ever repay him? She sobbed. She had failed. *Lost.* For the first time in her life, someone else had taken control. A shadow or spirit. A djinn perhaps? No, the djinni were rumored to be evil spirits. A guardian? Sent by Agarra?

A soft voice spoke behind her. "An *Aikashi.*" She turned and saw Gujun the Slayer gazing at her, his eyes raw with emotion.

"What?"

"The stranger you saw. He was part *Aikashi.* I knew him once."

Arraleen brushed hair from her eyes and blinked at him. "A spirit?"

"Perhaps now . . ."

She glared at the Shen, her face numb with shock. "That red-haired stranger helped me in the woods, near where they killed Grodu and the villagers. Said he owed the Sangala a debt of blood."

"The Sangala were there when she died, as was I."

"Who died? What are you talking about?"

"The empress of Shen."

She noted the pain in his eyes, the guilt. He seemed so different than before. Gone were the arrogance and cocksure confidence. He appeared vulnerable, culpable even. "I don't understand. Who is he?" she asked.

"Vian of Rundali. He was Empress Rasnei's lover. He vowed to avenge her death on all those involved."

She shook her head, confused. "He was . . . *is* a spirit, not a man. A djinn, rather, or demon?"

"An *Aikashi*. They're cousins of the djinni, way I understand it," Gujun the Slayer told her. "Vian was a dragon spirit from Rundali. A land in the east. Also, a man. A *hero*. He saved the city, Ta Shen. I was his enemy. But that was three months, and a lifetime ago."

"What happened to him?" She felt dazed, shaken to the bone, and wondered if this was all a nightmare, or witchery brought on by the Sangala's evil. The pain told her otherwise.

"I don't know." The Shen shook his head. "I didn't stick around long enough to find that out."

Arraleen stared at him for a moment, her eyes twitching and head giddy. She saw the big Yamondon sitting on a rock looking miserable.

"Are you hurt?" the Slayer asked her.

"My pride," she said bitterly.

"Where's your father?"

"Close by, hidden by rocks and screened from the worst

of the weather."

"Best we go get that arrow out," he said as the big Yamondon joined them. "This is Rogashi," Gujun the Slayer added, his eyes flicking across to the worried-looking Yamondon.

"You already told me his name."

"I did?"

She stared at them both. "My father's in a bad way. I'll need herbs and plenty of hot water. Can't mess with the arrow without those. I need to get him over there." She pointed to the mainland wrapped in cloud.

"There are boats a few miles from here," the Yamondon told her. "I can carry your father, while you and Gujun keep an eye out for Trendale and Xeeg's corsairs."

She shook her head. "There's a canoe. I could get across and bring something back." She realized she was rambling, her mind shaken and unraveled. *Get a grip, woman.*

"Come." She beckoned them follow her up the beach. She gazed at the ridge above and the gray wash of water over stone, curving into distance. No one around. But that snake Trendale was lurking somewhere. Reechers too. And not all of Kelgar's crew would be dead, unless Olgasha's hired corsairs had killed them in the fight at the camp. She doubted that. This island was big enough to hide several large groups and more.

"In here," she said, and she stooped under a shoulder of rock. She saw her father resting against the stone, his face pale and mouth slightly open. The Shen followed her inside the half cave, as the Yamondon kept a lookout.

She stopped beside her father. Tulomon Caze opened an eye. He appeared feverish, his face pale and damp with sweat.

"How are you coping, Father?"

"It hurts, love."

"I'll fix that, but we need to move. Get you to the mainland. These men will help us."

His feverish eyes saw the Shen for the first time. He coughed, seemed alarmed. "Father, relax, he's not an enemy today. The other's Yamondon. They helped me—"

"I know you . . ." he croaked as he craned his neck at the man behind her. "You came with Grodu. You were the spy they sent."

"That doesn't matter, he's helping us escape. And Grodu is dead." Arraleen wiped his brow. "Please calm yourself, Father, you need to be patient. We'll get you off this island and remove the arrow, once I have the things I need. First, we need to move you."

"Gujun the Slayer." Her father started chuckling. His eyes were wide, the fever was taking him. She needed to act fast. This dithering wouldn't do.

"Father . . ."

"He's a Shen demon, Arraleen. Come to steal our souls."

"No, Father. Just a killer like me." She glanced sideways at the Shen, who arched a brow.

Rogashi's head appeared from outside the nook. "Men coming this way, half a dozen. Maybe more."

"Which way?" the Shen asked him.

"From the north. 'Spect they're Trendale's thugs."

"Fuck," Arraleen muttered under her breath. "We can't move

my father that far, else the pain kills him. The shoulder's swollen with pus already. Damn this . . ."

"We need those horses, if we're going to get to the boats before they do," the Shen told Rogashi.

"I'll take the ridge and find a way to bring them down," the Yamondon said. "You stay with her in case they find this hideout."

The Shen shook his head. "Nah, you're wounded, Big Boy. And I'm quicker. I'll trot to the beach—stay ahead of them and lure them away. And if there's anyone asleep at the dock, they can help me grab a boat."

"You don't know shit about boats," the Yamondon said.

Arraleen noted, irritably, how both the men seemed to have recovered their wits better than she. But they didn't have Father to worry about.

"Xeeg's corsairs will help me," Gujun the Slayer said.

"You're insane," Rogashi told him, as he stepped inside and crouched low.

"Whatever you're planning, get on with it," she snapped at the pair.

The Shen grinned at his friend and glanced at her. "I'll go find us a boat," he said. "Don't kill my big friend, Dreamslayer. I'd be upset. And even you don't want that." He flashed her a grin and vanished.

Minutes later, she heard angry shouts and the thud of boots passing outside their hide. Moments passed and the big Yamondon took a look outside.

"They took his bait," he said. "Nine Dalcians chasing my

small friend."

"Trendale?"

"Nope. Think they were Kelgar's Reechers. Hopefully Gujun will introduce them to Xeeg's lot, so they can all kill each other while he purloins a boat." He flashed her a grin.

She looked bleakly at him for a moment and shook her head, not knowing what to think. His grin faded as he stared back at her, his heavy Yamondon face uneasy.

"Come here," she said.

"What?" He looked worried.

"Your neck. It's still bleeding."

"I hadn't noticed."

"Go find some kelp."

"What?"

"Seaweed. With bubbles. There's a ton of it out there."

"Why?"

"So I can staunch the flow, you daft prick. Go on. Bugger off, and let me watch over my father. His mind's wandering again."

Rogashi stared at her. "You're not what I expected, Dreamslayer."

"Don't worry, I'll return to normal soon as he's better."

He nodded, and vanished outside. Minutes later, he was back with a handful of bubbly looking weeds.

"Bladder rack." She sniffed it and nodded. He crouched suspiciously, and she pressed it against his neck.

"That stings."

"It's the salt. Hold it still, until the blood stops leaking out."

He did as she said, and kneeled beside her looking awkward

and very uncomfortable. Despite her desperate situation, she almost laughed at the state of him.

"You look ridiculous."

"I'm a Baha." He was offended again.

"Yes, and I'll kill you once we're on the level again. For now, we're allies, Baha. First, tell me what your king was planning for my father and I."

His face relaxed. "King Ulani has always admired your father as a worthy foe."

She laughed bitterly, but his eyes were serious.

"It's true, I swear it. My king always said that if the Yanturi listened to Tulomon Caze more than his cronies at court, we Yamondons would be in trouble." He looked down at her father, mercifully unconscious.

"*So?* Why would that matter to me? We're enemies. Ulani sent you and that sly Shen to find and kill Vendeli's Spymaster."

"Not kill. Apprehend. Take Tulomon Caze back to Cantacari. After Grodu failed."

"Grodu's dead, and good job too."

"Maybe he is."

"Olgasha killed him."

Rogashi looked at her and said nothing.

She was curious. "Why wouldn't your king kill us, if he could?"

"He didn't mention your name to me, but he said he wanted to talk with your father in Cantacari. I was tasked with fetching him."

"Why is Gujun the Slayer with you?"

Rogashi smiled. "He was a surprise visitor to our camp after we left Laregoza. My Tarkai found him wandering the shrublands like a lost puppy. We took him in because he looked useful."

"Now he works for your king, a spy like Grodu."

"Grodu has always been loyal to Ulani. Gujun is . . . his own man. He agreed to help us this one time. For gold, and more. And Gujun was worried about Grodu, who he met in Shen." He rubbed his neck and grinned at her. "It's stopped bleeding."

"Yes, it has." She sighed. Were all Yamondons this stupid? If so, Vendel should have conquered them years back. He was hunched, staring at her with that gormless expression. Like a large lazy hound relieved of its bone.

"What now?"

"I'm a touch weary, Dreamslayer. Think I'll rest. Those boys are long gone chasing after my Little Brother."

"Why do you call him that?"

"Because I'm fond of him."

"He's a murdering assassin, like myself."

"Maybe I'll grow to like you too."

"You won't get the chance."

"Guess not. Either way, I'm going to close my eyes and hope you don't stab me."

"You never know with me, Baha. Depends how fucking bored I get." She grinned for the first time that day.

CHAPTER 18|ESCAPE

Gujun raced along the beach, the Jians clanking on his back, the Reechers struggling to keep up behind. He was enjoying himself. The excursion had cleared his mind, and the horror and confusion had faded with the chase.

The Reechers were dropping behind, weighed down by their heavy furs and ringmail. He'd barely warmed up. He slowed his pace to lure them on. Needed them close and keen. Else those waiting at the docks would focus their attention on him alone.

Once he arrived, he'd worry about the boat. One thing at a time. He rounded a bend and saw the dock ahead, a group of men looking out at the channel. Gujun picked up his pace, drawing ahead again. Once out of sight of the men behind him, he diverted right and climbed the wet bank, reaching the lowest rocks. From there, he worked his way nearer as the Reechers rounded the corner behind. He saw them stop when they saw the men at the dock.

One of those shouted, having spotted the runners. Well hidden, Gujun almost laughed out loud as those pursuing him turned and looked for cover as a group of corsairs spilled from the dock and ran after them. Looking beyond, he saw three large ships had entered the channel and were making for the dock.

Blue Face Xeeg had come to join the fun. Gujun swallowed a curse. He needed that boat before the ships arrived, or his slim chance would prove impossible.

He waited as Blue Face's men ran past, intent on catching Trendale's, or whoever those were who'd chased him. Dalcians all looked the same to Gujun. He'd heard shouting off to the left, and the sound of steel clashing. The dozen left on the dock were still watching the approaching ships.

Gujun stood and jumped back down on the pebbles. He ran forward at a sprint until he reached the dock. A man turned his way and Gujun waved his hands frantically.

"Bandits," he shouted. "They're killing your men."

"Who the fuck are you?" The corsair glared at him, but Gujun pushed past and raced to the end of the dock where the main group stood, among them the men who'd run when the Rundali appeared.

"Kelgar's here!" he yelled. "Your men are dead."

Caught off guard, the nearest turned. Gujun's Jians were in his hands. He cut left and right, slicing and stabbing, killing three and pushing past.

The man he'd first passed was proving helpful, yelling back that Eagle Kelgar's men were attacking. In their confusion, Xeeg's fools crashed and jostled as Gujun killed two more and reached the nearest boat. There were three men on board.

He sliced through the mooring lines and jumped on deck. The nearest leaped at him. Gujun kicked him in the face, sending him sprawling. The boat was drifting out from the dock, the strong current taking it north. A spear crashed onto deck, and the two standing grabbed their swords and rushed him.

Gujun danced aside from a sword lunge and sliced across, severing one man's neck. The other one faced him with nervous eyes, as the one he'd kicked recovered to his feet.

"You want to live? I need this boat on shore a few miles up channel."

They stared at him. The men on the dock were shouting. One threw another spear, but it disappeared in the water as the boat drifted out of reach.

"Well?" Gujun watched their eyes.

They'd seen how fast he was, and with their comrade oozing his life blood, seemed hesitant to fight. Gujun jabbed forward with a Jian, stinging the armed one on his hand. He dropped the weapon with a curse.

"You know I can kill you both. If you want to live, get this craft under control and sail it north until I tell you where to beach."

The two glared at him. The bleeding one nodded eventually and took the bench, working an oar best he could with his impaired hand.

"You can join him with the other oar," Gujun said. "I'll steer."

The corsairs worked the oars in silence, and the craft picked up speed with the channel opening.

Keep her close to shore, Gujun told himself, and veered wide as rocks appeared from an outcrop ahead.

"You'll fucking sink us," the wounded one muttered, as the craft drifted out into the main current.

It's a fair point. Gujun slid away from the tiller. "You take over, shithead, and I'll man your oar. Don't get any foolish ideas. I'd sooner sink this ship than let you escape without me."

He took the bench and worked the oar furiously, as the other man glared at him. The wounded one soon got the craft under control by taking her out further into the channel.

Gujun saw men still fighting on the shore as they glided past. "Those are Kelgar's men," the one on the oar said.

"They are indeed," Gujun said. "Looks like your careless Sangala friend allowed a few to escape when you attacked his lair."

"That devil's not our friend."

"You'll be happy to know he's dead."

"You killed him?"

"Perhaps I did." He smiled, noting the fear and respect in their eyes.

Twenty minutes later, he glanced over his shoulder, recognizing the spur of rocks where the Dreamslayer had hidden her father. Past that, the tiny shape of the canoe still lay beached on the shore.

"Make for that canoe," he told the wounded tillerman.

Gujun stowed his oar as the boat drifted shoreward. Rogashi emerged from the rocks and waved at him. The big man vanished, and moments later reappeared with the woman and her father staggering between them.

Gujun's eyes flicked to the two Dalcians watching him intensely.

"You're taking us across to the mainland," Gujun told the pair. "Do that without any nonsense, and you can bugger off safely. Linger, and that woman will have your balls for supper."

They nodded. The oarsman stood and helped him assist the woman and Rogashi lift the wounded Caze onboard. The tillerman held the craft steady, as Rogashi grabbed an oar beside the other corsair. Gujun helped Arraleen Caze as she got her father seated in the stern.

He looked bad. Pale and shaky. Gujun doubted he'd last long. A shame after all this hard work to find him. He gazed back at the ridge and thought about the horses they'd tethered to that bush. They'd have got free by now, he told himself. Roaming happy.

The row took an hour. The current and strong wind pressed them northwards toward the far end of the island. But Rogashi's great strength, and Gujun helping, had the boat finally reaching the dock by the dead crofter's huts, where Arraleen had stolen the canoe.

Arraleen Caze stood and drew a scimitar. The Dalcians looked wild.

"Let them go," Gujun told her.

She glared back at him. "Why?"

"Because they've been helpful, and I like them." He waved a dismissive hand, and the pair took the hint, clambering off the boat and disappearing behind the huts.

"You've gone soft in the head, Shen. I'll only have to kill them later," she said, as she turned to assist her father to his feet.

"It's true, I've not been on form lately," Gujun said.

Arraleen pushed past, and Rogashi helped with her father. They sought the cover of one of the huts. The woman made Caze as comfortable as she could, while Gujun looked on and Rogashi messed with flint and got a fire going. After that he found a kettle and a well and brought clean water.

"Thank you," she said. "I'll need herbs. You go with him, Shen."

"I daresay he'll manage alone." Gujun smiled at her, and she shrugged indifferently.

"You should leave us," Arraleen Caze told him as Gujun watched her get her father as comfortable as she could.

"Why? I like it here." He met her gaze. The almond eyes were testing him.

"It's not your fight," she said eventually.

Caze had his eyes open. "He's involved." His face was pale and drawn, but he appeared alert, no longer feverish. "He helped Grodu betray us. It's why he was at that villa in Laregoza. You're a Yamondon spy, aren't you, little Shen? You worked for Chulan as a cover. I heard that you stabbed him in that palace."

"That was an impulsive moment," Gujun said. "I decided I didn't want Chulan as emperor."

"And instead you are an outlaw harbored by Yamondons." Tulomon Caze's eyes were hooded.

Father and daughter stared at him until Gujun smiled. *Seems you have your wits back, old man. Good. It will help me get that gold I'm promised. And the villa.*

"I'm glad your fever's gone," he said to Tulomon Caze. "Of course, it will return when she yanks that shaft out. Too bad. Pain must be crippling you. My reasons for being here are my own. And I get paid by whom I choose."

Caze glared at Gujun, and the woman mouthed a curse.

"I will happily kill you when we're done, Shen," she assured him with a cold smile. "We are enemies, and you will pay for what you and Grodu did to my father."

Gujun feigned a yawn. "We'll see. Not that I care a jot what you think, wench. But I didn't know Grodu worked for the Yamondons until later. And I wasn't interested, even when he asked me to assist with finding your father."

"You're a liar," she said, angrily. "And call me wench again, and I'll stab you now."

He smiled at her. *Go on, try, sweetheart. I'm bored.* She bared her teeth at him, and turned to her father as he groaned in pain.

"Where the fuck is that Yamondon?" she said, exasperated.

"Be dark soon," Gujun told her, glancing outside. "I expect he'll turn up before then."

As though in answer, he heard footsteps approaching. He rolled to a spot near the door where he could keep an eye on her and see who approached.

Rogashi appeared with a small bundle of green in his hands. "Arnica and lavender, yarrow too. And wild garlic. It's amazing what that bog provides." He passed the plants to Arraleen Caze who studied them, her face dubious until she recognized some of them, and nodded thanks.

"Time to take that arrow out," Rogashi said. Arraleen was already preparing.

"See anyone in your travels?" Gujun asked as Rogashi crouched beside the woman.

"No, but Blue Face's ships are on the move. I climbed a rise and got a good view south. Saw three raiders cutting up through the channel. My guess is they'll tie off at that dock we visited and range out searching for our Vendeli friends here. Xeeg Blue Face won't be happy you got away. He's missed all the fun so far."

Arraleen Caze ignored them as she heated the water in the kettle over the fire.

"What about Trendale?" Gujun asked the Yamondon.

"Dead?"

"We shouldn't count on that."

"You're right," Rogashi said, looking at the woman and her father.

Arraleen glanced at them both. The crafty Shen was up to something. She couldn't work him out. He seemed the sharper of the two. Rogashi was almost likable, apart from him being Yamondon. The Shen was devious, and she'd kill him first. But for now, she still needed the help.

Damn them.

She nodded curtly as they stared at her and turned to her father, prodding him until he stirred. Rogashi handed her a small stick he'd found.

"This is going to hurt, Father," she said. He nodded and opened his mouth wide for her to place the short stick inside. He bit down hard and nodded again. "You got his shoulders," she said as she glanced sideways at Rogashi, the Shen watching on behind.

"I've got him."

"On three," she said. "One . . . two . . . three!" She twisted and tugged the arrow free, and her father gasped and shook and fainted dead away.

Rogashi held his body firmly as she washed the wound clear of blood with hot water. She strained the herbs, mixing them with more water, adding the blend to the wound. Finally, she dried the area well before covering it with a clean piece of her shirt that she'd torn off for the purpose.

Her father regained consciousness moments later, his eyes wide with panic and legs kicking. Rogashi held him as she whispered in his ear until he stilled.

"The worst is over," Arraleen told him. Her father nodded and closed his eyes. Outside, the wind had increased, promising another miserable night.

The fire did little to keep out the chill. The smoke would be visible, but that couldn't be helped. Tulomon Caze slept fitfully in her arms. The Yamondon had ventured outside again to see if any Dalcians were about. That left the Shen staring at her with those dark cynical eyes.

"I don't like you," Arraleen told him after matching his gaze for a moment. "Why don't you go outside with your friend? You know my father's not running off anytime soon."

He looked at her curiously. "Despite what you think, woman, I'm not your enemy. You're a professional, as am I. I came here because of Grodu, and I'd heard that the Sangala were involved. I don't like the Sangala." He stood, flashed her a grin. "Get some sleep, Arraleen Caze. You're going to need it." He left them alone without further word.

Arraleen chewed her puckered lip. What had that been about? His manner puzzled her. Why bother with an explanation? It was as though he wanted her to see things his way. *Why?*

She berated herself. Why question it? It wasn't important. She'd kill them both at dawn and drag her father to the boat. Once onboard, they'd sail south and land anyplace they could. She knew how to handle sails and rudder. She'd cope. From there on, she'd find him refuge and fodder as they planned their return to Vendel, or wherever else he suggested they go. Truth was they had nowhere.

She thought about the Shen, his words. And his name, Slayer. Were they connected somehow? He knew the stranger who'd saved her. Perhaps Agarra the Huntress had sent Gujun too? A killer who would fight beside her. She closed her eyes.

Shut up, Arraleen. You're tired, that's all.

She must have slept for a while against her own advice. A crashing outside had her reaching for the swords.

The wind?

She stood and glanced down at her father. Still sleeping. That was good. Where were those two fools hiding? Perhaps the noise had been them. She stepped outside and closed the door behind her. A starry night. The clouds raced over the island ahead. It must have rained because the ground was wet. How long had she slept?

No one here. And yet, her instinct told her someone was close. She stole around the huts and saw the boat creaking against its ties.

A sound to her left. A rat? Some small animal, had to be. She turned back to the croft when something hard struck the back of her head and sent her sprawling.

CHAPTER 19|THE HOOKS

Gujun saw the dark shapes of men approaching through the gloom. He and Rogashi were crouched hidden in the boggy ground, his boots squelching with icy water.

"How many, do you think?" Rogashi asked, having stowed his spy-glass away, as it was misting up.

"Twenty, or more."

"We'd better get back. Been gone hours."

Gujun nodded, and together they rose carefully and crept back into the bare woods they'd left, after scouting the region for half the night. They'd been about to return when Rogashi had heard distant shouts. It seemed that Blue Face Xeeg didn't want to wait until morning.

The corsairs were making for the croft. There was nowhere else for renegades to hide, except the stores where Kelgar kept his boats. And Gujun assumed that's where they'd come from.

The scouting party would arrive at the croft in half an hour, or less. Once they were out of sight, the two trotted through the bog as best they could until the side creek and channel beyond spilled the moon's reflection, and the croft's roof trapped the moonlight.

They'd reached the store huts when Gujun grabbed Rogashi's arm and pointed to fresh tracks in the mud.

"Someone's been here," Gujun said. Rogashi nodded, and they made for the croft door, which had been forced wide open and was banging in the wind. Both Caze and his daughter had disappeared.

"The boat?" Rogashi asked him.

"Still there," Gujun said, as he took a look outside again.

"Can't be Blue Face. Perhaps one of Kelgar's lot?"

Gujun heard distant shouts from the hill. "Doesn't matter at the moment," he said. "Blue Face's scouts will be here in a minute. Best we move on. We can think while running."

"But which way?" Rogashi stared at him. The shouts were nearer, more excited. They must have guessed someone was here. "Their tracks lead back to the dock," he added, pointing. "Whoever this was must have suspected Caze would have returned here."

Gujun shrugged. "If they're more of Blue Face's boys, I doubt they'd risk crossing back to the island tonight. And, if they're Kelgar's, they'd stay away knowing Xeeg was coming."

"What do you think?"

"I think it's Trendale's work. He must have returned to Kelgar's lair and stolen a boat. He'll know the corsairs are on the mainland, and he would have to act fast to apprehend Caze. Now that he's got the prize, he'll try slipping their nets by going inland, further up the channel."

"Hmm, makes sense. Best we do the same," Rogashi said, as they made for the boat and cast off, even as the shouts got nearer and Gujun saw shaggy shapes arrive in the croft. Xeeg's scouts yelled as they saw the boat drifting out. The pair he'd spared must have run back to report. The woman had been right. He should have killed them. But sometimes it's good to keep a promise. *I'm getting soft.*

Rogashi steered the craft as Gujun worked the oars. To their right, the sky paled as morning approached.

"If it's Trendale, he'll make for the Hooks," Rogashi said. "Blue Face won't follow him there. Too many rumors, and Reech Corsairs are a superstitious lot."

Gujun grinned. "But we will."

"I was worried you would say that," Rogashi muttered.

Arraleen's head felt like an exploding melon. The rocking rhythm of the ship had her spewing air every few minutes. She'd emptied the last contents of her stomach a while back. Her hands were lashed behind her back and she was lying face first on the wet planks of the ship. Her father beside her, his breathing ragged and hoarse. Her wrist hurt badly again, the flesh swollen and throbbing. She tried flexing her fingers, else they grow numb.

As the light grew, she shifted on her side enough to look up and see their faces. She cursed, recognizing Trendale. He saw her and walked over, kicking her in the ribs.

"Twice captured, Dreamslayer. That must be a record for you."

She muttered a curse as he crouched down beside her.

"I needed to get your father away from that area," he said, smiling. "It's crawling with Xeeg Blue Face's people, who are not my friends. Of course, they'll follow us, because that Sangala would have told them how much you're worth. I did consider killing you, but why waste a good prize?"

"Fuck you." She spat at him.

"Don't be bitter. It's not personal, Dreamslayer. Things got hot on that island after Olgasha arrived. I needed a way out, and when I saw you'd been at my boys on the beach and got away, I figured I knew where you'd be. Not many homesteads along the strand. You'd best get some sleep—you're in for a rough few days."

"Up yours, Weasel." She spat again.

"You've a Reecher's foul mouth, woman. I'll have to wash that out." He left with a sly grin smearing his whiskers.

The day drifted on. Sometimes he came and goaded or kicked her. Arraleen bided her time, allowing her body to recover. She wasn't hurt badly, but the blow on the back of her skull throbbed—as did her wrist, the fingers turning blue. At least the motion sickness had passed. She jostled and shifted, forced her body over to one side, and managed to half sit up.

Trendale saw her and came over. She guessed the number of his men at a score, perhaps more. A large ship with a single red square sail. Stolen. One of Kelgar's, she suspected, though these were Trendale's bandits. She saw no Reechers among them.

"My father needs attention," she said as he stared down at her, his smug bearded face grinning. "He'll die if I don't help him."

"I only need his head."

"You'll get double the gold if he's breathing. The Yanturi will see to that."

Judging by his eyes, he was weighing up if she was lying. It took a moment. But as she'd guessed it would, greed won him over. He untied her wrists and stood over her.

"See to him, and be quick about it. We're mooring soon."

"Where?" She flexed her fingers and clenched her teeth at the racing pins and needles as the blood flowed freely again.

"You'll know soon enough, and you're not going to like it." He laughed and moved away.

She jostled close to her father, after spying her swords tied to a rail. The bandits were armed with spears and short swords, the odd ax. She saw no bows. She'd have to wait until they were ashore. First, she needed him strong enough.

"You awake?" she whispered.

He cracked an eye open and forced a smile. "Rough few days. Sorry, love. Not much help, am I."

"We'll get through it," she told him, as she untied the blood-soaked makeshift bandage and inspected his wound. There was some swelling as she'd expected, but no puckering flesh. The herbs had worked. She silently thanked the Yamondon for that. He must be dead, the Shen too. Caught out by this slippery bandit and his men. So much for being a professional, Gujun the Slayer.

"Can you sit up, get out of the wet?"

"Think so."

She helped him as he shuffled against her. Trendale watched them with greedy eyes, until one of his men said something and he turned away.

The moment she needed.

Arraleen slid the tiny knife from her sleeve sheath and slipped it inside his tunic.

Her father smiled at her, knowing she'd another sown inside the hem. "We'll wait until we're ashore," she told him. "Can you walk?"

"Yes, I feel stronger. That Shen was wrong, I've no fever."

"He didn't know how tough you are."

"What happened back there? Trendale—"

"Will die soon," she said, viewing the bandit stooped in conversation with two of his men.

"The Yamondon and his—"

"Already dead. Just us left. I'll work something out. If you can do for Trendale, I'll keep his men busy, maybe lead them astray and circle back, free that skiff tied on the stern. We'll need them off guard—perhaps when they make camp this evening. Hopefully they'll have grog and make themselves stupid." She looked at Trendale, pointing off to his right. "Looks like they're heading for the shore here."

She stretched her neck to see the land across to her right. The sea was rougher past the island. They'd reached a headland, and dark cliffs loomed ominously close. Beyond those, high on a cliff, she saw strange rocks. A structure, or work of nature? Man-made, it had to be. But ancient and unsettling to the eye. A castle or tower, with what appeared as giant horns, jutting and curving up from each end. Arraleen couldn't grasp how such a baroque monstrosity could exist. The sheer size of the horns defied her senses.

"What's the matter?" he asked as he saw her puzzled look.

"I don't know. There's some kind of giant animal building on a cliff. Doesn't look real."

His face took on a look of terror. "We can't land there."

She noted the fear in his eyes and chewed her bottom lip. "Looks like we are. Trendale's pilot's making for the cove," she told him. "I see steps carving up through that cliff. Must be what they've got in mind."

"Arraleen, we cannot go near that temple."

Temple? She felt her cheeks twitch nervously. What cruel gods had those ancient people worshipped? She imagined twisted sacrifices and blood rituals, and she shuddered. *Get a grip!* Pointless dwelling on such morbid fancies. Not when she had work to do.

"Hopefully we won't have to," she added, half to herself.

"The Hooks," he was mumbling, and she worried that the fever was taking hold again.

"You don't think they'll follow?" Gujun asked the Yamondon.

Rogashi stood, guiding the craft. "They might, but not if he takes them to the Hooks."

Gujun rested his oars as he gazed back at the channel. They'd reached the north end. Kelgar's lair was briefly in view on the windward side, as the island's stark hills slipped behind. Ahead lay open water. Greeting that wash were dark cliffs jutting out.

The strong current was helping. Craning his neck again, it wasn't long before he recognized the same giant, horned, stone ugliness he'd seen from Reechers Bay.

"Remind me about the Hooks," Gujun said. Those cliffs had an ominous feel. The Hooks were closer than he'd seen them from Reechers Bay. Brooding and alien. Dominating the skyline above the high cliff.

Rogashi spat. "Just old ruins, Little Brother. Rumored to be haunted by Aralais wizards. Probably just wind and bollocks, but sailors have always avoided the place. Trendale isn't a sailor. Up there amongst all that stone, he'll see what Blue Face is up to. And will doubtless scan Reechers Bay for their ships too.

"My guess is he'll study what's out there and return to Kelgar's ship, round the headland, and loop past the Razor's mouth, making for the forests we crossed last week. Once in Dalcia, he'll disappear."

Gujun nodded, his eyes still on the Hooks while working the oar. "Until he turns up in Vendel, with Caze's head in a sack."

"Trendale's greedy," Rogashi said. "He'll want them both alive for the extra gold. I daresay he'll find an agent to help him get them up to Omala City."

"He won't kill her?"

"He's rash. A gambler. Could prove his weakness."

Let us hope so. They approached the cliffs, the wind buffeting, and an icy chill coming from the stretch of water to their west.

"I see them," Rogashi said, pointing.

Gujun rested the oars and turned. They'd reached a lee, and the craft bobbed gently toward the shore. He saw the red-sailed raider moored against the rock. There were strands of pebbles leading up to a cut in the cliffs. Gujun saw stone steps visible at the bottom.

As they glided closer, Rogashi produced Dasco's glass and searched.

"There they are," he said after a moment. "Trendale leading. Twenty men with him, perhaps more. The girl's there, and her old man struggling in front. They're making for the steps, got the prisoners ringed by spears."

"Can't see her escaping anytime soon," Gujun said, after taking his turn with the glass and spotting the tiny figure of Arraleen Caze being prodded by a spear as she helped her father up the first few steps.

"We'll see," Rogashi said, and he guided the craft toward the raider.

"Anyone on that ship?"

"Doesn't look like it. He's confident Blue Face won't land."

"Bad wager on his part." Gujun was looking back.

"What?"

"Corsairs behind us, and they're approaching fast."

"For fuck's sake...why are we always so popular, Little Brother?"

Gujun saw the three vessels cutting through the chop as they cleared the island, the dark-red square sails bright in the sunshine, as the gloom of clouds shifted further off shore.

They reached the moored ship and tied off alongside. Climbing up, Gujun found a spear rack with weapons to hand. Rogashi and himself took two each. Shame there were no bows, but careless of Trendale leaving any weapons behind.

They waded across to the shore and scanned the beach, the gray combers washing in driftwood. It seemed even colder here, and the cliffs loomed dark and menacing above, the Hooks no longer in view. Trendale's climbing party was also hidden above in the fold of rock.

A glance back revealed Blue Face was intent on landing, the corsairs' lust for gold quelling their dread of this place. Trendale had miscalculated. His problem, mostly. But it would complicate an exit plan.

They reached the stone steps. Narrow, treacherous scoops cut like skims into the cliff. They'd be slow getting Caze safely up there. Gujun and Rogashi started up, using the spears as aids. They reached a ledge and rested halfway. He heard voices. Trendale's boys must be on top of the cliff. Below, the three corsair ships were drifting closer to Kelgar's stolen craft.

"No way back." Rogashi grinned down at him as they

continued the tricky ascent.

"Seems so," Gujun said. *But I've never liked retreating.*

They reached the flat windy top and crouched low in the cover of gorse. Close by, the ruins of stone walls loomed black and forbidding.

"Trendale will have seen the corsairs and be seeking refuge. He'll wait and see what they'll do, before moving on."

Gujun smiled at his big companion. "It's obvious what they'll do. This Blue Face seems like no fool. He'll send men overland to that headland, cutting Trendale off, while the rest remain on the ships. That way the bandits are stuck on this cliff."

"As are we, Little Brother." Rogashi slapped his back so hard it made him cough.

"There is that." *Thanks for reminding me.*

Arraleen squatted against the cold wet rock, her heart racing and head pounding. She'd got her father up safely, but the climb had proved long and difficult, with him stumbling and nearly falling twice. He lay beside her, sweating despite the cold. She was angry. With Trendale, his bandits, but mostly herself. The Dalcians were surveying the terrain and had left them be. Trendale was lurking over by the cliff edge.

She was almost spent and needed time to get her head together.

"Can you speak?" she asked her father, her voice hoarse.

He looked at her, nodded. His face was pale, and the blood was seeping from his wound again. *Damn them!*

"They look edgy," she said. "Trendale's planning something."

"It's this place ..." He forced the words out between his teeth.

"Just grim ruins. You need to rest, Father. I told you we'll get through this. And we will. They seem distracted. Trendale's worried. I can see it in his eyes."

As though he'd heard her mention his name, the bandit chief wandered over and stared coldly down at them.

"We're not lingering here," he said. "You need to make sure he's fit to move before nightfall."

"My father's sickly after that climb. You should have left us by the ship."

He laughed at her. "You've got an hour's rest, no more. After that, we're moving on. I'd prefer the two of you alive, but if that's a problem, I'll cut my losses and settle for your heads. Up to you, Dreamslayer. Best keep him awake, else he croaks in his sleep." He turned away.

"You fucked up coming here, didn't you?" she yelled back at him, and dodged the responding kick when he rounded on her. "Things aren't going your way, are they, Trendale?"

He spat at her and left them.

Seething inside, Arraleen gazed at the stone monstrosity close by, studying the strange shapes half hidden by fallen, cracked rocks and crumbles of scree. An ancient temple, her father had said. But built by whom? She couldn't imagine people worshipping in such a place. Perhaps they'd been mad like the ancient Ptarnian Emperors, who she'd heard her mother mention in her childhood days.

The tower stones were worn and shiny. She couldn't see gaps where they'd been laid upon each other. It was like one vast solid lump of glistening rock. Carved by many hands with unimaginable skill. The weird horns arching, dominating. Reaching and curving hundreds of feet above, their hooked grayish tips tapering inwards like bull horns, piercing the dark racing clouds far above.

She chewed her bottom lip and returned to gaze at her father. He was shaking badly, the sweat frozen on his face. She covered his body with her own and hugged him tightly.

This is my fault. I fell asleep in that croft. I've failed you, Father.

Her head throbbed, and she found her mood turning morose. It was this place. The grim atmosphere. He was right, there was something unclean about these ruins. She saw it in the bandit's faces. They were jittery and wanted to leave, but Trendale was waiting for something. He and several of his men stood gazing down at the sea.

On a whim, she kissed her father and stood shakily.

"I'll be just a minute," she told him, and crept off to a spot close to where Trendale watched with his men. She saw three ships down there, bouncing next to Trendale's. She smiled coldly. They had company. The corsairs were back.

She turned and crawled back without being seen. A slight cough stopped her in her tracks, the shadow of ruins blocking the pale sunlight ahead. Someone was watching her from inside. She glimpsed a face. Pale, the white eyes slanted and orbless and full of malice. It flickered and faded. She saw a bat-like creature flutter leathery wings and glide up from the ruined crenulations.

Imagination.

She shook herself and returned to her father, blinking in disbelief upon seeing Gujun the Slayer crouched next to him.

Instinctively, she reached for her hidden knife, stopping when he placed a hand on his lips. She turned, saw Trendale returning with some of his men.

"The ruins," he whispered. "Soon as you can get away."

She heard shouts, and the Shen sloped off behind a rock.

"Trendale's coming," she hissed after him.

"Stay alive. We'll work something out," he said, and slunk out of view. She glimpsed his shadow flitting off into the ruins as Trendale appeared, his face redder than usual.

"We're out of time, Dreamslayer," he said, angrily. He scooped his short sword free of the studded belt. "I've decided I'll settle for your heads."

He jabbed down hard. She rolled instinctively and lashed out with a boot, catching his belly and knocking him back as the sword swung wide.

She jumped to her feet, kicking out. He swung again, but she got in close and bit his ear. He slipped and dropped the sword while regaining balance. She kicked the blade away, but he ran at her and cuffed her, knocking her to her knees.

She clawed up hard into his face, both hands striking out, ten fingers taut in a tiger claw. He dodged, struck at her again but missed. His men were shouting and rushing this way. She stood, grabbed her hidden dagger, and made to slash his face, but Trendale's boot caught her leg and hooked her from her feet.

Should have seen that one coming. Arraleen rolled and dodged as he reclaimed the sword and stabbed down at her again. The bandits had her hemmed. Her father was choking close by. She ran to him and crouched low.

Trendale followed, panting heavily. He untied the double-headed ax lashed across his back. Grinning, the bandit chief loomed over, ax gripped in both hands, ready to finish them both. She placed her knife against her father's throat.

"I'm sorry, Father. I'll make it quick."

She made to stab into his neck, stopping when a sudden violent jolt caught Trendale off balance. She saw the men around him jumping back in alarm. Another thud. The ground shook, and she saw stones crack and fall from the ruins. Trendale stared at her, his mouth gaping, sucking in air.

"The curse, it's true!" one of his men was yelling. "The Golden Ones have seen us trespassing. They are coming for us!"

They started running for the cliff, and within seconds Trendale joined them.

"Good riddance," Arraleen Caze yelled after the cowards, her eyes half crazed with fear and rage. She reached across and grabbed her father again. "We've got to get under the cover of that stone."

Another rumble and boom, the ground shook around them. She bit her tongue and made it bleed.

"No, not in there . . . Arraleen . . . *please!*"

"Come on!" She dragged his body across until he staggered to his feet with her supporting his shoulder, forcing them both under the dark shadow of rock. She saw what resembled a gate—more like a mouth turned down in a scowl. The wind cried chill from inside, and shadows were flickering against the rock.

"Daughter, we can't . . ." He coughed as she forced him toward the mouth gateway. They passed within, and the walls seemed to press in upon them.

She almost screamed out loud when a hand grabbed her arm. Gujun nodded through the gloom.

"There's a tunnel," he said. "Rogashi made torches. We need to leave before those Dalcians rally."

"What caused those tremors?"

"Acoustics." The Yamondon emerged from a shadow with a brand in either hand.

Gujun passed her a spear, then took a torch from his comrade. He looked sideways at her father. "Is he okay?"

"We'll manage," she said. "And thank you."

"For what?" He blinked at her, the brand blazing bright above his glove.

"For being here."

He looked at her for a moment and shook his head, clearly puzzled by her manner.

"This way," Rogashi hissed. "We need to get through to the other side before the demons wake at dusk."

"Demons?" She looked anxiously at Gujun.

"Yamondons and their imagination," the Shen said, as they entered the narrowing gloom of a passage leading down to another leering mouth gate.

It had been Rogashi's idea. He'd seen the loose rocks, poised like teeth on top of one of the crenulations. Gujun had gone to check on Arraleen and her father, and to see what Trendale was up to, while Rogashi climbed up there. When Gujun signaled as Trendale came after the girl, the Yamondon started heaving hard, pushing the rocks free from their tenuous perch. Like rotten teeth, they'd twisted and crashed, thudding to the ground. The crashing noise had been magnified by the echoes and weird acoustics of this uncanny place.

He'd climbed back down and recovered the torch material they'd gathered when they'd first got up here.

Before that, they'd scouted the inside carefully, after seeing Trendale preoccupied and his prisoners resting. Gujun had found the tunnel leading down and out to a daylight hole in the hill on the eastern side. There was usually another way out if you took the time to look. No doubt the ancients had their secrets too.

They entered the gloom of the shaft. Gujun urged the woman lead her father behind Rogashi, who held his torch out in front. The tunnel squeezed narrow, like a shrinking round hole—or the belly of a snake, the black oily stone pressing down on their heads. They had to crouch, and he helped her drag her father in the tightest spots.

They'd been walking for twenty long minutes, descending

inside the hill, when Gujun heard shouts coming from behind and above. Trendale must have rallied and was on his way, having realized this was his only escape. Fool had got himself cornered on the cliff. The corsairs were most likely chasing him.

"You hear that?" Arraleen Caze's eyes were wild in the dark.

Gujun grinned at her. "It's only Trendale shitting bricks." They needed to clear this tunnel fast. Get under cover of gorse and out of sight, lie low until the cover of darkness aided their escape. That way they could watch the corsairs catch up with their bandit friends and kill each other happily in one big Dalcian love fest.

The tunnel had leveled out. Gujun spied a faint light ahead. "Almost there," he said, but stopped when Rogashi gasped.

"Ugh, something bit me, Little Brother. Flew at my face."

"Probably just a bat." Gujun kept moving forward, stopping abruptly when something slimy edged out of the tunnel wall. *That's not a bat.*

"There are creatures in here." Arraleen Caze's face looked stricken by torchlight, as they protected her father from a slimy creeping creature hopping toward him. Gujun's mouth dropped in horror as he saw a wrinkled face with pointed ears, sharp tiny reddish eyes, and razor-filed teeth, snarling. It resembled an ape, but had leathery wings pressed limp into its sides.

It hopped toward the woman, seeming more interested in her. Gujun batted it away with the torch, but others emerged like glaring gargoyles, and soon they were surrounded.

CHAPTER 20|RECOMPENSE

Arraleen clutched her face as the gargoyle horror bit at her. She struck it away, and Gujun swept the brand around as best he could in the limited space.

Her father had collapsed, and Rogashi helped her drag him to his knees, while Gujun batted more of the monkey-bat creatures away. The tunnel end glinted a hundred feet away, tempting them with daylight. They pushed forward, as the hopping, flapping horrors snarled and bit. Gujun's arm was bleeding, and Rogashi's face was smeared with blood. She hoped there was no poison in their fangs, as one had bitten her neck, which was stinging badly.

A side hole appeared. A vent. The things crept in there when Gujun caught one with the torch, frazzling it like an overripe fruit in a campfire. They didn't like the fire. The ghastly things were cowards.

Her father came to as they dragged him. Rogashi let him rest for a moment, as the creatures had withdrawn and were sulking in the vent hole. The Yamondon wiped blood from his mouth and cursed.

"What the fuck are those things?"

"Soilfins," Tulomon Caze muttered between wheezy breaths.

"What?" Arraleen stooped over her father.

"Winged demons from the nightmare years." He glared up at her, as though expecting worse. "Flesh eaters. They served the Shadowman in the ancient god wars."

"Easy, Father. More likely, they're some kind of mutated bat-gibbon," she said, and almost laughed at their predicament. She was shattered, and needed to hold herself together. Get through this . . . madness.

"Whatever they are, we seem to have scared them off," Gujun said, looking back up the tunnel. "Hopefully they'll prey on Trendale's lot."

"Doubt we'll be that lucky," she replied as they moved forward again, making for the tease of daylight ahead.

Reaching that, they squeezed out and sprawled on cold wet grass, catching their breath. The wind blasted Arraleen's face as she blinked and wiped blood from her neck. Shallow bite, more of an irritation than a problem. Still stinging, but less than before. Her father hadn't been bitten, but the others had, and Gujun's arm looked a mess. He didn't seem concerned.

"They were Soilfins," her father insisted, deliriously, as she sat beside him on the grass, wiping blood from her neck and getting her strength back. Ahead, Gujun and the Yamondon were scouting the slopes. Below where she sat, the steep hill fell away, wrapped in sighing purple heather and descending into the dark mantle of pines.

"Clear," Rogashi said on return. Gujun checked inside the tunnel. He grinned back. No sign of Trendale yet.

After a brief rest, they trudged on, Rogashi leading the way down and the Shen watching their back. Arraleen supported her father, who was still muttering curses about the gargoyle creatures. She pictured one of them feasting on Trendale's face. The thought made her smile.

Her hopes were dashed when she heard shouts from above, announcing the bandits had cleared the tunnel.

"I'll wait for you in the trees, Trendale," she muttered under her breath. They were nearing the woods and the promise of cover. She smiled at her father encouragingly. They'd almost made it, but Rogashi's raised hand had them stopping again.

"See that?" He pointed to the shadow of trees where she saw the glint of metal moving. Another sparkle further away, and more off to the right. That could only be one thing. Armed men clad in iron steel were waiting for them in the woods. Arraleen mouthed a silent curse.

"I expect that's Blue Face's scouts again," Rogashi said

cheerfully, as if he relished another fight.

"We daren't chance those woods. There could be a hundred hidden in there." Gujun the Slayer stood scanning the trees.

She heard shouting and glanced back up the hill. She recognized Trendale's rough curse, as he spotted them crouched below. "We should lure those bandits close, so the Reechers catch them," she said to the men. She let her father sit for a moment. He was shaking badly.

"Too risky," Gujun said.

She glared at him. "What other choice is there?"

"We should make for the cliffs on the north side," he replied. "We'll be able to skirt the woods and avoid the Reechers. Hopefully they'll see Trendale first. Agreed?"

She looked about. Almost dark, and Trendale's men were getting close. Scant choice, and they were wasting crucial seconds.

"Makes sense," she answered, jumping up. "Come on, Father, stay sharp." She helped him to his feet and supported him. They moved as fast as they could across to a goat track cutting through a break of gorse. Temporally hidden from above and below, they made good progress, stopping when the sound of distant waves announced the cliff edge close by.

Woah . . . and here it is. She almost slipped, and she hissed a warning to Gujun and Yamondon. They stopped, waving back they'd seen the drop. The cliffs fell sheer several feet to her left. No sound of pursuit, but the screaming wind could hide anything.

She allowed her father rest again, as she stood beside the cliff edge with the Shen gazing down at the distant shore a hundred feet below. She moved over and looked down. The waves formed dark ridges, and further out a cloud bank swallowed the rising moon.

As night closed upon them, the wind dropped and she heard shouts again, but further away. Maybe they'd got lucky and the corsairs were attacking Trendale. Dare she hope?

She glanced at Gujun, who nodded. *Best we keep moving.* She helped her father up, and they walked as best they could down the slope, the cliff to their left and dark shadow of woods flanking the other side.

They reached an overlook, with three tall pines marking the way. As they dropped down amongst the trees, Arraleen saw the shadows of men moving across to cut them off.

Gujun hefted his spear as Rogashi motioned for her and her father to stay back. The men below hadn't seen them yet, but a noise from behind warned her someone else had. She turned in time to see a figure emerge in the gloom and lunge down at her with a spear.

Arraleen blocked that thrust with her spear and, two-handed, twisted the blade up into his belly. He fell screaming, but other shadows came running out of the dark. Shaggy forms above the wild spring of heather. Among them was Trendale, his florid angry face lit by the brand he carried, the double-headed ax carving circles in the other hand.

"We have them!" he roared as the bandits dropped down beside them.

"Make for the woods!" Gujun hissed at her.

She struggled with her father, and he coughed. "Let me

go, Arraleen." She could hear blades clashing and saw Rogashi skewer a bandit.

Shouts from below announced the corsairs had seen them.

A bandit jabbed at her, and she sliced down at his feet, cutting half his boot away. He yelped and slipped aside. Another cornered her, and his comrade stood over her father with a curved blade.

She yelled a warning to him, but Gujun got there first, turning and dancing, a skinny blade in each hand. His back slice slashed the bandit's face open, and he tumbled over her father.

She couldn't get close, as Trendale's men had her pinned. The bandit chief pushed through them, his eyes wild, the brand cast aside and ax gripped firmly in both hands.

"You've fucking caused me some grief, bitch," he said. "Time to pay."

She stepped back and noticed her feet were on the precipice. *Best not slip.*

One of his men jabbed at her side with a spear. She twisted, trapping that thrust. Turning her spear, she reversed the weapon, sending him tripping and yelling into the dark. She held her balance, poised, braced, and waiting.

Close by, the sound of steel clashed and shouts continued. The moon rolled free of cloud, spilling silver light on the cliffs. She stood on a hummock of grass, the cliff falling away behind. Trendale and two of his men were above her, cutting off her escape.

The bandit chief waved the two back. "She's mine." He approached her, grinning, his double-headed ax held ready.

"Time to take your head, Dreamslayer."

The ax arced toward her neck. She ducked, but his iron-clad shoulder followed up and rammed hard into her chest. She dropped the spear and reached inside her cloak as her feet slipped on the rim. Somehow, she kept her balance. He shoved her, allowing room to swing again.

She heard Gujun the Slayer shout something.

Trendale swung hard at her midriff. Arraleen jumped forward, inside the swing, as the ax blow went wide. She clung to his mail and stabbed up into the leather under the armpit, twisting the knife blade, and jabbing again until the point sank deep.

Trendale choked and stumbled at the ledge.

"Die, dog." She spat in his face.

As he tumbled, his boot tripped her ankle, and she collapsed on top of him, falling through freezing air.

Fuck you, Trendale . . .

Far below, she saw the stony beach and combers rushing up to greet her.

I'm sorry, Father . . .

Arraleen Caze closed her eyes.

Gujun cursed, seeing Arraleen Caze fall alongside the bandit captain. Two of Trendale's men stood there gaping. Gujun dispatched the pair before they noticed his approach. He looked down, seeing nothing but stone and sea.

He sighed, turned, and saw the huddled shape of Tulomon

Caze crawling toward him. Close by, Rogashi finished the last of the bandits but warned more men were coming up from the woods. Xeeg's scouts would be on them soon.

It was over. Gujun approached the weeping man. Tulomon had seen her fall too. He sobbed and shook. Gujun leaned on his Jian and stared at him.

"Your daughter died well, Caze. You can be proud of her."

Caze was inconsolable. "Kill me, *please*. Finish this agony. You're the *Slayer*. Do it!"

"I was paid to fetch you, not kill you."

"Please," sobbed Caze.

"It doesn't matter." Gujun smiled at him. "We'll all be dead soon." Rogashi joined him as a group of shaggy figures emerged and surrounded them. It was fully dark again, as the moon had vanished.

"Get on with it, Blue Face. Or whoever the fuck you are," Rogashi growled, as Gujun gripped his Jians.

"Now that is a rare insult," a deep amused voice said.

Gujun jolted, seeing Grodu emerge from the gloom. Closer inspection revealed that the men with him were Yamondons. Among them the Tarkai, Agashi.

Rogashi laughed and ran to embrace his leader.

"You survived against the odds, it seems," Gujun said to Grodu.

"As did you, Gujun the Slayer. The world is full of wonders."

"The corsairs?"

"We caught Xeeg's louts in the woods. Our arrows did for most of them, but the Tark will mop up the rest. After that,

Agashi here will commandeer their raider ships our scouts spotted in that cove below the Hooks."

"How is it possible you are here?" Gujun dropped to his knees as exhaustion filled him. Close by, the miserable hump comprising Tulomon Caze sobbed and shook.

Grodu glanced at the Vendeli spymaster and grinned. "I got more help from the healer. I'll tell you about it later. And after that, the village woman, Misala, proved a friend. I recovered swiftly, as she was skilled."

Gujun looked at Caze, knowing that they'd need to stop him trying something rash. "You were saying?"

"A horse took me to the Gray River," Grodu continued, waving a casual hand. "I was happy to meet my good friend, the Tarakai Dolusa, and some of his Tark waiting at the ferry. Seems the king wanted his favorite soldiers, the Third, to keep eyes on events in the south. They left Cantacari a week after you and have been stationed by the river since."

Gujun smiled wryly, his eyes still on Caze. *Doubtless sent as insurance, in case Rogashi and I failed his king.*

"You listening to me, Slayer?"

"I am."

"I told Dolusa that you were in the Reech, making for Kelgar's lair. He let me drag this Tarkai and his boys away on this wild goose hunt. Proved successful." He grinned and walked over, staring down the weeping Vendeli. "This one's a mess. What about the girl?" Grodu asked.

Gujun shook his head.

"*Ah* . . . I'm sorry. She was a spirited lass. I liked her."

"She didn't much care for you," Gujun told him.

Grodu shrugged and returned his gaze to the weeping man. "Tulomon Caze. Spymaster. We meet again."

"I've no words for you, traitor." Caze stared hard at Grodu. "Your Shen friend won't kill me, so you'd best do it, quickly. Else, I recover my strength and kill you both."

"That would disappoint my king," Grodu said. "Ulani's so looking forward to discussing past animosities with you."

"Kill me, damn you!"

"No, Spymaster. You misunderstand our intentions. We Yamondons are here to help you avenge your family."

Despite his protestations, Grodu had Tulomon Caze carried down through the woods. One of the Tark hunters saw to his wound and drugged him with warm water and strained poppy. Once he was unconscious, they moved on through the night.

Gujun and Rogashi questioned Grodu more, as the Tarkai led a party off to secure the corsairs' ships. Agashi returned later, announcing they'd captured the ships, and all the corsairs were either dead or had fled into the dregs of the night. Xeeg Blue Face was missing, but they'd hunt him down, Agashi assured them. Gujun didn't much care. He thought of Arraleen Caze, and her drugged sickly father slumped over the back of a donkey.

Too bad.

They reached the Razor River a day later, crossing at a wide marshy section where the water was shallowest. He saw Reechers Bay glinting a mile to the left. From there, they rode horses up to the Gray River and crossed that at the ferry, before arriving at the river garrison manned by the rest of the Third. Tarakai Dolusa greeted both him and Grodu on arrival.

Once recovered, Tulomon Caze never spoke on that journey. His body mended, but he seemed resigned to his lot, his eyes snake cold and distant.

Skipper Dasco got word via pigeon and sailed down to Reechers Bay. Ten days after boarding, Gujun stood before King Ulani in the palace in Cantacari, with Grodu and Rogashi at his side. The king seemed in fine spirits.

"And how fare you, Gujun the Slayer?" Ulani stared across at him from his high table. A huge green parrot perched on a stand beside him, and three delightful young women giggled as the bird croaked insults at them. Rogashi had told him these were the king's favorite daughters. He didn't know about the parrot, but the bird seemed to like him.

"I am well enough, Lord King."

"Excellent. Rogashi has informed me that you wish to return east?"

"I do, Highness."

"I'd sooner you'd stay here. As an honored and occasionally *useful* guest. Young Rogashi here is simple-natured and fond of you. And Grodu says you have your uses. I would learn more of the east lands. Yamondo could use a Shen ally."

"I thank you, king." Gujun dipped his head. "But my heart is set on a place in Laregoza."

"Ah, yes. The villa outside Soloza. Grodu has spoken of this too."

"I like it there."

"As far as Yamondo's concerned, it's yours to take, Slayer. I'll send word to Cama of how helpful you've been. But it's up to him to decide, of course. And keeping it might prove tricky. Ran Genza won't be happy when he finds out.

"And your emperor, Lin Gu, will be searching that land for you. I hear that Cama has promised to help him find you. Tricky. Perhaps he could be persuaded to keep your presence a secret, if you helped the Laregozans in return?"

Gujun smiled. "With Genza."

Ulani rubbed his hands together and grinned at his lovely daughters.

"Something to think about on your journey, Gujun the Slayer. I'm sure General Cama will find you, so you'd best have a plan for that. Until then, and beyond. Stay alive, little Shen. Know you will always be welcome in my land.

"Rogashi and Grodu will accompany you to the mountain border towers, as they have other business to attend. From there, you'll cross by horse to Vendel, and reaching Kulshana, take a fast ship from the harbor."

"The Vendeli might not welcome me in their country, lord."

"I wouldn't fret too much about that."

Gujun had a thought. "You've made a bargain with Tulomon Caze?"

"Perhaps I did." Ulani stared at him, his sharp eyes revealing nothing. "For now, trust that the situation's soon to change in that land. I received two separate items of news from good people in Omala City, and Dalcia. Now leave us, and may the gods keep the skin on your back."

Gujun bowed and turned away. Next morning, he took the carriage east to the jungle mountains. Rogashi clasped his hand as they parted company at the border towers, half hidden by the swelter of jungle.

"I will miss you, Little Brother."

"As I will you, Yamondon."

Grodu stepped forward and slapped his arm, still sensitive after the Soilfin creature bit it in the tunnel. "I'll be in Cardalis keeping an eye on Genza. Why not join me?"

"Perhaps I shall." Gujun smiled. "You never know with me."

He watched them enter the closest watch tower, where they would gather news and rest for a day. No rest for him. Gujun guided his horse across the border and took the long winding track from river up to the high mountain passes. Two days later, he gazed down on the green slopes of western Vendel.

A few days later, in the city of Omala, a young woman watched diffidently, as the scantily clad ruler of Vendel leaned back, smiling, allowing the youth to work him over while resting idly upon his golden throne. Once sated, he pushed the youth away and glanced up. Saw her standing with head bowed. The veiled woman delivered by his newly promoted Captain of Guard. The previous two having been executed last month.

"The special slave you requested, Yanturi." The Dalcian bowed low and slipped back into the shadows. The woman gazed down at her beringed hands and noticed they were shaking slightly.

"How lovely." The fat man rubbed his greasy fingers together and sat up. "Come close, let me see what you've got hidden in there."

She obeyed promptly, with a rustle of silk and jingle from the tiny bells on her dusky ankles. She'd dressed immaculately, in scarlet and gold. This was her big day. Her nostrils twitched at his stale breath as he leaned close, pawing at her gown and fingering her black oiled hair. Tugging the neat braids. Her musky scent was exciting him. His eyes were hungry as he gazed down at her tattooed feet wrapped in green slippers, the bare toes ringed with gold. She remained still, awaiting his command.

"I've heard you've special skills. Time to show your face, woman." The Yanturi grasped her veil, pulling it off.

"I do, indeed," Arraleen Caze said. She smiled as she sliced his belly open with her curved dagger. "That's for my family, and my father's honor."

His screams echoed around the throne room. She watched him bleed, sob, and thrash for a moment. Then, bored, she whistled between her fingers, and three sleek black cats appeared from the gardens behind. Her panthers snarled and prowled and circled the throne.

The Dalcian appeared and clicked his tongue behind her. She joined him, as her cats took their leisure feasting on the dying man's flesh.

"The courtiers and court spies are dead, as well as their soldiers?" she asked.

The Dalcian nodded, his horrified eyes on the cats' grisly work. "Both city and palace are yours, Hareshe."

"Thank you, Crastus of Kamor. You've proved yourself a resourceful fellow."

He bowed. "I was pleased to help, Hareshe. The Sangala . . ."

"Olgasha's dead."

"That's good." He winced, hearing the crunch of bone. "Will you stay in the city or return to your country estate?"

"I think neither. My former maidservant, Gosha, is awaiting my return at the gates with the Yamondon slave she freed. Word is, she has news concerning my father."

"They're saying he's held in Cantacari, Hareshe. As King Ulani's prisoner."

"I suspect he won't be there long." She smiled and snapped her fingers, summoning her cats. They purred and slunk behind her, mouths dripping, as she strolled through the palace, ignoring the mess of corpses and carnage left from the recent coup.

Gosha dipped her head as Arraleen joined her servant and the Yamondon messenger she'd sent, who'd found her in the tavern in Dalcia.

"My brother has everything he needs to rule?"

"He does, Hareshe." Gosha bowed. "The Hashana, Cordeel, arrived in the city last night. He says he wishes to speak with you."

"I don't need to see him," she said. "You freed this Yamondon—was that wise?"

"Scaro's a good man."

"That he is. I've discovered that not all Yamondons are bad. I've learned so much, Gosha, since last we spoke. Think I might have grown up, finally." She touched her former maid's arm and smiled. "The country estate is yours, Gosha. I will inform my brother of all you've done. Cordeel will not intervene. May Agarra bless you and your Yamondon. Go now. Be happy with your life."

"Where will you go, Hareshe?" Tears were tracing Gosha's eyes.

"Oh, I don't know," she lied smoothly, smiling as the cats slunk by her side. "Find the next problem to solve."

Gujun gazed at the warm waves as they sparkled beneath the distant cliffs. Above, the villa gleamed pearl bright in the warm Laregozan late afternoon sun. He heard light footsteps approaching and turned, seeing the girl.

"You came back," she said, her honey-brown eyes worried.

"Said I would."

"Why?"

"To look at my home."

"Your home? That villa?" She saw where he had been looking, and she laughed.

"And I wanted to see your face again."

She crinkled her nose. "You can't stay here. Too dangerous.

There's been more men from your land asking for Gujun the Slayer. They're probably still some lurking in Soloza. And General Cama—"

"Come sit with me," he said. "You can tell me everything as we watch the sun set."

"Did you really miss my face?"

"I did." *More than I'll admit to.* "You are my friend, Kanny, and I've discovered how precious friends can be in this life."

He placed a hand in hers, and together they watched as the golden orb darkened to amber and red, and finally slipped beneath the sparkling ocean.

Gujun the Slayer and Arraleen Caze will return . . .

Would you trade your soul to save your life?

The Crimson Lady knows that's the only way to find the man she wants to kill—the mercenary known as Corin an Fol.

If you enjoyed Dreamslayers, you will love this new tale, *The Crimson Lady*. It's available free for newsletter members only. Don't miss out. Join our fun newsletter, the J.W. Webb VIP Lounge. Subscribe and pick up *The Crimson Lady* to delve deeper into this exciting series today.

https://bit.ly/CrimsonLady

The following is an excerpt from Blood Feud.

GUJUN ENCOUNTERS THE NORTHMEN

The Shen bowed stiffly when Calla strode to meet them. All save one individual, a smallish man Valgarn hadn't noticed before. This one looked confident, arrogant even, his dark eyes bored. He stood with feet braced and arms neatly folded, slightly away from the others. He caught Valgarn's gaze and smiled.

Valgarn whispered in the ferry captain's ear when he drew alongside. "Who's the little fucker with the evil black eyes, and those twin blades hanging from his back?"

"That's Gujun," the captain grunted. He shuffled and looked uncomfortable. "He's a killer." He turned away to attend his affairs.

"Welcome, ministers and secretaries, we are friends today." Calla spread his arms wide in greeting. The leading official stepped forward and bowed briefly again.

"Mighty Ran, I'm Secretary Ghee. I lead this conference party, and bid you sincere felicitations from Magister Chulan." Valgarn was still watching the killer Gujun. The small man looked amused by the secretary's words.

"He's one to watch," Valgarn muttered in Gorn's ear.

"More likely one to kill," Gorn coughed back. The man Gujun smiled again, as though he'd heard their words.

"Good to know," Calla said. "How fares the excellent Chulan? Is he busy preparing for our arrival?"

"He is, Great Ran—as are all his people, myself included. The empress and her regime are corrupt and decaying, like the ancient Ptarni who your noble ancestor destroyed. It's past time for regime change, and we will ensure the city is yours at the appropriate hour."

"Fine words." Calla's eyes were hard slots of violet. "But I'll need some assurance, a show of your loyalty to the cause."

Secretary Ghee stiffened uncomfortably. "Name it."

Calla smiled and turned to grab Valgarn and Gorn's cloaks. "Come forward, my friends, show yourselves to the good secretary here." They complied and stood towering over the nervous Ghee. The other officials looked shocked, terrified even, and the soldiers tensed, their steel gloves gripping those curious spears. Gujun was grinning openly, as though he was the only individual present who knew what was occurring here.

"You . . . have *Northmen,*" Soma Ghee said, his narrow eyes flicking over Valgarn and his brother.

"And more coming," Calla said. "The new king in Leeth has decided to aid the Cardalan cause. He no longer deems it appropriate to serve Shen, as his kin have for so many years. The loyal puppies have turned into wolves—isn't that right, Gorn? Valgarn?" Calla grinned across at them.

"We are here to kill Calla's enemies," Valgarn said, staring hard at Gujun, who shrugged indifference. *I'm starting with you, shithead.* Valgarn glared at the figure poised like a dancer at the end of the jetty.

Ghee seemed lost for words, so Calla continued. "So! Since we are discussing Northmen, can you prove useful by bringing me the head of one of yours?"

Ghee's narrow face looked pinched. "Lord Ran?"

"I speak of Hranic Finehair."

"The Auxiliary Captain?" Ghee looked openly shocked.

"I know who he is." Calla's eyes hardened again. "A constant thorn in my side, much like these men's cousin, whom your Magister recently outlawed, I believe."

"You mean Jaran Saerk? He's still alive?" Ghee's voice appeared on the brink of breaking.

"Roaming the Northlands, I believe." Calla laughed at the man's worried expression. "I've promised his head to their father. And you, Secretary Ghee, can go fetch me Hranic's."

"That will prove difficult." Soma Ghee whispered something to his fellow officials, who nodded sharply, their faces bleak. "But possible, yes. I will see to it in person."

"Excellent." Calla's broad face beamed mock joy. "I'll expect the trophy this time next week."

"I . . ." Ghee looked horrified, but Calla turned away and smiled at Valgarn and his brother. The party of Shen looked even more miserable, especially since a veil of cold rain had started spilling on the jetty deck.

"You can go back to your little fox holes." Calla waved a dismissive hand, and signaled the captain to ready the ferry for departure again. "That went as planned." Calla grinned at Valgarn and Gorn.

"Who is this Northman, Hranic Finehair?" Valgarn asked Calla as they left the jetty behind and made for one of the canteens, where the welcome smell of bacon meant breakfast. "Why not let us kill him? Why trust those little turds?"

"The Shen are crafty—don't underestimate them," Calla said. "But they are also cowards, and that man knows the lie of the land. Ghee wants to keep his head, and station, as does his master Chulan. Don't worry, they'll be plenty of Northmen for you to fight and kill, honorable foes, unlike the scrawny Shen."

They entered the canteen and were served immediately. A full steaming plate of bacon, sausage, eggs, and mushrooms—all washed down with small beer and fermented yak milk. A favorite among the garrison stationed here.

After they'd eaten, a soldier appeared and quietly whispered in Calla's ear. "Gujun the Slayer waits outside, Lord Ran."

"Ah, yes—so he didn't depart with the others." He turned to Valgarn and Gorn with a smile. "Come with me."

Gujun waited quietly, until Ran Calla appeared with the two Northmen alongside. Huge brutes, even for that ungainly race. Blonde shaggy hair and rough forked beards. Unkempt, so unlike the neatly styled Shen. Barbarian oafs for sure. These two were even uglier than normal, vicious looking and heavily armed, with bearded ax and sword at waists, shields across backs, and short spears clutched in fists. The pair glowered moodily at Gujun, the biggest looking like he'd strike him at any moment, or at least try to.

Gujun calmly registered their loathing and waited for the warlord to speak. Ran Calla was passing instructions to some of his officers outside the canteen, as the Northmen brothers and he waited. At last done with his administrations, Calla turned and awarded Gujun a wry glance.

"Thought you'd returned with Ghee," he said. Gujun didn't respond, but folded his arms and nodded. "This is Gujun," Calla said to the brutish brothers. "He works for Chulan, therefore is useful to me. A go-between, with special skills. Think you could kill him, Gorn?"

Calla winked at the biggest of the brothers who stepped forward and towered over Gujun. "Happy to." The Northman spat in the dirt before Gujun's feet. Gujun stared up at him with disinterest. "Cocky little bugger." Gorn made a show of grabbing his ax in one hand, tugging it free of the loop hole. "Can I split him in two, Calla?"

"You can try." Calla smiled at the other brother, who seemed the brighter of the pair, *though of course all Northmen are stupid.* "Maybe you'll get to splatter your first Shen, Gorn. What say you, Valgarn—want a go too?"

"I can wait," the other one said, mocking Gujun with his eyes and folding his arms, then adding with a grin, "I prefer fighting warriors my size."

"Ready to die, Gujun?" Calla said. "I'm sure Chulan can replace you easily enough."

"Dying doesn't bother me," Gujun said. "But that's not going to happen here." He smiled at the biggest brother. "Why are Northman all so ugly?"

Calla laughed, and the other brother swore, but Gorn's ax swung out, hard and fast for Gujun's neck. He danced aside and grinned up at the big man. "You're quite quick," Gujun said. "For a fat lazy slug." Gorn spat rage and swung again, from left to right. Gujun danced out of reach. Gorn stepped forward, panting with fury, face red and puffy. He swung up in an arc, and then brought the ax down with a wild, vicious slash that would have split a young oak in two.

Again, Gujun stepped aside, but this time he darted in close, spun on his right foot and launched his left, impacting Gorn hard in the belly. Gorn buckled and cursed. He tugged his ax free from the ground, where the head had buried itself six inches deep.

The Northman swung again, wilder than before, the weapon slicing hard for Gujun's head. He ducked, sent a foot out and hooked up behind Gorn's leg, twisting and lifting, sweeping the giant clumsy slug from his feet.

Gorn crashed onto his back with a clank and a thud. He tried to rise, but Gujun jumped forward and placed his studded boot on Gorn's neck, forcing him down until the man's face reddened with fear. To his right, the other brother reached for his sword.

Valgarn stopped when he saw the knife appear in Gujun's hand, balanced beautifully and ready to fly.

"Enough, Gujun," Calla said, waving a dismissive hand. "You've proved your point."

Gujun nodded to the Ran and removed his foot from Gorn's neck, allowing the Northman to cough and spew, regain his breath, and eventually rise to his knees. He looked furious, and stared at Gujun with a mixture of loathing and disbelief. The other brother looked more reflective. *Yes, this one was bright for a Northman*, Gujun thought. He bowed slightly to the Ran and stepped away, folding his arms neatly again.

"I told you not to underestimate the Shen," Calla said as Gorn rose and glared down at Gujun.

"I was just warming up," the brother spat at him. Gujun considered skewering the oaf for that insult, but decided against it. There were more important matters here.

"Chulan sends apologies," Gujun said. "Secretary Ghee has proved a disappointment of late."

"I'm sure he'll pay for any carelessness," Ran Calla said.

He turned to the towering Northmen. "You two go and find a wench or something else to do, and clean yourself up, Gorn. I will meet with you later." The brothers gaped at him for a moment, obviously perturbed and shocked at being dismissed so out of hand.

The younger, brighter one nodded. "Come on, Gorn, let's go get some ale and leave the Ran to his bust day." Gorn nodded and turned, after awarding Gujun a final acidic glance.

Gujun waited until they were out of earshot. "You have more of these clowns coming?"

The Ran nodded curtly. "Two hundred. I'll set them amongst Hranic's thugs. I've heard that Northmen like killing each other."

Gujun shrugged, bored with the subject. "You want me to deal with Finehair personally?"

"No, let Secretary Ghee sweat over that. I have a bigger task for you, assassin. Empress Rasnei—how fares she?"

"Frail and alone, save for ten thousand overrated guards." Gujun grinned. "Who can be bribed."

Calla laughed. "Can you reach her discreetly?"

"Of course, I can reach anyone, Ran. Though it might prove tricky staying alive afterward. So not much for me to get enthusiastic about, as I'd need considerable time to spend the vast amount of gold you'd be paying me."

"Hmm, yes." Calla nodded. "That's fair enough, and no need to rush things. But I want her dead and the family too—at your convenience. But no later than spring. When Pol Shen tumbles, I want no freedom fighters rallying around a ruler."

"No problem," Gujun said. "Chulan sent me primarily to ask for your aid in the countryside surrounding the city. The Midnight Cutting Crew have reemerged, those same thugs who helped the Tseole kill some of your men in Ferrytown last month."

Calla looked irritated. "Can't Magister Chulan deal with his own internal affairs? Why must I do everything?" Then he smiled. "Let me think on this, Gujun. It could be that I'll have a special task for those two brothers you just insulted. Send the Northmen across the river, let them fight each other, and then scour the lands for Gurtei's clowns."

"If you think them capable," Gujun replied.

"Tell Chulan to expect my army inside two months," Calla said. "That gives him plenty of time to arrange everything. I trust the Magister will ensure everything is accomplished with his usual attention to detail."

"I'll pass on your wishes," Gujun said, and he turned, making for the second ferry. He'd pole that one across himself. Hard work, but Gujun would enjoy the exercise. He vaulted onto the ferry and reached for the pole. "See you soon, Ran." Gujun waved at Calla standing outside the canteen, his brawny fists resting on sword and ale flask.

"I'll expect you, and news of your accomplishments," Calla shouted across, then vanished inside the canteen. Gujun poled out, allowing the craft ease into the steady brown flow of the Shen River. Once across, he'd report back to Chulan what the Ran had said.

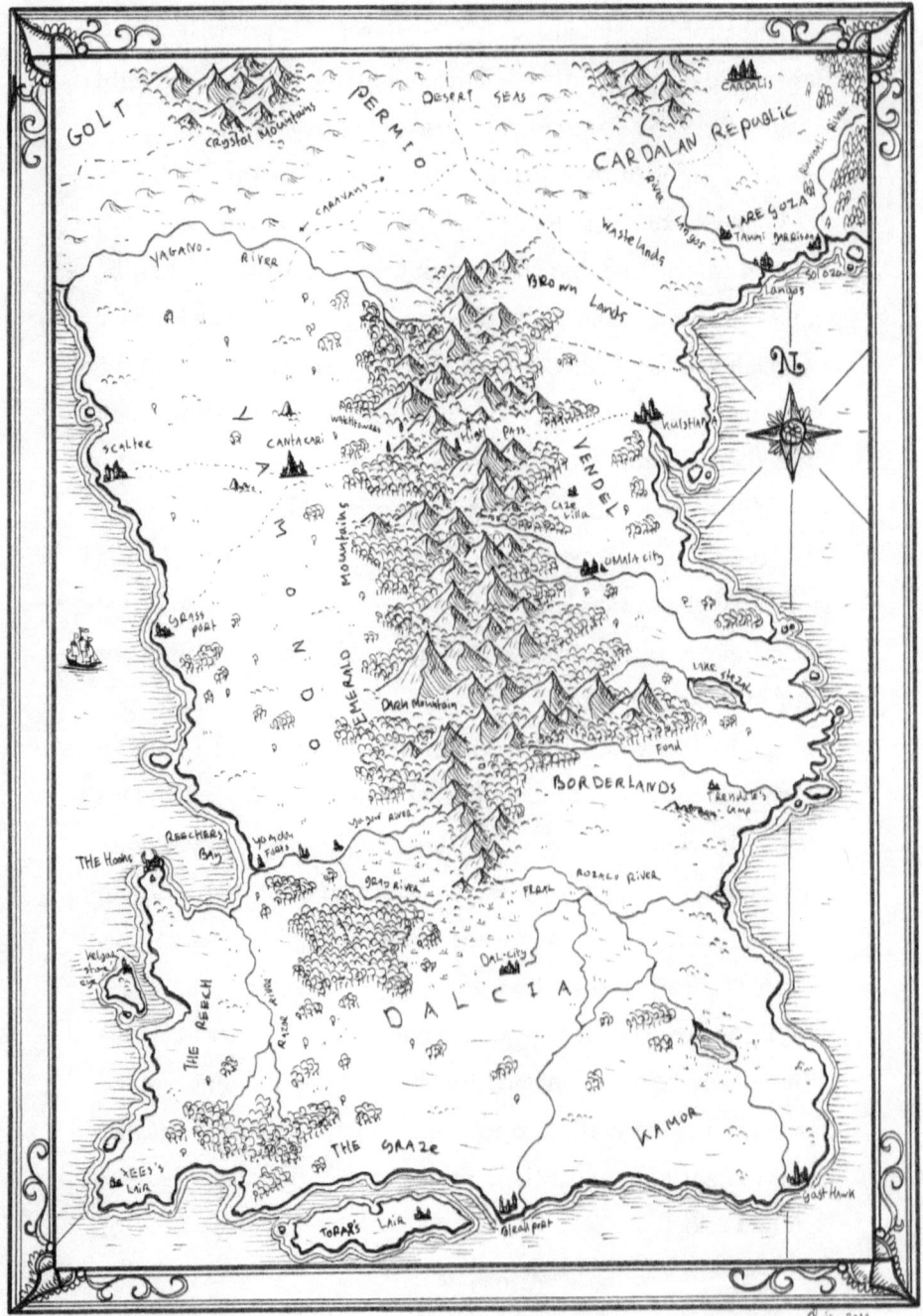

ENJOY THIS BOOK? THEN HELP SPREAD THE WORD!

Reviews are one of the most powerful tools in my arsenal when it comes to getting readers for my books. Much as I'd like to, I don't have the financial muscle of a New York publisher. I can't take out full-page ads in the newspaper or put posters on the subway.

(Not yet, anyway.)

But I do have something much more powerful and effective than that, and it's something that those publishers would kill to get their hands on:

A committed and loyal bunch of readers.

If you have enjoyed this book, I would be so grateful if you could spend a few minutes leaving a review, wherever you bought it. And I'd love it if you could email me a link to the review! ansureviews@gmail.com

Thank you so very much!

ALSO BY J.W. WEBB

THE LEGENDS OF ANSU
GOL: The Series Prequel

THE MERCENARY TRILOGY
Gray Wolf (Book 1)
Legends of the Longsword (Book 2)
Wolves and Assassins (Book 3)

THE CRYSTAL CROWN TRILOGY
The Shattered Crown (Book 1)
The Lost Prince (Book 2)
The Glass Throne (Book 3)

THE JOURNEYMAN TRILOGY
The Emerald Queen (Book 1)
The Voyage of Carlo Sarfe (Book 2)

THE BERSERKER TRILOGY
Blood Feud (Book 1)
The Giant's Dance (Book 2)
Shadow of the White Bear (Book 3)

ABOUT THE AUTHOR

J. W. Webb is an English writer living in Georgia. Mostly
he writes fantasy, though sometimes diverts in even stranger
directions. His epic saga, *The Legends of Ansu*, blends the mystic
grandeur of JRR Tolkien with the gritty realism of GRR
Martin. Webb's characters are three-dimensional and flawed,
their world a tapestry of vivid color and constant motion.
All the books feature beautiful bespoke sketches by the late
Tolkien illustrator, Roger Garland.